All that Glitters

AITA IGHODARO

CORVUS

Published in paperback in Great Britain in 2012 by
Corvus, an imprint of Atlantic Books Ltd.

10 9 8 7 6 5 4 3 2 1

A CIP catalogue record for this book is available from the British Library.

Trade Paperback ISBN: 978 1 84887 664 4
Paperback ISBN: 978 1 84887 665 1
E-book ISBN: 978 0 85789 711 4

Printed in Italy by Grafica Veneta S.p.A.

Corvus
An imprint of Atlantic Books Ltd
Ormond House
26–27 Boswell Street
London
WC1N 3JZ

www.corvus-books.co.uk

I'd like to thank everybody at my publisher, Corvus, for helping put this book together, particularly Laura Palmer whose advice was invaluable. Likewise thanks must go to Maddie West, Sara O'Keeffe, Corinna Zifko, my agent Sallyanne Sweeney and the many other talented members of the team who have worked hard on this.

I'd also like to thank all of my friends for contributing in different ways, from making me laugh and keeping my spirits high as I wrote to supplying scandalous stories and anecdotes. You know who you are. A special thanks must go to GC – who is nothing like Mr Sweet! - for that boat trip along the Amalfi Coast which provided so much inspiration. And to Ladi for lots of courtroom info – any inaccuracies are my own.

I must stress that this book is, if you hadn't already guessed, a work of fiction, and none of the characters is based on anyone, except when they are so famous they appear, fictionally, as themselves! Most of all, I'd like to thank my brilliant family for the love and support they've always shown me.

Prologue

First there had been the training.

'Open your mouth,' she said. 'No, really open your mouth and your throat, just like I showed you.'

Eventually Evita let the carrot pass right down her throat without gagging, and then she removed it.

'You're ready.'

'Really? You're sure?'

She didn't want to believe she was ready. She didn't feel ready. But then she looked in Gabrielita's eyes and felt choked with emotion. She knew she would do it.

'You are everything to me,' Evita said.

Gabrielita took Evita's hand and placed it on her own stomach. 'This love is real.' A tear rolled down her sunken cheek.

The darkened room smelled of damp and sweat. The furniture was a rickety table and two wooden chairs, upon which they both sat. On the table lay a Bible.

The next week she met the man. He didn't speak. Just sat there, filling the little balloons. Then he watched as she doused each one in oil and opened her throat the way she'd been taught. She swallowed one little parcel. And then another, and another, until before she knew it she had consumed fifty miniature latex parcels filled with crack cocaine. Her tiny stomach felt hard and bloated.

'That's enough,' she told him.

'More.'

'I can't.' She shook her head.

'Why? You did much more last time.'

She panicked. 'OK.' She opened her mouth again. She felt this one more keenly, as though she was suffocating as it passed through her oesophagus, and then a release when it reached her stomach. She wondered whether she might die on this trip.

He handed her the passport. 'Your name is Isabel Suarez-Octavio. You are eighteen.'

It didn't matter that she was fourteen; she could pass for eighteen.

He slid a piece of paper across the desk. 'This is your address.'

Then he handed her a bag filled with clothes and a pair of dainty high heels.

'Wear these clothes and these pearls, brush your hair and tie it back with this ribbon. You will wear no make-up except for mascara and concealer to hide the bags under your eyes. You're a posh girl. Elegant.'

The flight was the longest flight she had ever been on. And the only flight she could remember. She'd heard people say that her mama and papa had had a plane of their own but she'd been far too young to remember flying in it.

She closed her eyes as soon as she boarded the aircraft. She could not risk being drawn into conversation with anyone. But she also knew she must be seen to eat. They kept a special eye out on flights from South America. When the trolley approached her aisle seat she accepted her lunch and asked for a can of Coke. She took her first bite of the cheese and ham sandwich and chewed while the air stewardess was still within eyeshot. Then she coughed gently into a napkin; a more hearty cough would unsettle her stomach. Nobody knew that the mashed up sandwich was being transferred into the napkin as she did so. She rolled up the tissue and slipped it surreptitiously into her handbag. She took larger bites of the sandwich and coughed some more until it was finished. Then she slipped the can of Coke into her pocket. After a while she went to the loo and emptied the Coke down it. She slid the can back into her pocket and returned to her seat. When the stewardess returned to collect her tray, her food was mostly gone and the can of Coke was empty. Nothing unusual to report.

When the plane touched down she said a quick prayer under her breath. Then she disembarked and went through customs. She saw a security guard watching her. She assumed he was just like the men at home who watched her for no other reason than they liked what they saw. But she couldn't be certain. She made the decision to approach him.

'Hello,' she said loudly. 'Please advise me on the best way of getting to Bond Street. I'm wondering whether the Underground will be faster or whether I should stick to a trusty taxi?'

She was thankful for the countless English books she'd read and films she'd watched. They were her escape and they were her teachers. She'd known from an early age that if she wanted to learn then it would be up to her. Nobody would help her.

The distraction worked. The guard clearly figured that nobody with anything to hide would be stupid enough to approach him. So taken by her was he, in fact, that he personally escorted her all the way to the train, past the 'nothing to declare' signs and right past the two men holding out a sign saying 'Isabel Suarez-Octavio'. The men spotted her immediately but she walked right past them and they did not try to attract her attention while she was with the burly guard. One of the men had a knife in his pocket and had spotted the guard's metal detector. The other man had a face that was on the wanted list of every police department around the world and despite the plastic surgery he had had, he did not want to draw attention to himself. They would not follow her. Experience had taught them that if circumstances deviated from the plan then you cut your losses. It was dangerous to do otherwise. The 'accounts department' made allowances for this type of thing – mules who somehow slipped through the net. Often they died when a balloon or two split in their stomach, corroded by the acid. A few managed to escape. One or two misbehaved and had to be taken care of. They could lose somebody every now and then and still be in profit. They were never bothered by the ones who got away, as long as they did not step foot back in Bolivia. But they never came back to cause trouble because they were too frightened of what would happen to them, and they never went to the police because they knew that the police liked them little more than the men they worked for.

Evita smiled a small, triumphant smile and prepared for a life being Isabel Suarez-Octavio.

Part One

Chapter 1

'You are chosen.' The voice echoed around the ancient building. 'From the moment we select you, we begin teaching you to excel in life. From the Earl of Wilmington back in 1742 to Margaret Thatcher, Tony Blair and beyond, this university has produced more prime ministers of Great Britain than any other. We select you because we believe you are the best.'

Chloe Constance felt a mounting sensation of doom. Sweat trickled down the insides of her thighs, dampening the tops of her suspenders, worn to be sophisticated for her first day at Oxford. The woman's voice was giving her the creeps. And what's more, Chloe had a terrible suspicion she was far from the best. Looking left and right at the rows of attentive students, heads so full of knowledge they seemed to throb, Chloe felt sure she was about to find that out the hard way.

She was in the Sheldonian Theatre. The vast, circular building with its high domed roof was one of Oxford's architectural jewels. She gazed up at the painted ceiling. It was said to show truth descending upon the Arts and Sciences to expel ignorance from the university. Hastily lowering her eyes again she took a closer look at the people who were to be her contemporaries for the next three years. Lines of teenagers in their newly purchased formal academic dress for matriculation. The girls wore long black skirts and white shirts with black gowns over them. A black velvet ribbon was tied about their necks and they clutched at their mortarboards. The boys were also in black gowns and white shirts but with bow ties. Studying the row of earnest faces opposite her, Chloe reflected that none of the other girls would be wearing anything as risqué as suspenders beneath their gowns. As for the boys, they probably thought suspenders were things found in the science lab beside the Bunsen burner.

She brushed a flyaway strand of light blonde hair out of her face and tugged at the waistband of her skirt. She'd bought it too small in the vain hope she could lose a dress size before term started. Still, looking around, it didn't seem as though anybody would be on hand to pinch her extra inch.

The lecturer stopped speaking and everybody took their seats so Chloe followed suit. Noticing a couple of disapproving looks in her direction, she glanced down at her shirt and was mortified to see she was spilling out over the top buttons. She sighed at her attention-seeking curves. She couldn't help wishing she was taller and thinner and tanned.

Then, as if to taunt her, she spotted a girl in the row behind who was all those things and more. The girl stared back at Chloe before seeming to dismiss her with a haughty flick of her dark hair, averting her huge eyes to regard the lecturer with a curious, almost reverent stare. Chloe swivelled around to face the front. With a furrowed brow, she tried to pay attention but it was too late. She'd completely lost track of the ceremony and couldn't work out what was now being chanted in Latin, despite having been taught it at school since the age of five. She sighed and was heartened when her neighbour pointed to their place on the programme.

'Thank you,' she whispered.

Mercifully, slow organ music began playing to signify the end of the ceremony.

'Thank God! I'm dying of thirst,' Chloe said to no one in particular as she rushed out of the Sheldonian and into the glorious sunshine.

'Champagne, please!' she said to the bartender of the first pub she came to, a quaint cottage-like place with ivy growing up the walls and a pretty garden. She carried out her glass to a wooden table that overlooked the cobbled street. The other students streamed past, a sea of white and black. Shrugging off her gown and tossing it aside she savoured her first sip of chilled Moët. *Mmm,* she thought, enjoying the fizzy sensation in her mouth.

'A little toast to the city of dreaming spires? Or should that be dreamy esquires?'

Chloe jumped at the sound of the husky female voice. It was the girl from the row behind and she was holding up her glass for Chloe to clink. Chloe did, speechless.

How could this girl possibly be a fresher when she looked so confident and sophisticated? Chloe felt dumpy and woefully uncool in her presence. She was sure the heat was making her complexion even more flushed and the suspenders, which had seemed like such a good idea earlier, only made the problem worse. The newcomer had ignored the strict rules and worn neither tights nor stockings under her skirt. She now crossed a slender, bare leg gracefully over the other as she took a seat beside Chloe. Her long dark hair fell in a silky curtain over one shoulder, almost reaching her waist.

'I'm Isabel Suarez-Octavio,' the girl announced, turning to face Chloe with an amused expression, giving her the full benefit of her fine-featured, olive-skinned beauty.

'How lovely and exotic, a lovely name for a lovely girl,' Chloe rambled. 'I'm Chloe Constance, not as exotic as you, not really exotic at all.' She laughed. 'Yes, I'm very English – as English as this Oxfordshire pub …' Chloe knew she sounded ridiculous but felt a desperate, irrational need to keep talking.

'I think we two were the only ones with our priorities right in there,' said Isabel. When she smiled her face lit up and her dark eyes flashed so brightly that for a moment Chloe was silenced.

'Wh-what do you mean?' she asked eventually.

'Come,' Isabel ordered, jumping up. She grabbed Chloe's hand and strode onto the cobbled street. 'We were looking for boys in there, so let's continue.'

'Where are we going?'

'The Club.'

'What's that? OK, well then, hang on a minute.' Chloe pulled Isabel to the side of the street and into a secluded area behind a wall. She checked nobody could see them before hoisting up her skirt, unhooking her suspender belt and rolling off her stockings.

'That's better – I was about to melt.'

Isabel laughed. 'Yes, much better. Put your hair down too; it's very pretty.'

Chloe let her hair fall out of its loose knot and cascade down her back, flicking it over one shoulder the way Isabel had.

'Right, now we're ready,' Isabel said, slipping on a pair of vintage sunglasses. 'This way.'

They glided past historic colleges, pausing to peer at Lincoln College, with its manicured, lush green front quad and scarlet creeper winding up the medieval stone walls, before reaching the high street. There they passed the Examination Schools – a huge building in the style of a Jacobean mansion, where many of their lectures were to take place. They stopped again at a bridge, catching their breath at the sight of Magdalen College. The pale-stone building was set on the banks of the River Cherwell. Palatial in scale and with its Gothic Great Tower, it was resplendent in the light of the setting sun. From there they raced through fields of the brightest blues, reds and purples of the luscious plants in the botanic garden.

'I feel as though I'm in a dream,' Chloe said, eyeing a pretty fuchsia and bending to inspect it more closely. 'Everything's just …so lovely!'

'Come on,' said Isabel with a grin. 'Here's a bit of reality for you.'

They'd left central Oxford behind and were veering towards Cowley Road on the eastern outskirts of the city, a happy bustle of noise, dirt and the din of customers dining at cheap restaurants serving food of every nationality. Most of the people here weren't students and the imposing, ancient buildings of the centre were nowhere to be seen.

'It's like we're in a different country all of a sudden!' said Chloe, eyes widening. 'How do you already know where everything is?'

'I came prepared.'

A homeless man staggered towards Isabel and fixed her with a drunken leer. Isabel sauntered past him and stopped outside a graffitied building.

'Here we are,' she announced.

'Are you sure?' asked Chloe, clutching her Mulberry handbag tighter and glancing around.

Isabel pressed a buzzer and a voice rang out from the intercom.

'Yes?'

'In the club,' Isabel said.

The door buzzed open.

As Chloe entered she heard a voice calling out behind her, 'Excuse me, we met briefly, I'm Piper …' Her accent was American, the tone warm.

Chloe turned to see the girl from matriculation who had kindly helped her out when she'd lost her place. The girl had an open, friendly face and Chloe took an instant liking to her. She tried to hold open the door but it was too late, Isabel had forged on ahead, grabbing Chloe's arm and ushering her excitedly into the venue. The door slammed shut before Piper could enter.

Though it was only early evening the lights in The Club were already dimmed. The room looked like the inside of a high-class hooker's boudoir: opulent, smoky, unkempt. Through the hazy darkness, the girls took in the nicotine-stained, velvet-upholstered sofas lining the walls and the long, mirrored, antique-looking table in the corner, piled high with liquor, wine and champagne bottles. A chain-smoking barman in a white vest and braces was pouring drinks for the bustling crowd gathered near him. At the other end of the room an old man sat at a shabby, but clearly once grand, piano. He turned his head as they entered.

Chloe stared at him and he parted his lips into a toothless grin. Then he turned back to his instrument and began to play. Stooped over the keys like the hunchback of Notre Dame, his nimble fingers worked a set of 1950's jazz hits with an electrifying fire and intensity.

Isabel ran into the centre of the room to dance. As she moved, her hair swirled around her face and her long limbs swayed. It was as if she were alone with the pianist. She twirled and spun, gradually increasing her speed. But she never lost control. By now she had the attention of the entire room, who noticed first her dancing then did a double take upon seeing her face. Young men began to break to away from the bar area and edge closer. Some moved to the sofas and watched from there. Two hipster girls tossed their messy hair and whispered comments about irritating attention seekers, but they too were mesmerized.

Then, as suddenly as it had started, the music stopped. Isabel continued to dance, spinning faster and faster, gathering speed with each turn. When eventually she stopped she surveyed the crowd blankly. Every onlooker seemed to exhale simultaneously as they applauded.

Chloe had shrunk back shyly and now stared at her strange new friend with barely concealed astonishment from the edge of the room. She glanced around, noticing that apart from the old man at the piano, they were all students – either that or the club had a strict scruffy jeans, T-shirt and five o'clock stubble policy.

She heard a quiet but assured male voice at her side.

'Chloe Constance, isn't it?'

'Yes, it is.' She turned, giggling nervously. 'Have we met?'

'No, but I think we're in the same college, although I'm in my final year. I'm William, or Will, if you prefer. So do we have your grandfather to thank for the college cathedral?' He looked into her eyes in an interested rather than flirtatious way. Chloe was grateful to him for looking at her and not Isabel.

'Oh.' She blushed. 'That wasn't my grandfather; that was my great-grandfather. Probably the only reason they let somebody as dopey as me into the university.'

'Don't do that,' Will said.

'Do what?'

'Don't sell yourself short. I'm sure you're very accomplished.'

'Chloe, come and have something to drink,' Isabel called from across the room where she now sat surrounded by a group of young men, one of whom was pouring the contents of a bottle of Moët into her glass. 'Bring your friend,' she added.

'Shall we join her?' Will asked, striding over to Isabel's table before Chloe could reply.

Her heart sank as she saw how little persuading he needed.

'Just off to the loo,' she murmured to Isabel when she reached the table, and slipped off towards a side door. By the time she returned, Isabel and Will were deep in conversation. Next to Isabel's expertly dishevelled radiance he looked like a preppy head boy who didn't quite have the authority he craved. But he had something, Chloe decided. He was tall with even features and the floppy hair that she kind of liked. But it wasn't really that. It was his manner. He was so attentive. She rejoined the group and he turned to include her.

'So I was giving Isabel the low-down, seeing as you two both appear to have missed out on freshers' week.'

'I know, it's such a shame; it all sounds so fun. Unfortunately I had to be in Wiltshire for a family anniversary. Isabel, where did you say you were?'

'Oh, I – I just wasn't around,' Isabel said.

'Where is your accent from, Isabel?' asked Will.

‘I’m Bolivian. But my family are citizens of the world.’ Isabel averted her eyes, gazing at a far away point beyond his head.

‘That sounds glamorous. I’m from Hampshire, not far from where the Constances’ li—’ He faltered.

Chloe smiled. She knew her family was known in certain circles. She couldn’t escape that.

‘Back to the low-down,’ William said. ‘Half my school came here so I’ve known most of this lot for ever.’ He gestured at the others at the table and around the room.

Isabel followed his gaze. ‘Was floppy hair on the curriculum at your school?’ she said disdainfully.

William laughed. ‘Not at all. Just wait till you meet my friend Ol. He’s a fresher too.’

‘Ol? Why? What’s so special about him?’

‘He’s just one of those annoying people in life. You know … effortlessly successful.’ Will smiled. ‘They say his parents sent him to Eton just to get him out of Nigeria and save the country’s economy. He’s so handsome he was disrupting business at the major bank his family owns there. The place became like Madame Tussauds, with girls queuing up around the block, just wanting to touch him to see if he was real. Women can’t resist him and he can’t resist them.’

Chloe laughed and rolled her eyes. He sounded arrogant. And most definitely not her type. Isabel looked thoughtful.

‘What college is he at?’

‘When he gets here, he’ll join Chloe and me at Hambley. He arrives tomorrow. But don’t you worry, I’m sure you girls’ll know about it. He’s in the habit of making himself known to gorgeous women.’

Chloe flushed.

Will added slyly, 'I mean, the flash bastard had his father's Picassos up on his dormitory wall when the rest of us had sensible things like posters of naked girls.' He glanced at Isabel in the hope she'd disapprove of such ostentation, but she was still lost in thought.

Tipsy and euphoric with the first thrill of student life, Chloe gladly accepted a lemon meringue vodka shot from a round being offered at random by somebody mad, merry and, most importantly, male. She'd spent her entire education in a series of progressively stricter Catholic girls' schools; now all she could think was boys, boys, glorious boys. Looking around at all these tousled geniuses destined for great things, she felt like little Charlie walking into Willy Wonka's chocolate factory. The shot-wielding guy rushed off, balancing the final shot on his nose while doing the limbo over to his friends. They cheered as he caught it just before it fell, downing it with a flourish.

The Club became busier and busier as the evening progressed, everybody chatting and mingling until late into the night. At the call of last orders, Chloe stumbled to the bar and ordered another bottle of champagne.

'I have to go,' Isabel announced as soon as Chloe returned with the ice bucket and bottle.

'OK, I'll come with you.

'Let me walk you back,' Chloe and Will said at the same time.

As they made to leave The Club, Chloe bit her lip. Thinking of the homeless man they'd seen hanging around outside, she reached for the bottle of champagne.

He was still loitering by the door where he'd taken up

residence. 'This is for you,' she said, handing it to him, slightly at arm's length. He snatched the bottle and Chloe ran to catch up with Isabel and Will.

As they staggered in the direction of Hambley College, they passed freshers throwing up, groups of girls in fancy dress and boys dressed in black tie buying food from a kebab van.

Will swung an arm around each girl, threw his head back and began singing. His ever so proper, almost operatic singing voice was absurd belting out Nelly Furtado's hit song, "Try", and the girls collapsed in laughter. But Will thought he also felt Isabel flinching. As though the song took her somewhere she didn't want to be. Or was it just the sound of his voice?

'Which college are you at, Isabel?' he asked, reluctantly realizing he needed to get her home.

Isabel seemed too preoccupied to hear him. She was looking intently at two figures approaching from the other side of the road – a casually dressed teenage guy and a peculiar-looking older man. With his wild mane of white hair, full beard, pointy nose and tiny shorts, he looked like a skinny Santa Claus crossed with an elf. He spotted her and stared back.

'That's Professor Crayson,' whispered Will. 'He looks like a sex offender but he's actually an unparalleled world expert in economics. That's Oxford for you, huh!'

They continued back towards the centre of town, strolling companionably under the night sky, until Isabel unhooked William's arm from around her shoulders.

'I want to explore,' she announced. And with that she was off, sauntering into the darkness.

Chapter 2

The helicopter landed on Hambley College front quad at 3.15 p.m. in the afternoon.

'What's going on here?' The college porter – an Oxford staple never seen without bowler hat or grumpy expression – was not impressed. He threw open the gate to his lodge overlooking the college grounds and ran towards the gleaming aircraft. He pushed his way through the gathering crowd. For a long time nothing happened. Then the helicopter door slid open and a flight of stairs emerged onto the manicured lawn. The jostling crowd fell silent as a handsome black man stepped out of the aircraft.

Some Hollywood actor come to speak at the Union? The enraged porter found his voice.

'What do you think you're doing, sir?'

'I'm here to enrol. I'm a fresher.' He raised his eyebrows in surprise and smiled warmly, a slight dimple forming in his cheek.

The porter was disarmed. He didn't want to like this fellow. And he wasn't American after all – his accent was more Establishment than that young British royal who'd graduated last year. The porter had long become used to posh voices around college, but he'd never grown to like them. And this? Well, he'd never seen anything like this.

'Who the devil are you?'

Another smile.

'The name's Osaloni. Olu Osaloni.'

'Do come in, girls.' Professor Crayson held open his door and beckoned his two tutees inside. He ushered them onto a battered but comfortable old sofa in the reception room of his modest residence. It doubled as a library and study. The aged brown carpet could barely be made out beneath metre high stacks of dog-eared manuscripts. Bookshelves lined the walls, where textbooks and set texts jostled for space with Nobel Prize winners.

Isabel Suarez-Octavio and her tutorial partner, Piper Kenton, watched him, stifling grimaces as he pulled up the top of his corduroy slacks, stretching the material so tight that they could make out the exact shape and size of what lay underneath.

'Economics,' he began, pulling out his latest critically acclaimed book on micro-econometric theory and its applications. He licked his lips and resumed. 'The result of twenty years of research and described by *The Economist* as the greatest achievement in the history of the world. Anyway, I digress.' He put down the book in pride of place on his desk and wiped a speck of dust from its cover, before removing his glasses, wiping them for a painstakingly long time and popping them back on the end of his pointy nose.

Isabel and Piper held their breath expectantly.

'Now,' he continued, 'I'd like to put yesterday's debate into a more understandable context. Mildred, can you try to summarize what was concluded in that discussion?' He pushed his spectacles higher on his nose and blinked at Piper.

She shot Isabel a confused look. Isabel shrugged.

'It's Piper. Piper Kenton.'

'Oh, so it is, so it is. Well, carry on.'

'Well,' Piper scrabbled for a second, trying to find the most succinct way to express herself. She had been greatly inspired by the previous tutorial, despite Professor Crayson's clear lack of interest in his students. She knew he would rather be locked in his study coming up with new theories and writing award-winning books, but she admired him nonetheless and was desperately keen to impress him. 'Well, I believe—'

'Do get on with it, please; we only have an hour for this tutorial. Why so much dithering?' He peered, not unkindly, at her and drummed his long fingers on his desk.

'I'm sorry!' Piper said, willing herself not to cry, which only made her do just that. She wiped a tear from her eye and stared unseeingly down at the frayed bit on the knee of her bleached jeans.

'Oh dear,' sighed Professor Crayson. 'You people. You're … you're just not rational. How you expect to even pass let alone do well in economics beats me. Conchita, can you try to better Mildred's attempt?'

Isabel ignored his confusion of her name. 'Your assertions at the last tutorial were fundamentally flawed,' she announced.

Professor Crayson stopped drumming. He leaned forward in his seat and studied Isabel very carefully. 'That's a bold statement. Why do you say that?'

'Because your entire argument was that the girl in the story had built her fortune out of nothing. You talked continuously about the economics of making something out of nothing when in fact she did not start with nothing. She was blessed with bountiful assets, from her quick judgement, to the way she looked, to her ability to attract people to herself. Perhaps a better way to describe the process of her rise is to look at it as a conversion – a conversion of her assets into power and money. Or a monetisation. A monetisation of her significant assets, not her *nothing*.'

'Hmm, well, it's not a conversion, as that would imply one thing becoming another, when those alternative "assets" you've just described would remain, regardless of her accumulation of financial assets.' He began rocking back and forth in his seat, his whiskery moustache twitching happily.

'I'm not sure about that,' said Isabel. 'I felt that the more she converted her assets, the less potent they became. The assets were underpinned by her spontaneity, energy, lack of self-regard and lack of fear of loss – all of which were eroded by the money.'

'Questionable, but you've taken a novel approach. I must say I noticed that last week too …'

They continued debating for most of the tutorial, Professor Crayson increasingly [illegible]g Isabel's nerve and conviction, while Piper kept tight-l[illegible] dabbing her moist eyes with a tissue as she slowly rega[illegible]er composure.

When the[illegible]al came to an end, Professor Crayson stood and held open[illegible]oor to his study.

'The [illegible] to be written and debated next week is: "No Economy i[illegible]e".'

P[illegible]er nodded and rushed out, silently berating herself for crying a[illegible] shooting an evil look at Isabel. Isabel went to follow her out.

'Isabel,' Professor Crayson said.

Isabel stopped. 'Yes, Professor?'

His white whiskers twitched again. 'You will become one of the great women of your generation.'

Chapter 3

Chloe looked herself up and down in the old mirror she had propped up in the corner. Her dark and sparsely furnished room overlooked the front quad and she had just witnessed Ol's helicopter entrance. His arrival was hardly low-key and she was determined to avoid him at any cost. He was appallingly flash. Dreadful. She couldn't stop thinking about what an arrogant idiot he was as she cast a critical eye over her reflection.

Chloe supposed her long blonde hair was OK, but that was about it. Ever since her mother had told her, aged seven, that she was never going to be a 'notable' beauty, she had hated her round face and curvy figure, and wished her twinkly blue eyes were bigger. Her mother's misguided attempts at comfort were hardly helpful.

'You'll be fine, though, darling,' she had said. 'Most of the great courtesans of the past and women who married into staggering, multi-generational wealth were rarely particularly beautiful. They simply knew how to make a man feel good about himself. The great looks came afterwards. After all, who could fail to look a million dollars with millions of dollars?'

At the time, Chloe had been too young to be repelled by her mother's sentiments. As she wiped strawberry jam from her chin and watched George Michael frolicking in fur-trimmed boots for his "Last Christmas" video, all that her chubby, seven-year-old self had thought was, *if George Michael would only marry me I'd be a freaking beauty queen!* With that she had kicked off, at a perilously young age, a tendency to fall for entirely inappropriate men.

She picked up her mascara wand and coated her top lashes, first on their underside and then again on their upper side, and wondered if Isabel would re-emerge at the famous Oxford Union, where she was about to go and see a formal debate. It was on the advice of Will, himself a past president of the Union. She dreaded debates and was terrible at debating, if her school reports were anything to go by: 'Chloe's style is passionate and unusual, but she must now learn to include fact in her argument. She must develop the beginnings of logical thinking. We also recommend a psychological assessment with the school doctor.'

One of the motions she'd argued was supposed to have been: 'This house believes rising rates of interest can benefit society'. It wasn't her fault she'd misheard and substituted 'incest' for 'interest'. She sighed at the memory. But Will had won her over by regaling her with stories of personalities and celebrities, from the late Michael Jackson to Judi Dench, who had spoken at the Union, so she had decided she ought to at least see one debate.

Today's guest speakers were to be the young Formula 1 whizz, Jack Grenson, and the singer Piers Bellevue. She had been invited by Will to the grand pre-debate drinks and dinner, too. The dress code was black tie and she felt butterflies flitting in her stomach as she squeezed into her mother's slender floor-length black velvet dress.

'Chloe, are you ready?' She heard Will shouting her name from the corridor outside and rushed to open the door.

'You're looking dashing,' she giggled. His tall, skinny frame suited the formal dress of black tux and bow tie, and with his light hair swept back he looked like a 1940's film star.

'I don't need to tell you how beautiful *you* look.' He grinned, offering her his arm so that she didn't trip on her high satin slingbacks.

They jumped into a black cab and made their way to Frewin Court in the heart of town where the Union buildings were located.

'Come on, I'll show you around first.' Will led her through manicured gardens full of pink rambler roses and studded with students milling around, drinking on benches and in the splendid main building itself. Once inside, Chloe could see that the Union was actually made up of a number of interconnected buildings. She felt lost, reminded of how small she was compared with the great height of the ceilings and vast windows of the ancient architecture.

'So here's the Gladstone Room, where we'll have drinks in a minute. This used to be the library; the Old Library with its pre-Raphaelite frescoes is even more stunning. I'll show you later,' he said proudly. 'And now here's the office for the Union president—'

'My god, is that a bed in there?'

'Yup, it's an overnight job sometimes – full on! As well as all the debates and speakers there's a ton of other stuff to organize, from huge balls and events, to member trips abroad and arranging discounts at establishments around Oxford and special perks for members. And don't forget most members are life members, which means there are a hell of a lot. And now here's where we'll have dinner – the Macmillan room.'

'Ooh, I love this room.' She took in the oak panelling and elegant barrel ceiling. 'Who are all the statues and paintings of?' she asked as they wandered around the building.

'Mostly past presidents of the Union, past prime ministers.'

They returned to the Gladstone Room. Like a library in an old stately home, this room, with its deep armchairs and plush red carpet, whispered rather than shouted of old money and grand traditions. Rows of champagne flutes gleamed on the sideboard.

'I'd better not have too much or I might say something stupid when they throw the debate open to the floor.'

'One man's stupid is another man's genius. Say what you like – just say it with confidence and you'll get away with it.'

At dinner they were separated and Chloe found herself seated beside Piers Bellevue, one of the guest speakers. She recognized him instantly and was beside herself with excitement. One of her earliest memories was of watching her lust-struck mother, in a man's suit and trilby, cavorting around the kitchen to his songs shortly after he'd declared in an interview that there was nothing sexier than androgyny. Chloe's mother had had a crush on him for years. Now he was ageing, but still a rock star.

'My mother's a big fan of your work,' she told him, trying to play it cool.

'Well, I'm a big fan of *her* work,' he whispered, staring at Chloe's cleavage. 'Well done *mummy*!'

Chloe blushed and laughed nervously. 'Are you ready for the debate?'

'I'm ready for anything!' He leaned in close to her, and she could smell the alcohol on his hot breath as he reached for her hand under the table and then placed it on his groin.

She gasped and pulled her hand away, fuming at the pink and brown slices of beef on her plate. She saw Will eyeing her curiously from across the table.

After the pudding – a gooey chocolate tart – had been cleared away, Will rescued Chloe and led her into the debating chamber.

So this is the famous Union, Chloe thought, gazing around the packed chamber. An ornate wooden gallery circumnavigated the double height hall. Everything about the décor was beautifully aged, from the wooden floor to gilt framed portraits on the wall. You could see and feel the centuries of history, seeming to bestow an extra importance and gravitas on the present. Involuntarily, Chloe stood up straighter. Students were seated on cushioned wooden benches facing a central table on which two antique despatch boxes were positioned at the point where the speakers would stand to debate.

'Those were a gift from Winston Churchill – originally from the House of Commons,' said Will. Several more students peered down at the proceedings from an overhead gallery. The chattering stopped as the Union president swept in with other student officials – a slight girl in a sweeping plum ball gown and the boys all in black tie – followed by the guest speakers.

Chloe suppressed a giggle as the president made a precious speech thanking various 'honourable members' for everything from his photograph in the widely read student newspaper, *Cherwell,* to his red socks.

'Now,' he went on, 'as you are all aware, the motion for tonight's debate is: "This house would limit the permitted level of press intrusion into the private lives of public figures". Our special guest speaker for the motion is legendary singer Piers Bellvue, and against the motion we have Formula 1 star Jack Grenzen.'

Lined up in a row alongside the guests were various other Union officers and students who would also be speaking.

Chloe wasn't really concentrating on the debate, preferring to check out the other students and the decadent surroundings. She did, however, pay attention when Jack Grenzen got up to speak. It was always fun to see how famous figures measured up in real life.

Jack was small and shy away from the circuit and less dazzling than he looked in his all-in-one racing outfit, spraying magnums of champagne from the winner's podium. He seemed reluctant to be a part of the debate but had no doubt been told by his manager that it would be a good PR move. He'd been the subject of a string of kiss-and-tell stories in the media and it looked magnanimous to have him advocating press freedom despite his own suffering at its hands. Not that he'd suffered that much; the glamour models involved had all sung his praises – his manager might also have had something to do with that too. At any rate, he'd evidently spent many more hours on the race track than he had at school, and he kept confusing his speech.

Chloe's heart went out to him as he summed up that: 'People ought to let the press write about the private lives of famous people like me because otherwise thousands of glamour models would be out of a job. Oh sorry, I meant thousands of gossip journalists would be out of a job, and then' – he scratched his head – 'and then the tax-payers' money would be wasted and everything 'cos they'd all be on benefits.'

'What did Piers say to you at dinner?' Will asked Chloe under his breath.

'Oh don't, I've been trying to forget. He's a bit of a perv.' She glanced surreptitiously at Piers sitting across from her and caught him pouring vodka into his glass of water.

It wasn't long before it was Piers' turn to speak, and he took to the stand with a swagger.

'When I started making music, it was all about anarchy. It wasn't just the sounds we were making; it was the message we were spreading. Urging kids around the world to stand up and question evil regimes. To fight for love, fairness and equality. I started a revolution with the strings of my guitar.' He paused for dramatic effect, taking a long swig of his concealed vodka. 'I started a revolution.' He went on in a similar vein for quite some time, stopping only when a girl with long eyelashes and cute ringlets put up her hand to ask a question out of turn. 'I'll be signing autographs afterwards, honey,' he told her.

'I was just wondering who you were?' she asked, pulling shyly on a ringlet.

The president jumped up, embarrassed. 'May I remind you that this debate can only be interrupted by legitimate calls of "point of order" or "point of information". That was quite out of turn.' He swivelled around and bowed his head piously in Piers' direction. 'Pray excuse the ignorance of this …honourable member.' Clearing his throat, he shot her a withering look before taking his seat again. 'How dare she ruin my debate,' he hissed at his treasurer. 'Make sure she's expelled from the Union.'

Piers continued sulkily, 'So, anyway, I started a revolution, and I knew what I was working towards. Something bigger than me, bigger than music – I was working to change the world for good. And then what happens? I get caught by some skanky entrapper from the tabloids who exposes me as – shock, horror – somebody who has sex! And somehow, all the good I'm doing, all the positive messages I've helped to promote, are shot down. Killed in the flash of a cheap, supermarket bra strap. She could at least have got some nicer underwear, seeing as she was expensing the lot anyway. And she gave me a cold sore, too.' Another swig. 'Bloody woman, bloody tabloids,' he muttered, struggling to hide the slur in his voice. As the chamber oscillated between shocked horror and astonished amusement, Piers' argument descended into an increasingly drunken ramble, which eventually led to the most recent incident of a leaked sex tape involving him and a washed up actress. 'Between you and me, she was rubbish,' he confided. 'She'd had too much bloody plastic surgery. Her breasts were so far away they were actually a different temperature to the rest of her body and she couldn't tell her nipple from her designer vagina 'cos she'd lost all sensitivity. I had to tug her hair each time she needed to fake an orgasm for the camera!' He shook his head indignantly.

'Point of information!' cried Will, jumping to his feet. 'As I recall, your star had so faded that by the time said actress leaked the tape herself, nobody gave a rat's arse as to who you were. And you were caught selling the remaining unsold DVDs to the Passionate Pensioners channel for 70 per cent off.'

Chloe gasped, holding her hands to her face. 'Will!' she whispered.

'What? He was out of line with you at dinner,' he retorted indignantly as he took his seat again.

Piers slurped down the rest of his tipple and stuck two fingers up in their direction, concluding what had been a rather unexpected debate.

Chapter 4

'Canapé?'

On the proffered silver tray lay row upon row of orderly white lines of powder. Jack Grenzen looked up at Artemis, a final year student who had sashayed over in faded jeans and a backless silver top. Jack was sprawled on the sofa beside another partygoer, drink in hand.

'I've got my Gulfstream outside. Let's snort our way to Argentina!' Jack bellowed, abruptly getting to his feet to jump up and down on the sofa.

Artemis set down the tray and spun around with her arms outstretched in an airplane motion. Then she pulled a face.

'I can't or they'll all trash my house.'

Chloe was watching the exchange with mildly drunken fascination. She couldn't remember exactly how they had ended up at Artemis' house after the debate in the Union. But her parents were out of town and about forty students, along with Jack, had hopped on trains and in cars to the Oxfordshire countryside where Artemis' parents' converted barn was now the scene of revelry, and had been all weekend. More and more people had been coming and going since the early hours of Friday and it was now Sunday evening, so the numbers had thinned to around twenty-five. Chloe didn't think she had stopped being drunk since the drinks after Thursday evening's debate.

And now here was Ol, who'd only arrived that morning. She watched him out of the corner of her eye. Everybody else was rumpled and dirty from days of partying, so when he'd turned up in faded, low-slung jeans and a preppy cotton shirt with the sleeves rolled up, effortlessly casual yet immaculate, like an advert in a glossy fashion magazine, Chloe had felt acutely aware of how dreadful she must look. But he was so flashy and good-looking that he was bound to be a stuck-up idiot, so it didn't matter anyway.

And now he was coming her way. It was getting harder and harder to avoid him but she was determined to do just that. Low music was playing in the background and Ol gravitated towards a group dancing to it, moving in time to the track as he walked in their direction. Chloe wondered how he could pull that off without looking cheesy. He just instinctively knew how to work his body. She waited for him to pluck the prettiest girl aside for a close dance and was surprised when he beckoned to a shy-looking girl with mousy hair loitering awkwardly by the window. After a while, Ol continued on his trajectory towards Chloe.

'Hi, I'm Ol. You're friends with Will, right?'

'Yes. Yes, I am. I'm …my name's—'

'Chloe Constance.' Ol smiled, taking in her sweaty, partied-out appearance. 'You know, Artemis has this incredibly high-tech electrical appliance in her house. It's called a shower.'

Chloe laughed, despite herself. He was still eyeing her sweaty body but he certainly didn't look disgusted by what he saw. Chloe found his gaze quite thrilling.

'Yes, I probably ought to. But you kind of get to a point where you're so far gone there's no point even trying to do anything about it. It feels like a festival here.'

'Why don't you compromise and come for a swim with me?'

'Yes!' Chloe said immediately. She followed him out of the drawing room with its low wooden beams and inviting log fire, through a maze of interconnecting, dimly lit rooms, which made up the substantial but cosy family home. They came to the back door and Ol held it open for her. They walked for a while, until they were alone in the darkness, surrounded by fields. Somewhere to the left were the grass tennis courts and the pool but Chloe couldn't remember where.

'Where's the pool?' She glanced into his dark eyes and felt a tug of excitement. 'I didn't bring a swimsuit.'

'I won't look.' Ol grinned, placing an arm around her to guide her through the darkness towards the outdoor pool.

He kicked off his trainers and was out of his jeans and shirt in seconds. Then he strolled over to the pool in his light blue boxer shorts and dipped a foot in the water. 'You feeling brave? It's not heated!' he called back.

'Hmm? What was that?' Right now, Chloe didn't care what temperature the pool was. Her own temperature was rising steadily as she took in Ol's lean, hard body, from his broad muscular shoulders to his rippled torso, pert rear and long, strong, manly legs. She pulled off her own dress and stood awkwardly in her skimpy lace bra and thong, holding in her stomach as best she could. She heard a splash as Ol jumped into the water and noticed with surprise, and maybe a little disappointment, that he'd been as good as his word and made a point of not looking at her so she wouldn't feel uncomfortable.

She ran after him and jumped into the pool with a scream. He splashed her playfully when she surfaced.

'So, how do you like Oxford so far?' he asked, treading water.

'I love it! Don't you? It's such fun!' *I'd love it even more if you'd make a move on me,* she thought to herself. She felt guilty for having assumed he was awful when, from what she had seen of him, he seemed lovely.

'Yeah, me too.' He grabbed a foam ball floating on the surface of the water and threw it at her. She hit it back and when he returned the hit it flew over her head, landing on the solid ground behind the pool. She forgot her earlier shyness and rose, slowly, out of the pool, wiggling a little as she climbed the steps. Bending to pick up the ball she realized he had a very clear view of her in her near nakedness. As their eyes met she read a barely perceptible glimmer of lust, but soon enough he began chatting politely about various new friends in college. Chloe slipped back into the water.

She tried to concentrate, to muster up some sparky banter but frankly, it was hard enough just stopping herself from jumping into his arms; she couldn't be expected to sound clever at the same time. She realized he'd asked her a question so she stopped staring at him and giggled.

Ol frowned before breaking into a loud laugh. 'You know, I didn't realize the anti-tuition fee protests were so funny …I don't think you've really been following. Must be true what they say about blondes.' He spun his finger around beside his head in a 'dizzy' gesture.

'Hey!' Chloe shouted, splashing him as hard as she could.

'Oi! That was cheeky.' Ol grabbed her and lifted her out of the water with one arm and threw her over his shoulder. He spanked her arse and she gave a delighted shriek but all too soon he'd deposited her back in the water. *Surely he'll make a move now,* she thought, swimming closer, bottom still smarting.

'Hey, should we dry off and go join the others?' Ol asked, climbing out of the pool.

'Oh, er, yeah,' replied Chloe despondently.

Chapter 5

Hungover and homesick for the first time since she'd got there, Chloe wandered through Oxford city centre and then over the bridge towards Cowley until, without even thinking about where she was going, she arrived at The Club. She stopped outside, contemplating the derelict door.

'Er, I'm ...in the club,' she faltered, then was buzzed in. She looked around but didn't see anyone she recognized, so she got herself a glass of wine and sank into a chair at a little wooden corner table, alone. She took out her phone and checked the history again, hoping it had all been a bad dream, but no, she really had called Ol eight times since that night in the pool.

'Oh, it's you, Chloe. Why are you crying?'

'Isabel!' Chloe's eyes lit up briefly. 'It's nothing, really. Just being a bit silly over a boy who hasn't returned any of my calls.'

'Aww, sweetheart, we've all been there,' Isabel said, sliding into a chair opposite her. 'It just takes some women longer than others to work it out.'

'Work out what?'

'When you're with them, act like they're the only man in the world, but as soon as you part, they don't exist.'

'Really?'

Isabel nodded. 'Try it. Then they're the ones chasing you down, reduced to needy wrecks.'

'Well, I don't want any men like that,' Chloe said. She stared into the distance.

'Up to you.' Isabel shrugged, beckoning the waiter. 'Champagne, please. It's an emergency!'

'Who is he, anyway?' she said, turning back to Chloe.

'Him!' Chloe wailed as Ol walked into The Club with his arm flung over Artemis' shoulder.

Isabel glanced casually around then turned back to Chloe with sparkling eyes. 'So *that's* Ol Osaloni.'

'Don't look,' Chloe hissed. 'I was way too forward. All those phone calls. I know it's not very becoming to beg, but I can't help it; I've always liked boys. When I was little I refused to eat vegetables, apart from carrots, turnips and cucumbers. Mummy said it was a sign. Then when I was eight I refused to let adult guests stay over at our place in Hampshire unless they shared a bed like Mummy and Daddy. I felt it was so wrong for adults to sleep alone that when the Mayor of London came to stay without his wife, I took the cat, put one of my dresses and a frilly cap on her and snuck into the Mayor's room where I left her to sleep snuggled beside him on the bed. I just remember an almighty shriek when my mother discovered them in the morning. We've never seen the Mayor since. My parents nearly murdered me when they found out what I did.'

Isabel hooted with laughter. 'You just didn't want him to be lonely – your parents should have known that.'

'What do your parents do, Isabel?'

Isabel's eyes went dull.

'Did I say something wrong? I—'

'No,' Isabel said. 'Nothing's wrong.' She thought of the crash. She had been only three years old, just a toddler. She couldn't even remember most of it. *'Mama, Mama! What is happening? Why is everybody screaming? Mama, why are you praying? Mama, kiss, kiss, kiss, Vita.'*

That was all she could remember saying. But she could still hear the moment of impact. The sound of squealing breaks and cracking glass. A scream, a whisper. And then nothing.

'Mamaaaaaaaaaa!'

Isabel heard the sound of the crash every day. It had taken her parents from her. And after the crash had come the recovery, the homes, the journeys and then 'the flight'. She thought of the patronising, pitying, abusive people she'd come across in her short years. There would be no more.

'Isabel, are you OK?'

'Yes, yes, I'm fine. My parents – they're diplomats.' The words came easy and she could look Chloe in the eye.

'Cool.' Something in the way their eyes met told Chloe not to ask any more. They were silent for a few seconds.

'OK,' Isabel said with a wicked smile. 'Why don't you do something to take your mind off Ol …I was watching you at the Union the other day.'

'What? You were—'

'And I was thinking, *you* should run for president.'

'What, me? But I know nothing about debate or foreign affairs. I'd—'

'Darling, you'd be perfect. You'd be a sweet and charming breath of fresh air, and you've grown up around important people. You're the perfect hostess – you'd be brilliant at looking after all those politicians and celebrities that come to speak there.'

Chloe flushed happily and sat up straighter.

Isabel smiled imperceptibly. 'And we'll get Will to help us with our campaign. I'm pretty sure I've got him where I want him.' Isabel winked. 'And he knows the ropes – he was president in Michaelmas Term of his second year.'

'So I found out,' Chloe said. 'Somehow it didn't surprise me. He's very good at making you think you're the only person in the world when you speak to him, isn't he? It's that soft voice which really makes you listen, and then the gentle creasing of the forehead, which really makes you feel he's listening back. Classic!' She laughed and then leaned closer to Isabel. 'You know what, it might be fun. Nobody would ever believe it if I made it! Yes, it could be very fun indeed.'

'Two dangerously hot women in a corner, whispering. I should stay away if I know what's good for me.' They heard Ol's voice before they saw him pull up a chair.

Chloe looked down at the table to avoid the moment when Ol and Isabel first saw each other properly. She might as well just go home now. When she looked up, though, Ol was gazing at her. She smiled.

'I enjoyed our swim, Chloe … sorry I missed your calls, by the way. I do this thing at night. It's called sleeping.'

Isabel snorted and Chloe grinned sheepishly.

'So tell me, what are you guys plotting?' Ol said, after he and Isabel had been introduced.

'Chloe has decided to run for presidency of the Union,' Isabel announced.

'How can I help?' Ol asked.

The girls looked at each other, eyebrows raised.

'Really?' said Chloe.

'Yes, really. And you can't just run; you'll need to work your way up first. You know, take on boring, standing committee roles first. You might become treasurer or librarian first, if you win enough votes. I don't know much about the Union, but I gather these are more administrative roles where you can learn the ropes and show your stamina and commitment. The real excitement and prestige will come at the next rung, if you make it that far, when you can run for president. It's the world's most prestigious debating society. It's a life-changing role. Ah, and here's the man to tell us more.'

'Hey, kids.' Will sauntered across the floor to join them. 'So how long has this mothers' meeting been going on for? Some of us *finalists* actually have work to do.'

'We're talking about the Union. Chloe wants to run for president.' Isabel pulled out a chair for Will and patted the seat.

'I see.' Will slid himself in beside her. 'You're gonna need a hot-shit campaign for starters. You do know who you're up against?'

'Who?' the three of them asked eagerly.

'Piper Kenton.'

Isabel scoffed. 'She doesn't have any friends – who's going to vote for her?'

'She keeps to herself socially,' Will replied. 'I guess she's shy in some ways but I've seen her around lots and she's involved in a lot of activities. She's smart and she seems super focused. Don't underestimate her.'

'Let the game begin.' Isabel raised her glass of champagne and the boys raised theirs.

Finally Chloe gave a resigned and muted 'Cheers, I suppose!' She felt terrified.

Chapter 6

'Hi, I'm here to enquire about working for *Cherwell*?'

'OK, what do you know about us?' asked the editor.

'Well, I know that you're one of the oldest student publications in the UK and you've launched the careers of a number of my favourite journalists. That's what I want to go into after Oxford.'

The editor, a bespectacled twenty-year-old with an unruly mass of curly auburn hair, gave a welcoming smile but didn't say anything, so Piper felt the need to say more.

'I was going to try to be an attorney, but, that's what my brother, Tyler, is trying to do back home in the States. He's one of those enviably moral people who genuinely does want to fight for justice, not for money. That's probably why things haven't been going so good for him! Anyway, he's pretty brilliant and if *he's* struggling with work then I'm not even going to try to compete. I really hope I can make a difference this way instead. If the potential of the media is harnessed by people with integrity, it can be such a force for good in society.'

The editor finally spoke. 'What other aspects of university life are you involved in? I like our journalists to be active within the student body – you know, plugged in to what's going on.'

'Well, I do a lot of sport, like tennis, and I've just got into more unusual sports like parkour, which is essentially finding the quickest and most efficient way to navigate physical obstacles in one's surrounding environment. So, like, if I was doing it now I might vault over your desk to get to the door. I'm not too good; I've only just started, but it's fun.'

'Very cool!' The editor looked impressed.

'And, actually, I was also hoping to run for a position in the Union.'

'Is that so? And what is it about the Union that interests you?'

'Its incredible power to disseminate useful ideas. On a huge scale. Much like the power of the media.'

'That's very noble of you. I'm not sure many share your selfless motivations. The last *Cherwell* staff member who got involved with the Union had a nervous breakdown and was hospitalized from the stress of all the bitching, backstabbing and politics.'

'I'm no saint.' Piper laughed.

'You seem pretty saintly to me right now – just what I'm looking for! So, what sort of writing have you done before? If any? Most students start out here, so don't worry.'

'Well,' Piper hesitated, 'I did some journalism on the side while at school – back home in San Francisco.' She handed the editor a portfolio of her articles, some of which had been published in newspapers across America, including *The New York Times*.

'Wow! Serious drive. Serious talent.' The editor finished reading a piece headed: "Seek new friends for success. Why those closest to you are the most likely to underestimate your ability." 'This is interesting. Fresh.' She looked up. 'Welcome to *Cherwell*.'

Just then a dishevelled, long-haired guy sauntered into the

editor's office, cigarette hanging out of the side of his pouty mouth. He carried a huge canvas with both hands and deposited it with remarkable care against the wall.

'Can you put that out in here, Sam?' said the editor.

'Yeah, sure,' he said, making no effort whatsoever to extinguish the cigarette.

'This is Piper Kenton. She'll be writing for *Cherwell*,' said the editor. 'Piper, Sam Smith studies fine art at Ruskin. He's kindly agreed to guest edit a special art edition of the paper.'

'Nice idea.' Piper extended her hand.

Sam shook it firmly. 'Really nice to meet you.' Piper noticed that the rain which had been falling incessantly on the window-pane let up and a smidgen of sun shone through.

Sam dashed for the door, almost tripping over his beloved painting in his haste. 'Sorry but I've been waiting days for the sun – I need to paint.'

The editor shook her head fondly. 'He's astonishingly passionate about his work.'

Chapter 7

Chloe, Isabel, Ol and Will were sprawled on Chloe's unmade bed. 'OK, step one of our plan,' declared Isabel, 'is to dance.'

Ol and Will were too busy admiring the softness of her lips to take in what she was saying at first.

'Sorry, what?' Will asked after a while.

'Dance,' she repeated. 'We will go out every night and make a lot of friends. And all of those friends will vote for Chloe.'

Chloe cringed. 'I'm terrible at chatting people up.'

'Just dance,' said Isabel. 'Dance every night like it could be your last.' She cast down her eyes.

'Are you OK, Isabel?' asked Ol. 'You look sad.'

'Whatever,' Isabel said, oblivious to the glances the other three were giving each other. She stared out of the window. 'What? Can't I look out of the window for one damned second without having my every move scrutinized?' she snapped, immediately covering her mouth as though she had surprised herself.

Ol took her in his arms and hugged her. 'Look at me,' he said sternly. To deflect attention from her embarrassing outburst, she looked up at him in a way that usually crippled men and he looked down at her in a way that usually devastated women, and they both saw straight through each other and laughed. But they still held each other, letting one another go reluctantly.

Feeling awkward, Chloe gave a nervous laugh. She put down her notepad and pen; she hadn't taken any notes on strategy anyway.

Isabel brought the conversation quickly back on track. 'It's not really about friends,' she said. 'It's about "what can you do for me if I vote for you?" It's about alliances. But you need to make these alliances with as many people as you can.'

'Well, anyways, sounds like you have the plan under control,' Chloe remarked. 'My brain's hurting with all this strategizing. Shove off all of you so I can get ready for round one at Piers Gaveston's Halloween party tonight.'

Isabel stretched out a willowy leg and rolled her fishnet stockings higher up her thighs. Over them she pulled on a black, shiny, latex catsuit with an inbuilt waist-cinching, breast-enhancing corset. It was so tight that it was a gymnastic feat just getting into it, but little by little she inched it on.

'Breathe in,' Chloe called from behind her, glass of prosecco in one hand, the hooks of the corset in the other. Isabel reached back and extracted Chloe's prosecco glass.

'You'll need both hands for this.' She grimaced, downing the rest of the glass herself.

'One, two, three, in!' Isabel held her breath as Chloe gathered all her strength to fasten the corset. 'There, all done.'

Isabel spun around. 'What do you think?'

'Wait a minute.' Chloe ran to the corner of her room and grabbed a pair of towering stilettos studded with silver spikes. 'Put your shoes on.'

Isabel stepped into the killer heels and the two girls stood looking at their reflections in the mirror.

'Fuck! I am so nervous!' Chloe giggled, extracting a deep red lipliner and drawing fake droplets of blood on her chin. 'I'm shaking like a pair of double Ds on a bumpy ride.'

'What was that? I can't hear you properly with that gag through your mouth.'

Chloe pulled the gag aside and repeated, 'I am *so* nervous.'

'Just think of all the hot guys.' Isabel turned around to check out her latex-encased butt.

'Yeah but they'll all be so much cooler than me,' Chloe wailed. Piers Gaveston was another of Oxford's exclusive men-only societies and she'd heard that only a select few guys were invited to join. 'I've heard they blindfold you on the way out so you don't know how to get back to town and then they won't take you home until you've tried every drug available and had sex with at least three Piers Gaveston members!'

They stared at each other and Chloe gulped loudly. Then they picked up their prosecco glasses and clinked.

'Let's go!' Isabel said, flashing a confident smile as she ushered Chloe out of her room.

They made their way through the college grounds and into the centre of Oxford, where rows of specially commandeered buses were waiting to transport the select group of 200 or so invited students deep into the woods where a fetish-themed Halloween party organized by the Piers Gaveston society was to take place.

As they arrived at the buses they gasped at the spectacle. What at first appeared to be a sea of black leather became, on closer inspection, an array of students in a variety of customized fetish wear. Chloe gawped in awe as Artemis rode in on a gleaming chestnut horse, parting the crowds as she progressed. She wore only a black leather bikini that showcased her perfect figure, Titian curls flowing behind her.

'I'll follow behind the buses,' she was shouting to a strapping fourth year English and French undergrad who Chloe had often spotted and lusted after while pretending to read a book on post-war feminism at the Bodleian Library. Two six-foot-plus Classics students, who had both won Blues for representing Oxford at boxing, strutted past wearing pink tutus and red lipstick. Their lunchboxes bulged obscenely in their tutus. They pushed theatrically at strands of loose blonde hair falling from their wigs as they looked Isabel up and down approvingly. She ignored them.

'Where are Ol and Will?' Chloe fretted.

'Jesus!' Isabel burst out laughing as, just at that moment, their friends descended on them wearing only rubber underpants and copious amounts of black eyeliner.

The girls clutched their stomachs in laughter. The final part of their costumes had arrived. Isabel reached into her bag and pulled out two leashes, attaching one to each of the boys, who both dutifully got down on all fours to be yanked along.

'Here you go.' Isabel handed Will's leash to Chloe and kept a tight hold of Ol's for herself.

'Thanks, I can see what you're doing there,' muttered Chloe, gazing longingly at Ol's broad, strong back. It begged to be stroked.

Isabel smirked.

The Piers Gaveston members were easily identifiable as they were all wearing floor-length furs left open to reveal bizarre costumes ranging from full drag to hardcore gimp outfits. A rabbit fur-clad hottie with a military accent and a commanding manner waved the group onto the nearest bus.

'I don't like fur,' Isabel retorted, shooting him a dirty look.

Once on the party bus, the already carnival-like atmosphere was turned up a notch. The driver cranked up Kings of Leon on the stereo and the Piers Gaveston members at the front of the bus began passing back bottles of beer, wine and plastic cups.

By now evening had set in and it was getting dark. Two couples were already snogging furiously in the back of the bus and there was so much excited chatter that it was almost impossible to be heard above the noise. Just as the bus was about to set off, the door opened again and ten more whooping students jumped on so that there were no longer enough seats.

'You're gonna have to get cosy,' shouted the boys at the front of the bus and Chloe wasted no time in leaping onto Ol's rubber-clad lap.

'Another seat here,' she called breathlessly down the aisle, pointing out her vacated seat. Her large breasts quivered gaily in the cups of her corset as she brandished them under Ol's nose each time she turned to gaze up at him. Isabel climbed onto Will and various others did the same until everybody was seated, then the engine fired up and the bus roared out of town.

'Forget the woods,' Chloe said to Isabel, 'this is enough of a party already.' She didn't want the journey to end and was enjoying writhing around in Ol's lap. He put his arms around her waist, apparently to stop her from falling if the bus came to a sudden stop.

'You look delicious,' he murmured in her ear, taking in her tight, short leather skirt and enchantingly inadequate top. As his firm hands began to slowly caress her body she felt incredibly turned on.

All too soon, the bus reached the party site in the middle of the woods. It had been meticulously prepared earlier in the week. Two gold marquees lit with flashing lights housed a disco and a 'massage parlour', staffed by volunteer Gaveston members.

Outside, a commercial-sized cinema projector screen had been set up under the stars and was now showing porn. Chloe gasped in shock as a particularly graphic image was zoomed in on. Buses that had arrived earlier had already offloaded their passengers and some were milling around, drinking and laughing. Others were dancing feverishly both in and outside of the disco tent where a DJ was spinning modern remixes of 1980's classics.

'Come and dance!' yelled an ecstatic girl Chloe had never met before, grabbing her hand.

'Maybe later.' She laughed, looking curiously into her dilated pupils. She suspected the girl was high on more than just life. She turned to say as much to Isabel but she had disappeared in the throng, as had Will and Ol. Surrounded by worldly, older students, high on drugs that she had never used, Chloe's heart began to beat a little faster.

'Come!' the wild girl ordered again.

Chloe followed helplessly, feeling like Samson without his hair now that her tight new group of friends had vanished. She grabbed a vodka from a tray being circulated by another Piers Gaveston host, swaggering in chinchilla, and drank it quickly to give her courage. A pimply physics nerd grabbed her and muttered something about the laws of attraction as he thrust a sweaty hand up her skirt. She tried to stop him but he became aggressive.

'What are you even doing here dressed up like a fat slut if you don't want to have any fun?' A garlicky stench hit her nostrils as he hissed at her and she blinked back humiliated tears.

Suddenly the jerk was flung aside by a furious Ol who towered above him. He rushed to put his arm around Chloe. Will was hot on his tail.

'Anyone would look fat beside you, Horace, you anaemic little runt. We all know you only got an invite to stop you from snitching.'

Greatly relieved to see her friends, Chloe perked up. Even the 'fat' comment had stopped stinging now that Ol was cupping the soft curve of her stomach and whispering that she 'was so sexy he hardly knew what to do with himself'.

By now, drunk and horny as hell, Chloe felt like telling him exactly what he could do with himself. He could throw her down on the floor, take off her clothes and make frantic love to her like she'd imagined every day since she'd met him.

Instead she giggled and murmured 'Really?' in his ear, brushing his earlobe with her mouth.

'Yes, really,' he repeated. He bent his head and brushed his lips over hers. Immediately she pressed herself against him.

'Take off your knickers,' Ol whispered to Chloe as he slipped an arm around her waist and guided her into the disco tent.

'Excuse me?'

'Take them off. Now. Go to the loo.'

'Alright!' Chloe ran, hopelessly excited, to the loo, and in a cubicle she slipped off her thong and put it in the side pocket of her skirt. She squatted on the portaloo and was surprised at how long it took for her to empty her bladder. She'd drunk more than she realized.

She washed her hands and put more mascara on her already make-up clogged lashes. She never put anything much on her skin but she now wished she had something to lessen the redness of her face. She made her way back to the centre of the disco tent and found Ol.

She and Ol began to dance and she let him lead her as she wiggled in front of him. Some leggy final year students in short trench coats belted at the waist jumped up onto the podium and began to dance and fool around, cooing with delight as the guys in the tent positioned themselves so they could watch.

'Why don't you get on up there, too?' murmured Ol into Chloe's ear.

'I can't – it's so high and I'm not wearing any undies.' Chloe was appalled.

'Nobody will see if you don't attempt anything too athletic. No karate kicks! Now up you get.' He patted her rump and pushed her up onto the podium.

She began to dance, embarrassed at first, but loosening up when she realized the world hadn't stopped and everyone was just getting on with having a great time. On the podium it was a bit of a mad free-for-all. Ol had never taken his eyes off her, and now he moved right up to the podium so that he was directly below her. He gazed up and she knew that if she parted her legs just a fraction he would be able to see. She shimmied down to the floor to bring her face opposite his and kiss him, giving him an X-rated view in the process.

'And you seemed like such a sweet girl,' Ol said. 'It's always the demure ones.'

Ol had come to the party prepared and had pre-booked a suite at the six-star hotel near to where the illicit party was taking place.

He arranged for a car to pick him up and, as he paid the driver double to hurry, it didn't take them long to find it.

While plush and grand with antique-looking furniture and plumped up pillows and cushions, the gleaming suite was also surprisingly homely. There were floral curtains, comfy rugs and a sprinkling of fresh flower arrangements.

He pulled Chloe to him and began kissing her, but she pushed him away.

'How can you kiss me like this? I'm sweating like a pig. I feel disgusting.'

'This is becoming quite a theme. Let me wash you, then.'

He undressed her and threw off the jeans and T-shirt he'd changed into for the ride back. He tried not to smirk as she drew in her breath involuntarily at the sight of his girth. Taking her hand, he led her first to the steam room to get her even more hot and sweaty, enjoying the slickness of her skin, before carrying her to the marble bathroom, where he soaped her under the shower. She loved the feel of his slippery hands sliding all over her body. He caressed her from the crevices of her fingers to the tips of her toes. He lingered at her breasts, soaping them down lovingly and then bringing her to a climax with his fingers when he reached her clitoris. Just when she thought he'd given her all the pleasure she was capable of, he dried her with a fluffy white towel and laid her on the super king-sized bed where he reached for a condom and began, tantalisingly slowly, to make love to her.

'Fuck me hard,' she shouted, thrusting against him, unable to bear it.

'You asked for it,' he groaned, giving her all she wanted and then some.

It felt like they were at it all night, but eventually they drifted off, waking at intervals to make love again, until Chloe fell into a deep, exhausted and highly satisfied sleep.

When she woke, jolted by the sound of weeping, she reached out for Ol and realized with a start that it was Isabel's slender waist in her hands.

'Isabel,' she whispered. 'Isabel, are you OK?' She prodded her friend gently but she was fast asleep. Eyes still clamped shut, Isabel moaned and rolled over to face the other direction while Chloe looked on in puzzlement, trying to piece together the night's events.

'What happened?' she asked as soon as Isabel woke up. 'Where's Ol?'

'Oh, Ol went back to the party. He found me there and said you were sleeping in the hotel he'd sorted. I was shattered so I asked if I could go and sleep there too, so he sent me here in a taxi. He and Will are still partying hard, I should think.'

'What? He shags me and then runs back to the party?!' Chloe was outraged. 'Let's get out of here, go back and see what they're up to. It's ten a.m., for Christ's sake.'

By the time Chloe and Isabel had returned to the woods in a taxi, having twice got lost en route, the party was much more subdued, with only a few hardcore revellers still dancing. One of those was Ol in a corner, and riveted by his conversation was a petite Chinese girl in a black all-in-one and a black cat mask over her eyes.

Spotting the girls, he beckoned them over gaily. 'Hey, have you met Lin Li?'

Will appeared at their side with – incredibly at this hour – more drinks. Noticing Chloe's crestfallen face, he slung an arm around her and whispered, 'I'm sorry. I did warn you what he was like. He's a lovely guy but he's just not mature enough for a relationship.'

'I see you've already heard what happened then,' muttered Chloe.

She looked around for Isabel but already a circle of guys had gathered around, closing in on her, offering drinks, dances and even a hand in marriage in the case of one boy. Isabel's eyes were shining, as though she had not been up partying and hardly slept all night. She laughed uproariously, flirting and bantering, seeming in her element. It was hard to stop watching her.

Chloe wandered off out of the main area and through the trees, hardly caring if she got herself lost again. She was all alone now, or at least she thought she was, until she spotted a scruffy guy with days' old stubble and long brown hair leaning against a tree some way ahead. He was looking at her intently. She stood very still, peering at him out of the corner of her eye. He stood completely still. She moved very slowly to the left, only for him to repeat her movements. She ran a hand nervously through her hair. The boy did the same and he looked so strange that she couldn't help but laugh.

'Chloe, what are you doing? Why are you on your own?' Isabel appeared behind her out of nowhere with Will and another pal in tow.

'Will, do you know who that …' Chloe turned around to see if she could spot the guy but he'd disappeared. 'Oh, that's weird.'

In the distance the sound of the buses kicking into gear could be heard. It was time to head back to the city centre.

The trip back was a much quieter affair, with nearly everyone sleeping. Chloe spent the journey tormented with images of Ol and the catsuit girl swirling in her mind. So great was her jealousy and despair, she didn't notice the strange young man following her all the way back to her college.

Chapter 8

Sam Smith turned up the Rolling Stones really high and sang along as he painted. Another girl had told him he looked exactly like Mick Jagger had done at twenty and now he couldn't get this song out of his head.

He flung the paint at the canvas, which he'd laid down on the floor. He was only wearing jeans and he took these and his underpants off, then threw himself on the ground. He smothered himself in the paint, rolling around over the canvas, going into a meditative state where, despite his frantic movements, his mind was completely clear. Eventually he fell asleep.

When he woke up two hours later, the canvas was stuck to him. As he annihilated it in the process of extracting himself, he felt the satisfaction of seeing a piece come together. The beastly work that he had soiled was a thing of beauty. He hung it beside other works in his studio near where he studied at Oxford's Ruskin School of Drawing and Fine Art. As an afterthought, he picked up a small paintbrush, dipped it in some matt black paint and scrawled 'beast' across it. Now it was finished. He cried a little bit. He would deliver it to her when he had washed all the paint off himself.

'What are you doing?' Chloe peered over Isabel's shoulder at the list she was writing, face fixed in deep concentration.

'What list could possibly include fashion designer Clemency Clementine, billionaire investor Warren Buffett and human rights activist Shami Chakrabarti?'

'These are some of the people I think you ought to invite to the Union when you make president.' Isabel squeezed Chloe's hand. 'I know you'll make it! This week you'll be elected librarian and by the end of next term you'll be president.'

'You know, I'm really not sure I can be bothered with all this anymore, and I'm not that keen on anyone there – it's all so pompous and aggressive.'

'Nonsense,' said Isabel. 'You're always saying that, but you'll love it when you're there presiding over everything and your mother comes to watch one of the debates. You'll show her.'

Chloe sighed and switched on the TV in her room. The biggest of their rooms, they tended to always hang out here. A man in his thirties flashed up on the screen. The caption seemed to indicate that he was a newly appointed cabinet minister in the ruling Lib–Con Party. Archibald Arden, Secretary of State for Business.

'Is he handsome?' asked Isabel.

'I was just trying to work that out. Not handsome as such but … he draws you in, doesn't he? And he's got expressive eyes.'

'But hungry; they're hungry eyes. He knows what he wants.' Isabel bared her teeth as though they were fangs and growled.

'I know what *you* want,' giggled Chloe.

'No I don't,' snapped Isabel, jumping up to gently clamp Chloe's mouth shut. But when she returned to the desk she added Archibald Arden's name to her list and underlined it. Chewing on her pen she contemplated her list, deep in thought. She picked up the day's newspapers and began skimming through them once more, searching for more figures of interest for her list.

She stopped to look closer at a story headed: "Charles Sweet sues *Newsfunnel* for defamation following his acquittal on people trafficking charges". Mega rich entrepreneur Charles Sweet's name seemed to pop up in the news every now and again, usually for his business prowess. This time it seemed he had been accused of a heinous crime of which he was found in court to be innocent. He was now suing *Newsfunnel* for suggesting that anybody with evidence which could prosecute him was simply too frightened to come forward, hence why he was acquitted. The picture of him was particularly creepy, which was the reason she'd stopped to read the article in the first place.

About to point out his unsettling photo to Chloe, she was interrupted by the sound of something sliding slowly across the floor.

'Aarrgh!' Both girls jumped in surprise.

'OK. What the hell is that?' Isabel reached down and picked up the canvas that had been slid into the room. She rushed to open the door, looking left and right down the corridor, but there was nobody to be seen.

'I knew I should never have got involved in the Union.' Chloe shook and trembled as she eyed the huge, mutilated painting which had been ripped and stabbed and finally scrawled all over with the word 'beast'.

'It must be because I've been elected librarian.' She'd known an election would make her a few enemies alongside all her new 'friends', but who could hate her this much?

'I actually think it's kind of stunning.' Isabel propped the picture against a wall and took a step back to contemplate it. She didn't speak for a few minutes, just staring at it. 'It's beautiful.'

Chapter 9

The pit of Piper's stomach felt hollow and her throat was dry. She knew what she was about to do was dangerous. Although Michaelmas term was now over and it was officially the Christmas vacation, Piper had decided to spend an extra couple of weeks up at Oxford. Eight week terms were just not enough time to fit in all her work at the Union now that she'd been elected treasurer, as well as keep up on her sport, ace her essays and investigate for *Cherwell*. Now she was taking advantage of a less crowded city to score her biggest scoop yet.

She began planning her route. She would go the least busy way so that she could use her parkour moves without being gawped at. Practising the sport always helped her deal with stressful situations. She approached it like chess. As a mind game where she pre-planned her moves, as much as a physical one. She first worked out the best and most efficient way to shift her body from A to B, constantly sharpening her technique and fine-tuning her spatial awareness.

Jogging to the gates of her college she vaulted over them, doing a body roll on landing to lessen the impact. The porters watched her from their lodge but didn't bat an eyelid. Piper continued on at high speed, swinging, cat-crawling and vaulting wherever she could. As she flew through the air she temporarily forgot that she was on her way to what could be the most terrifying experience of her life.

Within minutes she heard the rumbling of trains and the station became visible. Entering Oxford Station, she glanced at the clock suspended high above in the main atrium. It was 8 p.m. She boarded the train to London. Her timing was perfect. She would be at King's Cross shortly after 9 p.m. Settling in her seat she reached into her bag and extracted her copy of an old *Cherwell* article dated 10 December 1990, then began reading:

> *The naked body of 19-year-old Oxford University student Laurelie Fairlie was found in an alleyway in the red light district of London's King's Cross at 4.55 a.m. this morning. The victim had been strangled following what appears to have been an uncommonly violent and sadistic rape. A man was captured on a nearby CCTV camera fleeing the scene of the crime and police are appealing to anybody who may be able to help identify him.*

Once more, Piper was irrevocably drawn to the grainy image of the suspect. His sallow appearance and lips twisted into a thin smirk were unappealing, but what chilled her to her core was the evil of his piercing eyes. She quickly folded up the paper to remove his face from view and ignored the sick feeling threatening to overcome her. The man's face made her feel that way every time she saw his picture but she knew how unreasonable it was to form any sort of critical opinion based on the look in somebody's eye.

She tried to forget him. After all, subsequent reports at the time had concluded that the suspect had been identified but released without charge. And now, on the same date years later, the murder was still unresolved.

When the train reached Paddington Station it didn't take Piper long to transfer to the London Underground and arrive at King's Cross, her final destination. She searched for a sign indicating the nearest washroom and found that it was just yards to her left. Taking a deep breath she marched towards it, paying the twenty pence necessary to cross the barrier. Once inside she headed to the furthest cubicle, pushed open the door and stepped in, bolting it shut behind her with a shaking hand. She rummaged around in her bag and pulled out the tight white cotton skirt she had bought for next to nothing at a charity shop. Swiftly wriggling out of her J.Crew jeans, cotton T-shirt and battered leather jacket, she squeezed herself into the skirt and a tight, low-cut lycra top. Not bothering with tights, she stepped into white PVC shoes, with the highest heels she had ever worn before. Finally she threw her leather jacket back on and, taking out a small compact, kohled her eyes, put on too much foundation and smudged on some cheap red lipstick. She knew she was going to freeze but she was prepared to suffer for her story. Besides, the December weather was the least she had to fear.

Clutching her bag she marched back out into the main station and then outside through the nearest exit, heading for the famous red-light district. She hurried to escape detection by any circulating police officers, half hoping she wouldn't succeed. Her nerves had turned to sheer terror as she found herself alone in the dark, cold night.

Although much of King's Cross had been cleaned up since Laurelie Fairlie's fateful tenure there, there were still areas where prostitution and crack abuse were rife and one of those areas was the very same alleyway in which Laurelie's body had been found. Piper slowed down as she approached it. She was struggling to breathe. All she wanted to do was run as fast as she could in the opposite direction. Seemingly out of nowhere a feverishly scratching junkie in dirt-encrusted clothes and a wild, unshaven face staggered past her into the alleyway, stopping at the entrance. He didn't seem to notice her in his haste. He unbuttoned his jeans and let them fall to the ground. Piper froze, unsure of what he would do and too frightened to react. The man was now naked below the waist and he opened his clenched fist to reveal a syringe. He injected it purposefully into his groin. Immediately his eyes glazed over and he collapsed back against the wall, where he remained for what seemed to Piper like an inordinate amount of time.

And then he saw her.

Piper did what she always did at times of grave uncertainty. She waited. The junkie looked her slowly up and down. She bit her lip and was all set to make a dash for it back in the direction in which she'd come when he nodded convivially and gazed in the opposite direction, finally pulling up his jeans. She was of little further interest to him. At that moment Piper remembered that to him she was not an Oxford undergrad but a dime-a-dozen hooker simply going about her business. She felt a surge of adrenaline and sauntered past him into the alleyway and began walking down it.

At the other end stood a thin, knock-kneed girl with hair scraped back into a tight knot. She puffed on a cigarette as she walked slowly back and forth, her shiny knee-high boots and mass of gold jewellery glinting in the dim light of the streetlamp. Her puny bottom was encased in a tight mini skirt not unlike Piper's. She kept as warm as she could with a bulky black puffa jacket.

As Piper approached she was shocked to realize that the girl, if you could still call her that, was much older than she'd appeared from afar. Or was premature ageing just another hazard of the job?

The prostitute scowled at her. Perhaps she was protecting her territory. She took her eyes off Piper only briefly to reach for her cigarette packet, scowling again to see that it was empty. Piper grabbed the opportunity, silently thanking her foresight in buying the wretched things. She pulled from her bag a pack of Marlboro Lights and held it out.

'I'm not 'ere to cause trouble,' she offered in her best *Eastenders* accent. 'I'm, err, I'm new on the scene and just trying to get to grips with the area.'

'Yeah. I ain't seen you an' all.' The woman stopped scowling and grew thoughtful. 'It's dangerous here,' she added after some time.

'I know,' agreed Piper. 'What about that crazy murder all them years ago? Laurelie somefink or uvver.'

'Sweet,' the woman muttered.

'Sorry? Sweet?' Piper was confused.

'That was before my time; there's been many more murders since. But none half as sick as what that nutbag did to her. You know, I could tell you a—'

A car slowed to a halt just outside the alleyway and its headlights momentarily illuminated the narrow space.

'I'm off,' she told Piper, stubbing out her cigarette with the worn toe of her boot. 'You better be gone by the time I get back.

Good luck.' She smiled and wiggled outside to meet the car. Piper watched her grimacing at something her punter was saying. She seemed to know him. She got in and the car drove off, leaving Piper all alone. She peered through the darkness in the other direction. Yes, the junkie too had disappeared.

She began pacing up and down, just as the other woman had. She tried to imagine how Laurelie would have felt, on this very night in 1990. How nobody had known about her secret life.

Then she felt an arm around her waist and a hand squeezing her neck.

And everything went black.

Chapter 10

Piper was not the only student spending most of her Christmas vacation at college. The finalists knew that this period was make-or-break time. A time to make up for too much fun in previous years, or to secure that coveted double first, before checking out of university with passport intact. A passport to a life of great success and high esteem.

Will sat stiffly in Professor Crayson's study and waited for the great man's verdict on his dissertation.

Professor Crayson spent even longer than usual wiping his glasses before picking up the essay and clearing his throat.

'Flashes of brilliance, William, but ultimately lazy. It needs improving. You're too fond of a shortcut; a glib phrase here to distract from a gaping hole there.' He crossed one skinny leg over the over and looked up with a smirk. 'You know, you'd make an excellent politician.'

'I want a first class degree,' said Will.

'I'm not sure you deserve one.' The professor looked him challengingly in the eye.

'I'm sure I don't.' Will grinned. 'But you know as well as I do that our world is not a meritocracy.'

Professor Crayson took out a pen and ran his beady eyes over Will's dissertation once more. He drew the pen across the entire thing and then back again so that a gigantic cross marred the work.

'In that case, start again.' He closed his eyes and looked up at the ceiling as though deep in thought and concentration. 'And give me something that not only *flashes* brilliance but is so blindingly bright throughout that it inflicts *pain* upon the reader. A tortuous sense of profound incomprehension that such genius is possible. Rather than the mere boredom and occasional pitying laughter that your current work mostly induces.'

'I'm going to miss you, Professor!' Will got to his feet with a fond smile for the eccentric man.

'Now get out of my sight. I've got work to do.' Crayson hunched over his writing desk and picked up the hefty tome he had been reading when Will arrived.

Will strolled back across the quad and out through the college gates to pick up a sandwich from the nearby deli. Beside the deli was the medical centre, a trove of medical information and the surgery of a number of campus doctors. As he approached he thought he saw the back of a familiar figure emerging from the medical centre.

'Isabel? Isabel, is that you?'

The figure hurried away but Will could tell it was Isabel just by the way she walked.

'Isabel, hey, wait for me!'

'Oh, er, hi Will.' Isabel turned sheepishly.

'What are you doing here over Christmas? I thought you were going to the Caribbean?'

'Oh, I, er, needed to get some stuff done. Oh my god, did

you see Piper's story in *Cherwell*?' she asked, quickly changing the subject.

'Yep, she's fearless! Retracing Laurelie's footsteps all these years later. That was ingenious, and she wrote it up so well. A really spooky, riveting story. I can't believe she even roped someone into blindfolding her and pretending to attack her. She really experienced the whole thing.'

'A pity she couldn't shed any new light on the murder though.'

'Yes, but she did her bit to raise awareness of it. These things can't just be buried. She's gutsy and persistent …'

'She'll be harder than we thought to beat,' said Isabel with a nod.

'You can say that again. You know I worry about Chloe; I'm not sure she's cut out for the Union. She's not tough enough. She's too sweet.'

'Why?' grumbled Isabel. 'Because she giggles? Just because I giggle less than her am I any more likely to throw myself in front of a train to save a friend?'

Will pulled her close, stroking her hair. 'You're amazing,' he said. 'Mad, but amazing.'

'I have a plan – to help Chloe, anyway,' Isabel said.

'You do?'

They strolled arm in arm towards the deli.

Chapter 11

Chloe had just joined Will and they were sitting at their usual corner of The Club, gulping down coffees.

'Welcome back, Miss Librarian. Now for the real challenge. Beating Piper Kenton to president! I've liaised with Ol and he's organized a car to take us all up to London and talk election strategy with a top public affairs consultant – they're the same people his father is using for his overseas expansion.' Will grinned triumphantly.

'What? You're mad! And anyway, there's no way I'll beat her – consultation or not. She's practically famous now, with all those scoops she's been getting for *Cherwell*. I mean, discovering before any national paper that the US defence secretary was planning to stand down and finish his PhD here was pretty amazing. And more annoyingly, I kind of like her – she's a really cool girl!'

'Well, everyone knows who you are too, and they've seen you, met you in person. Piper's always working too hard or playing sport or at the Union debating to actually go out and secure votes. Anyway, don't worry. Isabel and I have … don't worry, you'll be fine.'

'What? Have you done something? Something dodgy?'

'We want the best person for the job in place; what's dodgy about that?' He picked up his phone as it rang. 'Hey big man. OK, cool!'

'Right, let's hit the road!' Will said to Chloe.

'What, right now?'

'Yes, come on.'

'Can I go like this, in jeans?'

'Course, it's a Saturday.'

'Why didn't you tell me earlier?'

'Because we knew you wouldn't come if we gave you an option. Up you get.'

'I've got so much work to do,' moaned Chloe.

'Well, you've only got your prelims to worry about; think of me with my finals. Anyhow, we both know it's not as if you were actually going to get anything done sitting here.'

Chloe giggled her assent. 'Whoop! Let's go to London!'

They paid up and left The Club where, to Chloe's shock, a dazzling black Bentley was waiting outside for them.

'Why do we have this ridiculous car?' she asked.

The uniformed chauffeur walked around to open the front passenger door. Will ushered her towards the front and then climbed in the back beside Isabel who, Chloe could see, was already settled in, cracking jokes with Ol.

'Come on in,' beckoned Ol. 'It's my father's car and driver for when he's in England. I was going to drive us down myself but this way we can work out what we need to get done on the way to London.'

'Get in! Get in!' shouted Isabel, leaning over Will who had climbed in on her other side. Will's face flushed bright red and he seemed to stop breathing as her upper body hovered over his thighs.

Chloe climbed in front. 'I'm nervous, guys.'

'Don't be!' everyone chimed.

'I wonder what Piper's doing now?' she fretted.

'Probably talking to her made-up actor boyfriend,' drawled Will. 'Nothing useful at any rate.'

'You really need to get your confidence up, hon,' Isabel added. 'The Union will be good for you.'

As the car set off, Ol began skinning up a spliff on his lap.

'Ooh yes, I need to relax.' Chloe's neck was already hurting from turning around to poke her head between the two front seats and remain part of the conversation. She watched the progress of the spliff greedily.

The driver frowned at Ol in the rear-view mirror so he leant forward and slipped his father's employee a wad of cash. 'Dad doesn't need to know, right?'

Ol offered the spliff around but Isabel turned her head away. 'Keep that thing away from me,' she said coldly.

Will got out his folder, announcing 'strategy time!' and Isabel gratefully reached for her own notes.

They arrived in Victoria a couple of hours later and marched with youthful confidence into the offices of Babcock & Jones, where Dolly Babcock was waiting for them. When he saw her, Will wished that the others had dressed a little smarter and put on a suit like he had. Chloe and Isabel were both in jeans and casual sweaters. Ol had a button-down shirt on with his jeans at least, but he still looked too laidback. Only he and Dolly looked the part.

'You're late,' Dolly said.

Dolly Babcock was a bitch. A curvy, platinum blonde in a sharp suit and dangerous stilettos, it was her forty-eighth birthday. But you wouldn't have known it to look at her unlined face and plump lips. She registered the arrival of the group with curt, business-like handshakes. She didn't smile. *She isn't what you'd call warm, but,* thought Will, catching Ol's eye, *she oozes sex.*

Dolly had been brought up on a council estate nick-named 'Half' because only half the people that went in ever came back out to function in society; the other half were murdered, died or imprisoned. But Dolly had been lucky enough to get a grant and then a scholarship to good schools. From there it had been Cambridge, where she'd graduated with a first in political sciences and headed straight to a promising job with a big American consultancy firm. She had risen up the ranks to become its youngest ever female UK head. Her speciality was public affairs. In 2004, she had set up Babcock & Jones with a colleague and was now a millionaire many times over. Divorced three times, she declared to any would-be suitor that she was married to her work, but he could audition for a job as her mistress.

Looking at her now, her suit jacket nipped in at her hourglass waist, Will could see where she got her fearsome reputation as a killer in the boardroom and a thriller in the bedroom.

Will threw her a charming smile. 'Ms Babcock, how kind of you to give us your time. I know how busy you are.'

She didn't smile back. 'I made time for you because I was curious. Curious as to how some floppy haired pipsqueak like yourself could have the confidence and audacity to bother me. Come with me,' she said to the group, but looking only at Ol.

He read this as a challenge. Not 'come with me' but 'keep up with me.'

'With pleasure,' he replied, letting the awestruck girls pass in front of him before he and Will filed into her office. They were meeting there, even though it was a Saturday, as Dolly had work to do and would be there for a long time yet.

'Erm, I don't know why we're here, really. I'm so sorry we're wasting your time ... you're obviously so important ...' Chloe, petrified of Dolly and babbling with nerves, was doing her best to ruin everything for them.

Dolly held up a hand in Chloe's direction, cutting short her prattling. She glanced briefly at a fascinated Isabel, winced at Will and turned her gaze again on Ol, where she let it rest.

'We'll do this quickly.'

Something in Ol snapped. He wasn't her bitch.

'Can you show me to the gents first?'

Dolly sighed with irritation. 'OK, follow me.' She added, 'I've jotted down some notes on effective campaign tactics and I'll talk you through them, but then you all need to be out of here by two-thirty.'

Ol followed her out of the office and shut the door behind him.

They passed a plush conference room en route to the toilets.

'The gents are over there.' As Dolly signalled down the hallway, Ol took her outstretched hand in his and pulled her to him.

She let out a scream, quivering against his chest.

'Nobody speaks to me like that.' But he smiled as he held her. The warmth of his regard counterbalanced the roughness with which he handled her.

Dolly Babcock didn't get to head up a global consultancy and discard three husbands by being easily intimidated. She loved a challenge and thrived on the unexpected.

'I'm sorry,' she breathed. 'I'm just stressed; I've got a lot on.' She was clearly enjoying the role reversal.

'I don't care,' Ol said. He kissed her roughly and then stroked her face. 'We're going to go back in there, have our meeting, and then I'm going to send them back to Oxford in my car. I'm going to give you an hour to tie up any unfinished business here and then we'll get a suite at Claridges and I'm going to make love to you.'

Dolly struggled for breath. *How old was he, anyway? He seemed like just a boy.* She reached down and felt his erection. *Fuck!* It took a lot to shock her but what she now had in her hands nearly gave her cardiac arrest. If he was a mere boy he was suffering from the world's most staggering growth spurt.

'Don't ever order me around,' were his final words before he took her hand and led her back to her office and let her re-enter first. He waited a minute or so and then sauntered in, relaxed, calm and smiling.

Chapter 12

Chloe screamed, shocked to see a homeless person sitting cross-legged outside her bedroom door, smoking a cigarette. A very striking homeless man with wild dark hair and stubble around his sulky lips. His eyes were brooding, dangerous. She gradually realized he looked a little familiar. Did she know him?

'Oh, you're the guy from the woods. You were mimicking me!' Gosh, she hadn't noticed his looks then – so far away and in the dark. 'Erm, well, can I get to my room, please?'

He stood up. 'I'm Sam. Did you like your present?'

He spoke in a gravelly faux-cockney accent, like someone in a Brit gangster movie.

'What present?'

'The painting. I left it under your door.'

'*You* did that?' Chloe was horrified.

'I thought you'd like it. It's my favourite piece.'

Chloe slid her key into the lock and went in. She turned around to face Sam, still hovering outside her door.

'Well, who are you?'

'I'm Sam Smith.'

'Oh. I think I read about you in *Cherwell*.'

'Can I come in?'

'Yes, I suppose so.'

Chloe reached under her bed and pulled out the painting, glad that Isabel had forbidden her from throwing it away.

She laid it out on her bed and gazed at it, before turning to look at him, all dishevelled and stunning. Now she understood. The beauty behind the mess.

'It's like …you,' she smiled. 'Thank you.'

They stared at each other, neither of them looking away, neither of them talking.

'I knew I would find you,' Sam said eventually. 'Can I paint you?'

'Now that is a chat-up line no woman can resist.' Chloe's face lit up.

'Do you meditate?' Sam asked.

'Err …no.'

'We can meditate together.'

'Um, perhaps.'

'And do you communicate?'

'Sorry?'

'Do you communicate? With nature? How do you make sense of your relationship to nature, and the world? How can you communicate without understanding? Without listening? Hearing?'

'I don't understand.'

'Sometimes I don't talk.'

'OK.'

'I just listen.'

'Right.'

'Let's go!'

Sam beckoned towards the door. Chloe hesitated and then followed him out. They strolled in amiable silence through the bustling town until they reached the River Cherwell.

'I don't know why I'm doing this!' Chloe giggled. 'I barely know you. This is absurd.'

'But it also feels very natural, right?' He looked at her.

'Actually, it does,' Chloe said, surprised at the realization.

'So tell me about yourself.'

'Well, what do you want to know?'

A couple of hours later, they were still talking and Chloe had told Sam pretty much everything about herself and yet she knew little about him. She petered off.

'Your turn, Sam.'

'I'll paint you here,' Sam said by way of reply.

'But there's no paint.'

'Let's go back to nature.'

He walked over to the river and knelt down beside it. He was silent and unmoving for a while and Chloe wondered whether he was praying. Then he washed both of his hands in the water before gouging out handfuls of muddy grass from the bank beside it.

He walked over to Chloe and smeared his own face and then hers, so that they were both covered in mud.

'May I paint you?' he asked again.

'You're …crazy …' But Chloe pulled off her sweater, so she was standing in just jeans and a vest top. She held out her bare arms and raised her face to him. 'Paint me.'

He took her hands in his, gently massaging the mud into her fingers. Then he took her left arm and ran his hands up and down it, stroking and massaging her flesh. He scurried back to the river to wet his hands once more and gather more earth, which he carefully spread over her shoulders and smoothed up and down her other arm. Finally he took her face in his hands, leaving five brown finger marks on each cheek. When he had finished he took a step back and contemplated his work.

Chloe contemplated him. Compared with his artist's passion and depth, Ol seemed like a puppy running around on heat. Their night together had been amazing, but her fever for him now seemed merely an itch, which she'd already firmly scratched and rid herself of.

'I totally love you!' Chloe laughed.

Piper pulled her hair into a perky ponytail high on her head and picked up her tennis racket. She knew she was overdoing it with all this sport and the Union as well as keeping on top of her studies but she missed her boyfriend, Chad, so terribly she had to keep herself busy.

She stretched out a well-toned leg and frowned. What had Isabel Suarez-Octavio and William Austin been doing at the *Cherwell* offices as she was leaving? She thought of the brilliant articles she had coming out in week seven, the week of the presidency election, and smiled. She had killed herself for them. It was her best stuff yet and perfectly illustrated how dedicated she was to the Union and debating, and that she was the best candidate for the job. Piper genuinely liked her opponent. Chloe was sweet. But she was woefully ill-equipped to run anything other than a big house in the country.

Chapter 13

Chloe looked down at her tight jeans – bought pre-puberty when she'd been two stone lighter and ripped everywhere, including just under her bottom from years of wear and tear. Her blue shirt, covered in paint and missing the top buttons as a result of one of Sam's fits of inspiration, now showed far too much cleavage. Hot with anxiety and nerves, she had piled up all of her hair in a mad bird's nest on top of her head and shoved a pencil in it to hold it up. Her cheeks were flushed and she felt disgustingly sweaty.

'Well, I'd better change into something smart before we do the rounds.'

'No, go like that – you look like you've been making love non-stop for five days,' Isabel said.

'Eeew,' squealed Chloe. 'Anyway, Sam and I haven't …yet. I think we will soon, though.'

'Forget Sam. Don't you realize how important today is? You need to look approachable, non-threatening, but still sexy. Today is your last chance to make an impression and you need all the votes you can get.' Isabel looked her friend up and down approvingly.

'Oh, come on, that's so tacky!' Chloe replied.

'Look, sex makes the world go around – neglect it at your peril.' When Chloe looked sceptical, Isabel went on. 'Let's think of, say, school as a microcosm of the world. Who were the kids who wielded the most influence over the other kids? They weren't the brainiest, were they? No, they were the sexiest.'

'Yeah but we were so young and naïve then. I mean, look at presidents and things – they're not sexy.'

'Oh I don't know – I'd definitely give Obama one. But anyway, they don't get there alone, do they? Why do you think presidents ally themselves with celebrities to get votes? Do you think anyone would care that Angelina Jolie adopted a baby if she didn't have bee-stung lips? Come on, get your baps out and let's go!'

'You're sick, you know that?' Chloe laughed. She felt sick herself. Sick with nerves.

They started at St Hilda's. The exquisite setting on the River Cherwell, with its lush, grassy banks resplendent with the last of the meadowsweet, made up for the new, unattractive concrete building of the college. It had been the last all-girls' college in the university before becoming co-ed a short while ago.

'Let's appeal to the feminist element,' whispered Isabel as they closed in. Together with William, Ol and an army of obedient fellow students and other wannabe Union hacks, who had been promised favours of all kinds should Chloe be elected, they had divvied up the thirty-eight Oxford colleges, so that at every single one there were people chatting up the boys and girls on Chloe's behalf and finding ways to remind them that today was election day and they should 'Vote Constance for Constant Thrills'.

On hearing that, Sam had said that the Union and everybody involved could 'suck my dick', which Chloe had duly done. There was no way Sam was going to help out, but otherwise they had a buoyed-up supportive team and everyone was raring to go. To overtly canvass for votes was technically not allowed, so they had to be inventive.

They'd sent Ol to the left-leaning Wadham and told him to leave his chauffeur behind; meanwhile Will was welcomed with open arms at traditional Christ Church, where everyone already knew him from school.

Back at St Hilda's the girls debated whether Thatcher would have had the confidence to become the first female prime minister had Somerville been co-ed while she was there. And they questioned why men had traditionally obtained a higher proportion of firsts than women at Oxford.

'I think it's 'cos they work harder than us,' sighed Chloe.

Isabel shook her head. 'Apparently we actually spend more hours revising. They did a study a few years ago and came up with the "bullshit factor". Basically men often have a more confident style, so their answers are deemed worthier of a first than our generally more cautious, balanced answers.'

At the legendarily academic St John's, they argued over calculus and laughed conspicuously at the absurdity of a variety of mathematical conundrums before soliciting an opinion on the matter.

Outside 'Rugger Bugger' Teddy Hall, they changed into their tennis whites – with extra short skirts – and jogged into the bar for a tipple and a flirt.

'Can you pass me that bottle of wine with your big, strong, rugby-player's arms? I need to quench my thirst and fuel up before heading to the Union,' tittered Chloe at the college scrum half as Isabel kicked her shins.

'A *bit* more subtlety,' she muttered.

'Oh yeah. Forgot about elections today,' said the six-foot-seven barrel of brawn. 'You'll be getting my vote …'

Exhausted from the day's hustling, Chloe lay her head on Sam's bony chest and held him tightly to her in her bed.

'This is nice, just holding each other. We don't have to do anything else if you don't want to,' Sam said.

'This is lovely. But tell me more about you.'

Sam flinched. 'What do you want to know?'

'I don't know. Why do you love painting and sculpting?'

Sam held her hand too tight, not speaking.

'Ouch, you're hurting me.' Chloe winced, trying to extricate her hand.

'Sorry, babe.' He was silent for a few minutes and then said, 'I used to wish I didn't love painting. It wasn't the done thing at my school. They used to laugh at me. Spit on me when they saw me in the playground drawing.'

'How awful!'

'They hated me because I never had the right clothes, couldn't afford the latest trainers. They hated my long hair. They used to kick me, and call me a faggot because of it – long before any of them even understood the words they used. Then, when I was ten, I decided to work on my first large portrait. My teacher gave me a special A3 sheet of paper and every playtime I would take it to a corner of the playground to work a little on it. After a month, when it was nearly finished, a group of boys cornered me and asked me for the drawing. I said no. That drawing meant more than I even knew. It was like a piece of me; a body part or something. At least that's how it felt when they ripped it from me. I physically couldn't move. I was crippled without it. Then …' Sam paused and hit the wall with the side of his clenched fist. 'Then they threw it on the floor and started jumping up and down on it. Sullying it with their feet. And it hurt so much they could have been jumping on me.'

'Come here.' Chloe cradled Sam's head in her arms.

'What happened after that?' she asked gently.

'They said I had to stop drawing and painting because if I didn't, they would kick the shit out of me.' He spoke into her warm neck. 'I tried so hard not to but life was kind of unbearable without art. So I started to draw again and on my eleventh birthday they beat me so hard that I ended up in hospital. After that I went to a different school. But I kept playing up, being naughty. I didn't see the point of it. I was expelled from everywhere and told I had a filthy attitude. My mum's a single parent and life was hard enough for her as it was. I feel awful for what I put her through.'

'It wasn't your fault,' Chloe soothed.

'That's what my mum says. But it was. It was my fault. I didn't have to react like that. But Mum says she knows I'm gonna make it as an artist. She believes in me the way she used to believe in my useless dad. This time I won't let her down.'

That night Chloe slept soundly and happily, forgetting about the dreaded vote-counting ceremony the next day. Instead she dreamed of a life with Sam. She felt guilty for loving Sam's heartache, but his admission of it and his sadness had made her feel close to him. She felt like she had broken through a barrier.

Chapter 14

The next morning, Chloe felt bereft when she realized that Sam was no longer in her bed, but then she spotted a tiny charcoal drawing on a Post-it note stuck to her bedside table. It was of herself sleeping. She was struck by how profoundly talented he was. This, unlike the beast canvas, was the type of art she could relate to. She felt deeply moved. She picked it up and turned it over. On the back he had scrawled in pencil:

Had to get up and paint – needed the morning light. Come to my studio later and we'll have dinner.
Yours,
Sam

He'd forgotten that it was her big day today, so she wouldn't be free for dinner. Truth be told, he was completely uninterested in her involvement in the Union but Chloe didn't mind. He was an artist and that was everything to him. He couldn't be expected to bother with the day to day of student life. She floated out of bed and dressed quickly before heading to The Club for lunch to join Isabel and the rest of Team Chloe.

When she arrived the place was heaving. The toothless old man was hunched over the piano and Ol was leaning on the top of it, beer in hand, watching him play at close range. As the old man sped up, his back lurched up and down each time he hit the keys. The crowd began whooping and cheering.

Ol waved to Chloe and Isabel and the old man swivelled around. Spotting Isabel, and no doubt remembering her marvellous dance at the start of Michaelmas term, the pianist let out a strange noise. If he'd had teeth it would probably have sounded like a welcome cry but instead it was a frenzied gurgle. He sprung up off his stool and hobbled over to her.

Ol took over his vacated seat and began playing instead, as the pianist led Isabel to the middle of the room and began flailing his arthritic arms and legs in excitement. Unfortunately Ol only knew one song. A fast but simple number, which he played over and over as Isabel did her best to move in time with her partner's manic movements.

By now around fifteen girls had gathered around the piano, many of them draped on the instrument itself, others fussing over Ol, massaging his shoulders as he played.

'My card's behind the bar!' he shouted above the din to Will, who was being brought up to date on the previous day's canvassing by Chloe. 'Get some champagne in for everyone.' He turned back to the piano and played his song for the umpteenth time, grinning at all the incredulous and insincere marvelling at his musical prowess.

'Ol, you're amazing, where did you learn to play?' said the fawning girls.

Will led Chloe to the bar, asked for three magnums of champagne and began pouring glasses for everybody in sight.

'Are you sure you've got enough there, Will?' Isabel shouted, laughingly dodging the old man's attempts to give her a piggy back.

'We're not leaving here until the votes are counted this evening. Might as well make the most of it. Come here, this is for you.'

Isabel grabbed her new friend's hand and led him over to the bar. 'This is Aiden. He's played the piano here for over sixty-five years!'

Will handed Isabel and Aiden a glass of champagne. Aiden took his and winced as Ol began playing his naff tune yet again. He hobbled hurriedly back to the piano to retrieve his instrument.

'What the hell are you all celebrating for? How can you be so sure I've won? Because I'm pretty sure I haven't.' Chloe realized she was genuinely unsure whether she even wanted to win. She would only really know how she actually felt the moment the results were announced.

Isabel and Will exchanged looks. 'Whatever the vote, we can't change it now so we might as we well try to enjoy the day,' reasoned Will. 'Besides, we covered every college. Piper didn't.'

'She didn't need to. She's had access to every single student via her column in *Cherwell*. I've been putting it off but I suppose I really ought to see what I'm up against. Has anyone got a copy?' Isabel avoided eye contact and Will became suddenly preoccupied with a speck of dirt on the surface of the bar.

'It, er, didn't actually come out yesterday.' He coughed. 'There was a printer malfunction.'

He caught Isabel's eye and she tried to suppress a giggle, clamping her mouth shut with her hand for a few seconds before bursting out in fits of laugher.

'Oh god!' howled Will, trying not to laugh. This only made Isabel laugh more and by now she was wiping away a tear, doubled up, her hand clutching her stomach.

'Oh, you couldn't have! You didn't!' Chloe stared at her friends, stony-faced with rage.

'Chloe, let me tell you something.' Isabel stared hard at her friend. 'This is the real world. You need to grow up and stop being so naïve. There are people out there who aren't nice. Bad, truly evil people. Will and I are your friends. Trust us.'

Ol walked over. 'Hey, I've got an idea,' he said, to break the tension.

'What?' they all chorused.

'Er, cheers?' He thrust a glass of champagne into Chloe's hand.

'Down it! Down it! Down it! Down it!' chanted Will, until everyone in The Club was chanting along with him.

Chapter 15

By the time the excited group had made their way to the Union for the vote-counting ceremony, Chloe was already far too sozzled to notice Piper on her own outside, talking despondently to her long-distance boyfriend over the phone.

'I don't know, Chad,' Piper said into the mouthpiece, watching Chloe, Isabel and their raucous entourage with despair. 'It just didn't come out yesterday. All the printers were completely jammed.'

She listened for a while.

'No, no, I didn't do that. You're not supposed to go around hassling people for votes. Anyway, I wouldn't want to – it's creepy. Well, look, you should get back to your audition. I'd better go – they're about to announce the result. Me too, baby.'

She hung up then slowly tightened the laces on her running shoes. They were light with a good grip. As she bounced up and down on the balls of her toes she felt the polar opposite of light. She could finish her jog to her room, change quickly and be at the Gladstone Room in forty minutes. There was no point hanging around early.

Chloe sank into a deep armchair in the red-carpeted Gladstone Room and breathed deeply, trying to stop her heart from pounding.

She saw Piper make a late entrance, resplendent in a black velvet dress. Chloe still had on the simple white Reiss dress she'd worn all day. She'd thought it was pretty but amid the grandeur of the room she suddenly felt out of place. Piper looked perfect. Not for the first time, Chloe felt a stab of inadequacy. Meeting Piper's eyes she smiled. It was an awkward smile but Piper returned it. They shared a flash of understanding. Whatever would happen, at this fleeting moment in time they were in the same boat.

'Honourable Members, can I have your attention please?' The current president held up a hand. 'The votes have now been counted and verified, and we have a clear winner. The president-elect of the Oxford Union is …' he paused. Nobody spoke. There must have been sixty or so invited guests at the ceremony, but you could have heard a butterfly fart.

'Chloe Constance!'

The room became a zoo. Everywhere Chloe looked, friends, acquaintances, people she didn't even know, were dancing, kissing, toasting and shouting congratulations. Will grabbed her and pulled her into an embrace. She just nodded. She felt numb.

She had won a huge election without having any real desire or aptitude for the prize. What had seemed like just a game had become very real. She would soon be in charge of a mammoth institution, entertaining presidents, pop stars and politicians, when she hadn't the foggiest about current affairs, let alone even a summer's work experience in an institution of any kind. Isabel had wanted it for her more than she herself had. Why?

She peered over Will's shoulder at Isabel, looking radiant, tossing her hair with a triumphant smile. She had saddled Chloe with this massive burden but what did Isabel hope to gain from it?

Piper was also looking at Isabel. In her eyes was nothing but pain.

Chapter 16

When she was sure the others had all gone their separate ways for the Easter vacation, Isabel pulled on her thin coat and picked up her case. It was small. She didn't need much. With a heavy heart she set off for the bus stop. She would first get a coach to London. From there she would do a long Tube journey. It would take her right outside of expensive central London. Then there would be another bus and then a long walk.

She put out an arm to hail the approaching coach. Once inside, she took a seat beside a woman with a round face and friendly smile. The coach was hot and she soon began to sweat. At the next stop, ten more people embarked and the coach reached capacity. Now the heat was almost unbearable and the coach smelled of the combined sweat of all the people squashed inside it.

Isabel reached into the side pocket of her case and pulled out the well-thumbed leaflets the doctor had given her. She began reading through them again. She winced at the accompanying pictures. Of people contorted in pain. Of operations. Of the risk of death. She closed her eyes and repeated the words the doctor had told her. *The illness is not always terminal. Stay strong. Wait for the results.* She closed her eyes but that was a mistake as immediately she was back there, in her ugly past.

'Don't do it.'

'Why? What else is there?'

'Don't do it. Please, there are other ways!'

'I need to.'

'Please, don't do it!'

Isabel's eyes snapped open. She would never go back.

She surveyed the people on the coach, imagining their lives. Her heart panged at the thought of those students heading home to their welcoming families. She saw her neighbour reach into her bag and pull out a squashed pasty. She took a hearty bite out of it and a piece of onion dropped from the pie onto Isabel's leg.

'Sorry love,' said the woman, extracting the onion and putting it in the discarded wrapping which she let rest on her lap. In the process, she scattered crumbs all over Isabel's leaflets.

'Would you like some?' The woman smiled and brandished the pasty under her nose.

'Look what you've done!' snarled Isabel, brushing away the crumbs. She slid the documents back into her case and turned away from the woman.

On her other side a student opened an egg and cress sandwich. The coach was now punishingly hot, and smelled of sweat, egg and onions, but Isabel closed her eyes and tried to absorb the warmth. It would be cold where she was going.

Chapter 17

'Jesus, your house is like a bloody Oxford college,' grumbled Sam as he strolled hand in hand with Chloe through the acres of landscaped garden at her family home in Wiltshire.

'You don't like it?' asked Chloe, crestfallen. They had spent so much of the previous term with each other that Chloe had envisaged a glorious, romantic break together at her home. Chloe's parents had taken her sister, Pip, away for Easter so Chloe had the house pretty much to herself. She had invited Sam to stay for a week and she had begged the staff to take the week off, promising not to tell her mother. She'd had a sinking feeling that Sam wouldn't approve of the servants.

'It's alright, I guess. I'll have to try to get some painting done here but it's going to be hard to get going in this environment. I started on this set of canvases back in the dirt and bustle of East London and I'm not sure there's enough energy here. It's a bit sterile.' He saw how crushed Chloe looked. 'No, I mean, don't get me wrong; it's immaculate, and tasteful and charming here. I like it.'

'There's nature all around you!' Chloe exclaimed, pointing to the untouched woodland that extended beyond the garden. 'I thought that was what gets you going. There's hardly a decent square of green in East London.'

'It's not that simple, babe. You like everything to be simple, don't you? I don't know why you and Isabel are so tight – you couldn't be more different.'

'What does Isabel have to do with anything?' Chloe snapped, feeling hurt by his comment.

'Just that I was chatting to her about art. She's incredibly knowledgeable about it. Blew me away, in fact. That girl must have read a lot on the subject and has extremely complex views.' He kissed the top of Chloe's head and they carried on their walk in silence.

'I really wanted you to be happy here, Sam,' she whispered.

It was impossible not to feel sorry for her. Sam avoided looking into her hurt eyes as he drew her into a hug, her voluptuous body moulding into his hard, rangy frame, her soft flesh filling the spaces between his ribs.

'We're so different, aren't we? I think that's why we work,' she said, looking up at him hopefully.

'We balance each other,' Sam agreed. 'Everything should be balanced.'

After that conversation, they barely spoke all week because Sam was always painting. But he took regular breaks to eat and make love. Chloe loved taking care of him. She loved to cook and fuss over him, make sure he kept his strength up for long hours with his paintbrush. Sometimes she'd just sit there watching him as he painted.

'Shhhh,' he'd say, every time she tried to speak. He needed total silence in order to concentrate. She didn't even mind that he was a selfish lover. She could pleasure him all day and be perfectly happy. Most days they didn't even bother getting dressed. They drifted about the house naked, like two hippies in a commune. Like Adam and Eve.

On the last night she waited until they were in bed together before she asked him the question that had been playing on her mind for weeks.

'Honey?'

'What is it, babe?'

'It would really mean a lot to me if you would come to my first debate.'

'Flippin' heck, when are you gonna stop ramming that godawful place down my throat? Christ almighty. Fine. Yes, I'll come. Now can I get some sleep?' He picked up his pillow and pretended to suffocate himself. Chloe grabbed it happily and smothered his face in her minty kisses.

Chapter 18

Despite her nerves, Chloe felt like the Queen of England as she glided into the debating chamber in a sweeping floor-length black taffeta gown that she'd hired, paid for out of her budget as the newly-elected president of the Oxford Union. She watched the packed floor rise.

She'd never expected to enjoy this. Truth be told, apart from the week's interlude with Sam, she'd had a dreadful Easter since winning the election last term. The break had seemed to be over before it even began, and all she had done was worry that she wouldn't be able to do the job, which would start the minute she arrived back in Oxford for Trinity, the final term of the year. And now here she was, hosting her very first debate.

She kept her introductory speech purposefully short.

'Honourable members, as your new president, I welcome you here tonight to our entrepreneurialism debate. For the motion "This house believes business is not booming", we have the inimitable retail tycoon, Gabriel Paradis. And arguing against the motion, I'm delighted to introduce our guest speaker, the newly appointed Cabinet minister and rising star of the Lib–Con Party, Archibald Arden, secretary of state for Business.' She clocked

Isabel touching up her lipstick at the mention of his name and was grateful to her for her briefing on him earlier.

'But before the debate commences, I'd like to remind you of some of the highlights we have to look forward to at the Union this term. First of all, the fashion designer Clemency Clementine will be coming in tomorrow to talk to us about her transition from society girl to superstar businesswoman. Then we have a host of stellar speakers from all fields, including: the professor at the forefront of prostate cancer research, a top human rights activist and the most successful financial markets speculator of modern times.'

She glanced at Isabel, who smiled her encouragement. Her parents and even Sam had turned up and were sitting in the row behind Will, Isabel and Ol, who were all in the reserved seating at the front.

Chloe stepped down and took her seat next to her friends, feeling ecstatic when Sam mouthed *you look beautiful.*

'I feel like a complete fraud,' she muttered under her breath to Will.

'Why? You won by so many votes that *Cherwell* not printing doesn't even matter. You won by a bigger margin than its readership among Union members, so you'd still have won if it had come out.'

'Really?' She stared hard at him. She hoped he was telling the truth, but then Will was so persuasive that he could make a living selling hairbrushes at conventions for the bald.

She turned to Isabel for validation but Isabel had a strange look on her face. She was staring at the young politician, even though he was not the one debating. He didn't seem to have noticed her, being too preoccupied with his notes and keeping track of his opposition, but Chloe knew it was only a matter of time.

'Isabel's got a crush,' she whispered to Will, turning her head so Isabel wouldn't overhear. 'I was starting to think she was a lesbian. She hasn't been with anyone all year. At least, not that she tells me.'

'What are you talking about? What crush?' snapped Will, following Isabel's gaze, a scowl on his face.

Chloe turned her attention back to the debate with an envious sigh. She should have known that Will was just like every other man.

As the final speaker concluded his argument, Isabel finally caught Archibald's eye. Perhaps she'd soon be calling him Archie, as she knew his friends did. Her lips curled into the smallest flicker of a smile and then she looked away. There. Over to him. She ran her hands through her hair, tousling it a fraction and frowned, as if she were concentrating on the summation by the opposition guest speaker.

She tried not to look at him again, but she could see out of the corner of her eye that he was affected by her. She saw that he was less able to control his gaze than she was. She felt ecstatic. She allowed herself to meet his gaze again and this time she gave him a knowing smile.

At the end of the debate she got up to leave through the door that read 'Aye' above it and headed to the Gladstone Room for post-debate drinks. She avoided the rush of people who came by to chat, brushing each one off politely but quickly, because it would be harder for him to make his move in front of an audience. Helping herself to a glass of prosecco, she waited in a corner of the room and pretended to be reading emails on her phone.

Finally, Archie appeared in the room. Though the room was packed their eyes found each other instantly. Archie made his way leisurely around the space, stopping to converse and debate with various clusters of people. He didn't look at Isabel again but she knew he was still aware of her. After a while he moved nearer and was drawn into a conversation with a group of students directly beside her. They were in their final year and had finance jobs in the city lined up for after Oxford. They were keen to question him on his transition from the city to politics. He would occasionally glance sideways at Isabel as he answered their questions, never suggestively but always inclusive. She decided to make it easier for him and edged into a gap in the circle. There were handshakes and introductions all round.

And then his hand touched hers. He held it for a second longer than he had held everybody else's hand and she smiled and looked into his eyes a second longer than she had looked at the others. After that she didn't notice anything or anybody else in the room, but she didn't let it show.

She smiled and listened as he told his story. 'Really, the key is hard work. Hard work and seizing opportunities. That can be applied to most things, but never more so than in, er …'

He was struggling to hide his interest now. He was looking at her more and more frequently, unable to drag his gaze away, and each time she could see how much he wanted her. She too felt acutely aware of the most intimate parts of her body; tantalisingly conscious that she was a woman and he a man. His conversation was becoming less coherent. The invisible magnet that had drawn him closer to Isabel had ceased to be invisible and was now blindingly obvious. The rest of the party realized they were surplus to requirements, and, making polite excuses, wandered off into the crowd. Finally they were alone.

'So, what brings you to the Union?' he asked.

'Fate,' she replied. And then, 'I loved your arguments. I completely agree with your point about the current levels of tax relief for investors in SMEs.'

She could see that he couldn't concentrate.

'Are you listening to me?' she admonished lightly. 'I don't think you are.'

'Of course I'm listening to you. You're mesmerizing.' He was leaning in closer now and she sensed how urgently he wanted to touch her. She edged nearer too, knowing that when he finally did touch her it would be electric. Her whole body tingled with anticipation.

'So what did I say then?' she teased.

While Archie was falling hook, line and sinker for Isabel, there was one person who was definitely not being taken in by her charms. Piper had slipped undetected into the party and having watched Chloe doing absolutely nothing, despite being at the helm of the organization, she had turned away in devastation, only to spot Isabel.

She, of course, had the attention of the most important person in the room. Piper was sure that somehow Isabel had been the reason her special issue of *Cherwell* had not come out, and was the source of the torrent of mean stories that had been spread about her behind her back. There was even talk she'd made up her boyfriend. It was hard enough to make friends in a new city as it was; she didn't need everybody thinking she was a weirdo too. She liked the people at *Cherwell* and the people she did sport with, and they all liked her. But something was missing. Most of her *Cherwell* work she did alone, writing away in her tiny room. Parkour was not a team sport and the people she played tennis with she rarely saw off the court. She didn't have anyone with whom to enjoy that closeness that Isabel and Chloe and their little group had found. She was desperately lonely.

She knocked back an entire glass of red wine in five huge gulps, even though she didn't usually drink much.

'A toast,' she muttered, 'to getting even with Isabel Suarez-Octavio'. She put down the empty glass and escaped the awful noise and triumphant revelry of Isabel and her friends.

Chapter 19

Isabel felt a pounding in her heart and the thrill of adrenaline coursing through her body. She had not felt this way in years. Not since the flight.

'Houses of Parliament, please,' she asked the taxi driver. 'Portcullis House.'

She drew in her breath as they crossed Westminster Bridge. On the other side, on the north bank of the River Thames, stood the Palace of Westminster, also known as the Houses of Parliament. The great gothic building, astonishing in scale and beauty, was the city's thumping heart – the meeting place of some of the most influential and powerful people in the country. As they drew nearer, Big Ben, the Palace's clock tower that stood high over all of London, chimed out.

Portcullis House, a later addition built in a similar style to augment office space for the members of parliament and their staff stood adjacent, connected via an underground passage.

The taxi came to a stop at the entrance and Isabel paid the driver and jumped out. Her belted Clemency Clementine dress, in royal blue, swayed at her calves. Nothing about the way Isabel looked today said 'student'. Too glamorous to be mistaken for a politician, she might be the pampered wife of the president of an oil-rich country. She watched the Justice Minister as he struggled to exit the building while gawping at her at the same. Eyes bulging, he began to push open the door before taking a step back as if to hold it open for her, succeeding only in tripping on his own foot. He then stretched out a sweaty hand before pulling it back hurriedly to his side and beckoning her into the building with a shake of his head and a jumble of breathless words. She smiled. It was bizarre to watch these MPs on TV, po-faced and proud as they defended their policies, and yet here they were in the flesh, reduced to dribbling idiots in her presence.

Once inside the entrance, she froze as she was faced with a wall of police and security. Shaking slightly, she forced to the back of her mind the crippling memories that uniformed guards always dredged up. She put her bag and jacket in the tray to be scanned and then turned, as asked, to face a machine that would take her picture. She said a quick prayer that she would get safely through security.

A grainy black and white image, which completely butchered her face, emerged from the machine and a surly security guard tacked it onto a visitor's pass and handed it to her before guiding her through a body-scanning detector. She was then asked to wait until Archie or a representative could come and personally collect her. She relaxed – everything was fine.

She waited fifteen minutes for Archie to arrive.

'So sorry to keep you; I got called into a meeting with Hugh James.' Isabel nodded; Hugh James was the Prime Minister.

She stepped forward to greet Archie, flashing him a flirtatious smile, but he shook her hand in a business-like manner and led her brusquely into the main building where they would be having lunch.

She took in all the middle-aged men in suits, bustling about the vast atrium, some followed around by their younger aids and researchers. She overheard a journalist conducting an interview, running to keep up with an MP she recognized but could not name. She understood Archie's need to be business-like.

'Where are we going?' she asked.

'There is a restaurant overlooking the river but unfortunately we don't have time for that today so we'll go to the canteen.'

Isabel's heart sank as he led her to a large, bland canteen, not unlike that of any regular office block. Almost every table was occupied by grey-haired men in grey suits. Archie beckoned to a chair at the nearest table and recommended the roasted tofu salad, the thought of which made Isabel want to gag. Where was the meat devouring, red-blooded stallion she'd been fantasising about?

'Just one course as I can only spare twenty minutes,' he said, looking at his watch.

Fuming, Isabel asked for a pea and ham soup and ate it in silence as Archie took endless phone calls from a number of different MPs, journalists and even one from the Prime Minister himself. *Sorry*, he kept mouthing across the table at her as he listened, but he didn't seem sorry in the slightest.

She looked around and noticed a couple of other young women in the canteen among all the men. They were mostly wearing white shirts and plain knee-length skirts; she assumed they were all secretaries or PAs and then felt guilty for her assumption.

The moment she finished her soup, Archie got to his feet.

'Right, shall we make a move?'

'Now?' Isabel asked aghast. They hadn't even spent ten minutes together.

'Yes. I have to pop back to see Hugh at Number Ten soon, but I need to collect a document from my office first, so come with me and I'll show you around quickly before you leave.'

Isabel realized that any woman in Archie's life would have to put up with playing second fiddle to an overweight sixty-year-old with a comb-over.

Archie walked incredibly quickly down one of many long corridors but Isabel refused to run after him, so he was forced to slow down and wait for her. She peered into the rooms they passed on the way, all of which seemed to be filled with older men with plummy voices, laughing and conversing with each other in a sort of smug, gentlemen's club manner. The further along the corridor she went, the more intense the atmosphere became. Now she understood why the place was often referred to as 'the corridors of power'. Despite the aching dullness of everyone's appearance, there was an unmistakable feeling of excitement and expectation. Of laws being passed, of history being made. An atmosphere of power and privilege filled every corner of the building. A constant, beating pulse that was quiet but deafening.

At the end of the corridor she saw the Prime Minister emerge, deep in conversation with an advisor. She felt a surge of adrenaline to be a small part of this thing.

'Here we are. Wait here,' barked Archie, pushing her into his empty office before she was seen. 'I'll be back in a minute.' He shut the door behind him and was off.

Isabel took a look around his office while he was out brown-nosing and decided to shake him out of his indifference to her.

'What the *hell* do you think you're doing?' hissed Archie when he returned to his office. 'Do you realize the Prime Minister could have come in here with me?' He slammed the door shut behind him and walked over to where Isabel was sitting in the huge, deep chair at his desk overlooking the River Thames. She had her cone-heeled feet up on the table and her dress had ridden up to her waist so that her long, bare legs were exposed. On the desk were her black knickers.

Archie stared at her, shaking.

Isabel held her breath, petrified. She knew she'd gone too far.

Then he yanked her up by the arm and kissed her. He moaned and panted as all his pent-up sexual yearning overwhelmed him. He grabbed her bottom and forced his hands roughly between her legs. Then he undid his belt and dropped his trousers and underpants, then hoisted up her dress. He turned her around and pushed her forward, so that she was kneeling on the chair, bent over the back with her bum in the air. He plunged himself into her, hard, throbbing, groaning as he entered her. He penetrated her with merciless thrusts, clamping one hand firmly over her mouth to stop her from screaming, squeezing her breasts with the other. He was almost crying with the effort to suppress his groans as his thrusts became more and more frantic. He came hard and quickly and then collapsed on top of her, leaving her mad with lust and completely unsatisfied.

'I'm sorry, I had to come. Quickly get dressed. I'll make it up to you later.' He got up and handed her her knickers before speedily dressing himself and pulling out from his desk drawer a little mirror which he regarded at length, turning his head from side to side as he smoothed down his hair.

'Here,' Isabel said with a laugh, 'let me help you.' She patted an unruly lock of hair down flat and smoothed his tie. 'There, good as new.'

He took another long look in the mirror then kissed her quickly, picked up a folder on his desk and led her to the door. He opened it and glanced left and right to check the corridor was clear before ushering her out, half-walking half-running back to the main entrance. This time she did run to keep up with him. They made their way to the buzzing foyer and slowed down.

Looking far more composed by now, Archie turned to Isabel and said quietly, 'I'll call you later.'

She nodded and turned to exit the building with long, confident strides.

Chapter 20

The sun shone down on Isabel and Chloe, both flushed and happy, as they sat by the river watching the different colleges' rowing teams sail by for the much anticipated Summer Eights celebrations. Left and right, as far as the eye could see, the river was lined with young people drinking Pimms and rosé, the girls pretty in floaty, colourful dresses and the men in bright shorts or trousers with pastel-coloured cotton shirts, sleeves rolled up casually and shades on.

'So we've pretty much neglected our prelims amid all the fun and games this year.' Chloe grinned sheepishly at Isabel, who looked impossibly glamorous in a wide-brimmed sunhat, reminiscent of Saint-Tropez in the 1980's.

'Are you really bothered about your first year exams? You know full well you came to Oxford to get a husband not a degree,' scoffed Isabel.

'Well, I haven't seen you enrich your mind particularly either – just your contacts book,' giggled Chloe.

'How dare you!' Isabel retorted. 'My family knows everybody, anyway. Besides. I'm leaving Oxford.'

'What?' Chloe was stricken.

'There are things I really have to do with my life, and sitting around drinking Pimms is not one of them. Don't worry, you'll be finished with the Union next year, and I've helped you through all that. Of course Will graduates this summer but you'll have Sam and Ol to look after you and I'll only be in London – hardly far away.'

'But what are you going to do?'

'I'm going to build something big. Make a difference. There's no time to lose.'

'The world is not enough,' Chloe tried to joke, masking her despair.

'No,' Isabel replied, deadly serious.

There was no time for them to discuss Isabel's dramatic news any further as the next event in the insane calendar of activities that the Oxford summer season entailed was the fashion show, which Chloe had somehow managed to arrange at the Union.

'Between you telling me who to invite and my standing committee staff doing the organizing, it's actually been a lot easier than I thought being president, though I still get nervous at debates,' Chloe confided when they had changed into short, black cocktail dresses and were on their way to the show.

Isabel's dress was skin-tight and simple, to showcase her slenderness, while Chloe's had a lace-up ribbon front. She felt better about her appearance than usual. Nicely buxom and rather Marilyn Monroe-esque with her hair curled.

'And just the mention of such a historic institution opens up so many doors. I can't believe we managed to get a world-class supermodel to open our silly little show.'

'Wow!' exclaimed Isabel as they reached Frewin Court. A row

of Bentleys, Porsches and Rolls Royces were lined up outside. 'Our supermodel has clearly drawn a bit of an entourage.'

The Union had been converted into a winter palace as all the designers, including the fabulous Clemency Clementine, wanted to exhibit their winter collections in readiness for the coming year. In the courtyard the grounds had been transformed to look like a vast lake, its mock icy surface shimmering under lights simulating the setting sun, and flanked by a forest of real trees.

Inside, groups of people were gathered around, reclined on antique chaise longues and in armchairs, enjoying caviar and champagne.

'Wow!' said Isabel again.

'We got caviar and champagne sponsors,' Chloe announced with pride. 'Well, my librarian sorted it – but it was my idea.'

'I'm impressed. I wouldn't have had time to do all this. Not with the plans I've been making.'

'Ooh, hello! Not your typical student over there,' Chloe giggled into Isabel's ear as they passed a man in his late twenties with penetrating eyes and gently wavy auburn hair smoothed carefully back. He wore an immaculate white shirt open at the neck, a navy blazer and jeans that showed off toned thighs. His brogues shone as though never before worn and his imperious face was unsmiling as he checked his heavy, expensive watch. No doubt irritated the showroom was not yet opened up to the spectators.

'He looks mean,' Isabel whispered.

'I know,' Chloe said cheekily. 'Now, where on earth is my mother?'

People began to rise, chattering excitedly, and file into the chamber, the doors to which had been thrown open. Isabel and Chloe found their seats at the front, next to all the VIPs like Clemency and the other designers. The man they'd spotted outside took a seat nearby and Chloe checked her list to see if she could work out who he was.

She reddened as her mother arrived with a great deal of commotion.

'Madam President, Mummy's here!' she announced from the door, her loud, clipped voice reverberating around the room. She was dressed chicly in vintage Alaia and dazzling diamonds. Her glossy, highlighted hair cascaded down her back like glistening liquid exploding out of a champagne bottle. She tightly clutched by the arm Chloe's hyperactive little sister Pip, who had just turned six. Pip had somehow managed to grab a glass of champagne on her way in and was transfixed by the caviar-topped blini she had dropped inside it. Mrs Constance tottered to join them on the front row, but as Chloe hadn't known Pip was coming she'd only saved one seat, so her mother demanded loudly that everyone move down one, entirely unruffled by anybody's celebrity status.

'This is fun,' said Isabel, swaying dramatically in her seat in time to the slow burlesque music which had begun playing. She closed her eyes, seemingly consumed by it. Chloe cringed, hoping there wasn't going to be a replay of her performance at The Club. It was bad enough with her mother's entrance. But then the music stopped and the lights dimmed. The crowd fell silent. The feeling of suspense that had been steadily growing now held the room in its thrall. All eyes were glued to the catwalk and not a breath could be heard.

Just as it seemed the crowd would pass out from holding their breath, the music started up again and a sinewy, elfin-cropped peroxide blonde, draped in a feathered cape and a white bodysuit, appeared on the catwalk in a cloud of white butterflies. It was the international top model from Latvia, Natalya Ozolin. She walked moodily down the runway with slow and deliberate steps, never smiling, but with a hint of flirtation behind her pout.

'It's so weird to see her in the flesh. I've read so much about her in the papers I feel like I know her already. She's good, isn't she?' whispered Chloe.

'She certainly knows how to work the catwalk,' Isabel agreed, remembering the big exposé on her family that coincided with the model making her name in the fashion world two years ago.

Natalya reached the end of the catwalk and struck a pose, turning sideways in front of the cameras opposite and placing both hands on her hips to part the feathered cape, showing it off from different angles as the photographers snapped away. She made her way back down the runway, and her presence was such that it was impossible to look away until she had disappeared completely from sight.

Next up, a well-built man wearing nothing but silver shorts and a rabbit fur coat strode down the catwalk.

'Now that's more like it,' Isabel whispered to Chloe, licking her lips as she watched the way the shorts caressed his big bulge with each stride. 'I hate fur but that's one bunny I almost don't feel sorry for,' she said.

'No, I think you should feel very sorry,' retorted Chloe. 'I think you should stage an animal rights intervention right now. Jump up there and ambush that man – I'll be happy to help.'

'I'll help too,' shouted an indignant Pip, who was always loath to be left out. 'Let's jump on the naked man!' she screeched at the top of her voice. The surrounding spectators turned to gasp at her as her freckled little face scrunched up in laughter.

A number of other extraordinarily thin models and some hand-selected students completed the roster and then, in the blink of an eye, the spectacle was over.

'I started planning this at Easter. It's amazing how much effort goes into something that is over in so little time,' Chloe said.

'I know,' agreed Isabel, not really listening. 'Shouldn't we go and chat to people? You know, do your hostess bit?'

Chloe went to check her mother was OK. Seeing that she was chatting to another mother in the row behind, she joined Isabel, who'd gone to introduce herself to Clemency.

'I particularly loved your autumn 2011 collection,' she was telling the enchanted designer.

'My goodness, *you* should have been up there modelling,' said Clemency, returning the compliment. 'Do excuse me, I have to join Natalya as we have a dinner in London in twenty minutes, but here's my card. Keep in touch.' She handed the card to Isabel and rushed out.

'How are they going to get to London in twenty minutes?' Isabel asked, slipping Clemency's business card in her bag.

Moments later, through the mullioned windows, a convoy of helicopters carrying Natalya, Clemency and a number of their friends could be seen ascending into the air.

'That's how.'

Disappointed to have missed Natalya, Isabel looked around for their next target. Right on cue, Mr Mean drifted by.

'Please let me have him?' Chloe joked, knowing that, hopelessly committed to Sam, she was all talk and no trousers. 'You always get the boys' attention but this one's all mine.' She hadn't realized how loud she was until he turned and stretched out a hand to each of them in turn.

'Hi, I'm Hank,' he said with a stiff German accent.

'Hunk?' asked Chloe.

'Talk about nominative determinism,' added Isabel. She too showed the bravado of the not genuinely interested.

'I said Hank, not Hunk. And as for "let me have him" – well, I didn't realize I was a commodity to be traded. Last I checked *I* was the one who traded commodities. In fact, I was the most successful commodities trader in the world under the age of thirty-five.' He smirked. 'Now, can I get you ladies a drink?' He offered them an arm each.

In heels, Isabel was as tall as him. 'I don't want him anyway,' she stage-whispered loudly to Chloe behind his back.

'Why not?' Chloe laughed when Hank promptly released Isabel's arm in mock horror.

'I want to *be* him,' Isabel declared, marching ahead.

Chloe, always a sucker for a beautiful man, clung on to Hank's arm a few seconds longer, but when she spotted her mother beaming at the two of them she let go quickly so as not to give her any ideas.

Isabel had wandered off. *Probably to London for a rendezvous with her politician,* thought Chloe.

'Darling, I can't tell you how proud I am of you.' Her mother appeared at her side and gave her a kiss. Chloe felt very happy that for once she'd proved she could do it.

Chapter 21

Now that Isabel was preparing to leave Oxford and start building her empire, she wasn't able to claim a student loan for next year and all her savings had gone. She needed an interim job. Plus, she wanted a little more experience. There was only one place she wanted to work at until she got her own company up and running, and that was Serebar Sisters, the world's most powerful female-founded media consultancy. And there was one man who could get her in. It helped that she wanted him. Badly.

The circumstances in which Isabel would secure Archie's help getting her her first post-university job were less 'request' and more 'ambush'.

'Dinner's served,' she purred, striding into the sparsely furnished living room of the stucco-fronted Notting Hill mansion he lived in all alone. It needed a woman's touch, she noted, mentally adding fresh flowers and extra cushions. She set the two tender sea bass fillets on the table of his heavy oak dining table. It was long enough for big banquets. He obviously entertained a lot. 'Baked sea bass and vegetables à la Isabel.'

'My word, it smells delicious.' Archie sat eagerly at the table. He stared in amazement at Isabel, still standing there in her apron and elegant Clemency Clementine peep-toe shoes. 'I'll be asking you to move in soon.' He smiled.

'Please eat,' said Isabel. As he raised the family silver to his moistened lips, she untied her apron and threw it casually over a chair. There was a loud clang as the silver fork came crashing down, landing on the crystal plate. Isabel wore only the heels and a pair of white French knickers.

Immediately Archie was on his feet, reaching for her, but she jumped back.

'Uh-uh. Eat up first.'

She sat down at her place and calmly sliced into the fish. Chewing on it meditatively, she gave a throaty moan. 'Mmm, really rather good, if I say so myself.'

Archie was eating his so quickly that Isabel had to throw her head back and laugh. 'Please, slow down, you'll give yourself indigestion. And you've got a long night ahead of you.'

Archie choked on a parsnip and Isabel actually had to run around and perform the Heimlich manoeuvre on him to dislodge it, which threw the evening slightly off course.

When he'd calmed down, she sat on his lap and kissed him, bombarding him with questions about politics, hanging on his every word. 'I loved visiting the Houses of Parliament,' she said. 'Your world fascinates me.'

'You're amazingly well-informed for a student,' Archie said, cupping her small, delicate breasts in his hands.

'I'm an economist; I love this stuff.'

'A beautiful economist.' He kissed her and within seconds Westminster was a distant memory and Isabel's French knickers were on the floor. His hands and mouth moved so urgently over her body that it felt at times like he had eight arms, so desperate was he to get to each and every part of her, and so ready was she to give herself.

He pushed aside the plates and laid Isabel down on the table. Her peep-toe shoes fell to the floor with a thud as he positioned his face between her legs, bringing her to a deep climax, devouring her with even more fervour than he had her cooking. Overwhelmed and hypersensitive from her first orgasm, she tried to distance herself from him but he wouldn't stop. Like a man possessed, he grabbed her hips and buried himself deeper between her legs, bringing her to orgasm again.

'Let's go to the bedroom,' he said when she had finally recovered. His voice was hoarse with lust. Isabel glided towards the stairs but he seized her and carried her up, almost running in his haste.

She undid his shirt and removed his trousers and underwear. Then she teased him, stroking his trembling thighs, fondling his balls and pressing his special spot, before taking him in her hot, eager mouth. When his groans became dangerous, she slid herself on top of him, staring into his eyes with adoration and caressing his torso like it was the crown jewels as she writhed, enjoying him.

'I want to work at Serebar Sisters.'

'What?' he panted in dazed confusion. 'Oh yes!' he moaned. His penis throbbed, as if seconding the motion. He was about to come.

'So you'll get me the job?' she said.

His face contorted. 'Ohhhhhh. Yeeeeeeeeeeees!' He lifted his pelvis and head suddenly off the bed, jerking compulsively as his cock pulsed and he exploded harder and more passionately into her than ever before in the short, intense time in which they'd known each other. 'Oh yeeees,' he sighed. Then he relaxed and his head collapsed back onto the pillow.

'Great,' she said, climbing off him and planting a big kiss on his lips. 'I'll call to remind you about it tomorrow.'

'About what?' But Isabel was already on her phone, checking train times back to Oxford.

Chapter 22

The two girls were in Chloe's room changing into their ball dresses for the Hambley College ball that evening. A final celebration before they broke up for the year and went their separate ways for summer.

'Ta-da!' Isabel stepped out of the bathroom and spun around so that her filmy midnight blue silk gown flared up and danced about her knees.

'Oh, you look stunning!' exclaimed Chloe. 'Here, will you do me up? What do you think?' She wrinkled up her face.

She had initially loved her dramatic, bright yellow taffeta number, but now that she had seen Isabel's simple, elegant dress, her own felt fussy and bulky.

'You look as pretty as a sunflower,' Isabel said, doing up the dress and giving her friend a hug. 'It's a pity Sam won't see you like this.'

'Well he will, but only at the end of the night, when I'll be a complete mess. But to be honest I'll probably have more fun without him. I adore him so much but he just wouldn't enjoy this; he'd much rather be on his own painting. His drive completely humbles me. I mean, who do you know like that?' She attacked a photo of him on her phone leaving lipstick marks all over it. 'Mwah! Mwah! Mwah! You know, I don't want to jinx it, but I'm pretty sure he's about to ask me to marry him!'

The ball was already in full swing and the entire college had been lit up under a halo of gold from the towering lanterns and spray-painted tips of the buildings. Eighteen hundred students from thirty colleges were milling around. Twelve-foot tall stilt walkers, sprayed metallic purple from head to toe, stalked the lawn. Clowns performed backflips and human pyramids on plinths. A gigantic marquee housed a vast dance floor, which was sure to be filled as the night progressed.

'Thank you,' Isabel said, taking a margarita from one of the endless trays being circulated.

'Let's explore,' Chloe said, helping herself to a cosmopolitan along the way. 'Hi Jenny, hi Adam. Gita, how are you? What an amaaaaaazing dress! Hi Masha!'

Everyone had turned up, buoyant after the pressures of exams and conscious that tonight was the last night of the year. For the likes of Will, this was the last ball before he left the university. Everyone was determined to dedicate the night to nothing but pure, unadulterated enjoyment.

When the girls finally found Will, stuck deep in conversation with Ol and Artemis, he turned and grabbed both girls in an immense embrace and wouldn't let them go. Ol jumped on top of the group and then everybody piled on. Only an hour in and the girls' carefully crafted hair and make-up were already a thing of the past – not that anyone cared.

'It's almost midnight!' cried Ol. 'Let's go.'

They headed straight for the marquee. Folk-rock band The Inquisitive Beats was supporting Piers Bellevue and they wanted to see all of it.

'Are you ready, Oxford?' roared the lead singer from the stage.

'Yeeeeeeeessssss!' Right back at him came the collective affirmation of hundreds of young people. The stars seemed to shine only for them. They danced. They twirled and spun and leapt and flew until they were giddy with euphoria. This was their ball. This was their time.

The place heaved with students radiant and preening now that they were out of their scruffy jeans and in rarely worn finery. It felt like a cross between a festival and the sort of perfectly proper, very grand ball that Jane Austen might approve of.

'Good idea,' cried Chloe, seeing Isabel take off her shoes so she could really go wild. She followed suit and starting swinging her high heels above her head in time to the music. It was invigorating to dance barefoot under the night sky.

The Inquisitive Beats finished their set with their most well-known track so that everybody could sing along and then they disappeared off backstage to make way for the main act.

'Take a look at that!' exclaimed Will with a whistle as a trickle of girls with ball gowns dishevelled, or even tucked into their knickers in one case, emerged out of a side door marked 'Dressing Room – The Inquisitive Beats'.

They ran over to investigate and found there was a very organized system in place. A queue of incoming girls was waiting outside one dressing room door and then leaving out back via the other, all of which was being stage managed by the band's minder.

Chloe jokingly joined the queue but was grabbed by both Will and Isabel, who wanted to go and watch Piers Bellvue. Seeing him up there on stage, they had to admit he still had it.

After that, the night merged into a riotous blur until gradually, like a fairy tale, everyone seemed to fall asleep.

'Isabel, hon, wake up! What is it? What is it?' Chloe's face was creased with concern.

Isabel sat up with a start. 'What?' She rubbed sleep from her eyes.

'You were talking to yourself, moaning and crying in your sleep.'

'I was?'

'Yes, and it's not the first time. You did it before, that night at the hotel.'

Isabel was silent. She shook her head.

'Come on, let's go get breakfast.'

They picked up their high heels and ran barefoot through the dewy grass. In the dusky early morning light, the college looked like the aftermath of an apocalypse, with empty drink cans, food and discarded items of clothing scattered all over the grass. An odd shoe here, an earring there, a bra and, terrifyingly, a prosthetic limb beside the wilting marquee.

They queued up for hog-roast sandwiches and then sat on the grass and ate them in silence, taking in the pale, make-up smeared faces of the tired girls and the boys, shirts crumpled and untucked, bow ties drooping and hair pointing in every direction. They were all united in their mass exhaustion. Their disarray a badge of honour, like Armageddon survivors.

The sun rose and Isabel lay slumped against Chloe, chewing on her sandwich, washed down with slugs of warm, leftover champagne. She felt a rare twinge of contentedness, so sweet and stark it was almost painful. It was easy to forget in that moment. To think this was all there was.

Part Two

Chapter 23

Isabel glanced at the invitation for the fourth time. It was an oversized black box of matches embossed with bold white lettering. On one side was the address, and the other side stated simply: *Sam Fire Private View, in association with ISO Communications.* 'Isabel Suarez-Octavio Communications,' she said out loud, savouring the name of her newly incorporated PR and communications agency.

She could barely believe how quickly everything had happened since leaving Oxford six months ago and she couldn't wait to see the old gang all together again at her own exhibition, housed at her own immaculate townhouse. Chloe, Will, Ol and of course Sam, the star of the show, would all be there.

She'd taken a gamble by choosing to back Sam, but then he'd renovated and decorated her new house for free with the skill and craftsmanship of an exceptional artist, and it was now ready to be used as a gallery. Sam Smith was so convinced this would be the making of him that he'd even changed his name by deed poll to the more memorable Sam Fire. Isabel would help Sam out tonight by drawing all of her glitzy friends, as would his girlfriend Chloe, who would bring all her parents' establishment friends. Will, who had been persuaded to leave his coveted banking job in the city to come and work for Isabel, had even secured the attendance of the bigwigs and high rollers from his old bank.

Will's PR plan for ISO had so far been ingenious. Their trump card angle to hook the press tonight, aside from the guest list, was the fact that not only were all the works at the exhibition going to be on sale but that the entire 'art gallery' was on sale that day too. Isabel's plan was not only to sell the house, ISO Communication's first asset, but to work the room with Will and secure investment in exchange for a small stake in the business from the wealthy art patrons who were sure to be impressed by the slick event. Then her company would be good to go and she could kick phase two into operation.

She started planning her outfit. This was important. She'd long established she was not some bimbo for Archie to hide away at his home. This was ISO's first big public engagement and it was time people started taking her seriously. She opened Archie's closet and pulled out one of the elegant, knee-length dresses she had been given by Clemency Clementine, which skimmed her curves and was cut low, but not pointedly so, at the front. Isabel had taken the designer at her word and kept in touch after her visit to the Union. Since then they'd become firm friends.

She slipped on smart patent leather Louboutins with big bows at the toe and blow-dried her hair instead of leaving it natural and tousled as she usually did. Her make-up was mascara and a sharp red lipstick. She was ready to take on the world.

Beep. 'Am outside in taxi' read Archie's text message. She picked up her little laptop, two phones, her lipstick and the invitation. She slid it all into a crocodile skin Prada laptop case and skipped out of Archie's house and hurried outside to the taxi. Archie reached over from inside and held open the door for her.

'Wow,' he murmured, kissing her cheek as she climbed in beside him. 'On we go, please,' he told the taxi driver.

'Your campaign seems to be going well, Mr Soon-to-be-Prime-Minister-we-hope.' She remembered not to snog him in public now that he was so high-profile and had to watch his reputation.

He squeezed her hand surreptitiously. 'Your coming up with "PM for a day" for underprivileged children was a fantastic help. They loved their day at Westminster and the press loved it even more.'

'No problem. I have to say I thought you'd had it when you mistook that skinny cleaner for one of the orphans and posed with her in your arms for the press. She must have been, what, seventeen? Thank goodness Will had the presence of mind to tell the press that for some of the orphans, life was so tough it put years on their faces.' They both laughed.

'Watch the game?' asked the driver through the partition glass with a friendly nod.

'No,' snapped Archie, who didn't appreciate being interrupted.

Isabel turned in surprise. 'But I saw you on the telly today – laughing and joking about it and charming the pants off a couple of your rugby-loving constituents!'

Archie yawned.

'Oh, I get it ...the charm only comes on when the cameras come out.'

He stared at her. 'You are the most gorgeous thing I've ever met in my life, do you know that?' he whispered. 'And when I get you back home, I'm going to ravish you. I'm going to take off all your clothes one by one and massage you all over your beautiful body.

Then I'm going to kiss you everywhere. And then I'm going to lick you, your nipples and your cunt and your bottom … and then I'm going to take you right there – up your naughty little bottom.' He slid a hand between her legs and stroked her thigh, a light smirk playing on his lips.

Isabel resisted the urge to kiss him. She stared at this incredibly driven, powerful man. 'You know I'm so proud of you.'

She thought back to how, since Oxford, she'd got herself to this position. It all started with Nobu.

Ol's father, Chief Tunde Osaloni, pulled up outside the restaurant in his chauffeur-driven Bentley. He looked so much like his son – Isabel could see immediately where Ol got his height and profile from. She approached him and extended a hand. He shook it.

'My son has told me a lot about you.

She quickly introduced him to Archie. He pumped Archie's hand and looked hard at him for a while, as though searching for something.

'I'm a big advocate of what you people are trying to do with our banks,' said the chief.

'Between you and me,' Archie said, leaning in as though he was about to confide all of his most intimate secrets, 'I've been a proponent of the benefits of investing in emerging markets long before it became sexy. You might have heard of the "Bigger than BRICs" initiative? You have? Yes, that was one of my first projects on entering the cabinet.'

'Gentlemen, shall we go in?' said Isabel. The two men were so caught up in their conversation that they had quite forgotten they were outside on the pavement.

They made their way into Nobu and had an aperitif in the ground floor bar. Isabel enjoyed the buzzing atmosphere, its décor a concoction of iridescent surfaces, lit by muted sparkly lights and packed with pouty, leggy girls and Rolex-wearing city types.

They were soon led to their table in the restaurant upstairs. It was not often that Isabel felt invisible in the company of men and she quite enjoyed the novelty of it. She ploughed through the bowl of edamame beans as the two men talked business.

'So, you see, there are plenty of ways that a resident non-domiciled individual like yourself can become very involved in the life of the Lib-Con Party, and indeed the country.'

The food was exquisite. Scallop and lobster starter dishes gave way to a selection of fresh sushi and sashimi, followed by delicately flavoured black cod in misu sauce and some wagyu beef. By the time Isabel took a final sip of her hot sake, she was convinced something special had just happened.

When Archie left the table to use the gents, Chief Osaloni reached into his soft leather case and pulled out a chequebook.

'Shall I make this out to Isabel Suarez-Octavio or do you have a company name I should use?'

'Excuse me?' Isabel spluttered, nearly spraying the table with droplets of sake.

'I'd like to give you something as a token of my thanks, for your introduction. I pay all my fixers.'

'Oh please, no, I didn't want anything for it. I just thought you and he would be a good match.'

'Please accept it. I'd be offended if you didn't.'

Chief Osaloni slid the cheque for £500,000 towards her across the table. 'Get yourself a little pied-à-terre. Renting does not make good business sense in this market and I can tell you're a businesswoman.'

Now, in the taxi with Archie, Isabel remembered the feeling of buying her first home with that cheque, a repossession she got for a knock-down price and immediately sold for twice its value. Not long afterward she had reinvested in the huge but dilapidated Shepherds Bush townhouse, which she hoped would be sold at twice its value again.

'So remind me of what you're hoping to achieve with the investment drive tonight?' asked Archie.

'A lot of money,' was Isabel's dry response. 'I want to expand quickly, with the biggest clients – governments, heads of industry, leading lights in the arts and culture, and top entrepreneurs – so I'll need serious funds to run offices, pay staff and to fly around the world and woo big clients who expect the best of the best. We can't scrimp.'

'I wish I could officially hire you, you're so good. But imagine how it would look if any of those opposition spies or nosy newspapers discovered we're, well, you know. Conflict of interest if ever there was one.'

'Oh, of course I don't expect anything from you. Will and I have already identified some potential investors anyway. There's Divia, a hedge fund wife and serious art collector and patron; she gets off on discovering new artists and likes Ruskin grads. We found her through Sam. Then there are some hotshots at Will's old bank – though not his old boss Matthias, who hates him for leaving! Plus lots of other financiers. Oh, and Angus and Fergus. They're retired but they were pretty successful back in the day. Now they want to back promising young people – they came to the entrepreneurialism debate at the Union.'

'Sounds like you know exactly what you're doing.'

'Yes,' said Isabel, 'And I won't let anything get in my way.'

Chapter 24

Chloe propped herself up on her elbow on the floor of Isabel's swish new townhouse and watched Sam put the finishing touches together for that evening.

'Baby, can I have a piece of your art?'

'No. I'm selling everything at my exhibition. And anyway, I gave you *Beast*.'

'That was ages ago. And that was the only present you've ever given me. Not even for Christmas or my birthday.' Chloe pouted unintentionally.

'You're so spoilt, you know that?' Sam said. 'I've got my first exhibition coming up and all you can think about is yourself. I bet you got presents everyday growing up. I didn't.'

He finished varnishing a thin table he'd spotted in a charity shop. He reckoned the owner hadn't known its value. He'd intended to graffiti it and sell it at the exhibition but at the last minute decided to varnish it so Isabel could use it in one of the upstairs showrooms to showcase the potential of the house to prospective buyers. He couldn't resist graffitiing the underside though, and thought it was one of his best works.

'That's very classic and restrained for you,' said Chloe, looking at the table and trying not to cry.

'Yeah, I love it. I'll put it in the house and then when the exhibition's over I'll give it to Isabel. You know, as a thanks.'

Chloe's eyes were downcast.

'Sorry, baby,' Sam muttered, stubbing out his cigarette on an ashtray. 'Did I upset you?'

'I just don't like it when you snap at me. I only want to make you happy.'

'Baby, you do. You make me so happy.' He looked at her, red-eyed and vulnerable. 'Why don't you cheer yourself up, baby? I want to watch you.'

Chloe gazed up at him from where she sat on the floor. The way the light hit his head it seemed as though there was a halo above it. Why did they draw angels blond when Sam's face, studded with dark stubble and cheeks sunken with the weight of his intensity, was the most heavenly thing she had ever seen?

She parted her legs and began to touch herself.

'Darling ...' His voice thickened. She finally had his full, undivided attention.

'Make love to me?' she asked hopefully.

'Not now, baby, I'm working.' But he walked over to where she sat and unzipped his flies so she could pleasure him to a quick climax. Then he stalked off to do some 'communicating' in readiness for his show.

Since Sam, along with Will and Isabel, had left Oxford last year to concentrate on making waves in the London art scene, where he was quietly making a name for himself, Chloe had felt more and more isolated. She remembered what he'd told her last week when she'd turned up unannounced in London at the squat he shared with two other artists. The other artists were hardly ever actually at the squat, preferring the comfort of their parents' or girlfriends' homes when the weather got a little less congenial. But Sam was real. Sam stayed alone there, enduring the hardship because the break from convention brought out his creativity. He'd had only a towel wrapped around him and a cigarette in his mouth when he went to open the door absentmindedly, as if he were expecting a delivery. Certainly not her, at any rate. He started in surprise to see her. Then he kissed her but didn't allow her inside the building.

'I'm communicating,' he told her. She knew what that meant. That he was feeling at his most inspired. His most in tune with nature. Whenever that happened he refused almost all contact with humans, preferring only his ongoing communications with the birds in the sky, the fish in the river, the rats scurrying along the skirting boards of the squat and the lush green bushes which raged, wild and awe inspiring, through the enclosed garden at the back. It was at times like this that he produced his best work.

'Oh sorry, darling!' She left the eight bags of groceries she had bought for him from Marks and Spencer at the door and kissed him goodbye, as lingeringly as she could before he gently pushed her away. Then she turned and went back on the train to Oxford.

Chloe was interrupted from her reverie by the sound of Isabel's key in the door. She'd come early to help set up.

'Hey,' sang Chloe, always delighted to see her friend, who was all too elusive these days. 'You look amazing. Where's Archie?'

'He's had to nip back to his office but don't worry, he's coming. He'll be here in a couple of hours when everything gets going.' She looked around her glossy white house filled with stunning canvases. 'The place looks great. I wish Sam would tell us what his secret unveiling will be, though.'

'Even I don't know. He wants a completely authentic response when it's revealed. I know it's something extraordinary, though. I can sense it.'

'Of course it will be – he's a genius. He needs to hurry up, though. Things will be kicking off soon. How are you, darling?' she asked as if she were just seeing Chloe for the first time.

'I'm good, good. Uni is …OK. Hard. What about you? Are you keeping well? Are you in love? And Archie doesn't count!'

'Why not? But anyway, I'm not in love with him.'

'Liar. But he doesn't look after you properly.'

'I don't need looking after – you know that, hon,' Isabel said. 'Anyway …he did ask me to marry him.'

Chloe started to scream and had to cover her mouth to hold it in.

'We were in bed and he was telling me all about Hugh James, about how he'd started calling meetings they'd already had and that he'd started having to cover for him because he didn't want anybody to know that he had Alzheimer's—'

'How dreadful!'

'Yes, it's in its early stages but Hugh told Archie he wanted to leave office with his pride intact. He confided in him that he wouldn't be running again at the next election, and that he backed Archie to succeed him as leader of the Lib-Cons. So Archie turned to me and said he was going to do it. Going to go for the top job and run for prime minister. I knew he would and was just so proud of him. But then he said he needed a wife. Said who'd heard of a bachelor prime minister? And then, 'Isabel's voice faltered, 'and then he said that, mad as I was, did I want to spend my life with him and make our relationship formal and a lot more appropriate. Very romantic,' she added, to hide her emotion.

Chloe's jaw dropped. 'So what did you say?'

'I said no.' Isabel looked away. She thought of all the skeletons in her closet. All that was unknown about her. There was no way she could let anybody that close.

'I said I didn't love him.'

'How did he take it?'

'He was saddened, but for him the job comes first. He's practical. He said in that case we would always be friends but he would need to get a wife and be squeaky clean to get elected. This will be the last public event we ever attend together.' She turned so that Chloe wouldn't see the look in her eyes.

'Well, I think Sam's going to propose soon. And *I* will be saying yes. I can't wait—'

'Didn't you think he'd propose at the end of last summer?' Isobel interrupted gently.

'Did I? Well, I guess things need to change. But it'll be so much easier for us to be together, for him to do his art when we're living together. You know, at times like this, when he's feeling really … inspired, he could work and communicate, and I wouldn't dream of getting in his way, but at least I'd get to see him. At least he'd come back home to my bed at the end of the night. Oh Isabel,' she sobbed. 'What should I do?'

'You know what to do,' Isabel said after a while.

'No I bloody don't. I don't know anything.'

'You don't know it, but you do. Somewhere inside of you, some fibre, some tiny part of you, has figured out what you need. It hasn't reached your brain yet, but it will and you will find your path and the people you're meant to share it with.'

'I hope so.' Chloe sniffed. 'Have you found yours?'

'I hope it's this. The launch of ISO. Really, Will and I have amazing plans if we can just secure the rest of the funding.'

'I wish I could be more like you.'

'No you don't. Believe me.'

Chapter 25

Clemency Clementine arrived at the Sam Fire private view to the familiar glare of flashbulbs. Revelling in the blinking lights as though she were a sunbather basking in the sun, she turned this way and that, posing just so and then switching position again so that every angle and part of her body could be captured. Clemency was too thin and it aged her, but in photographs her angular features worked well, reflecting the light flatteringly on her face while her barely-there body allowed the clothes to fall freely, unhindered by even the slightest lumps and bumps. She stood up straighter and put out one leg to showcase the thigh-high slit in her gold Clemency Clementine maxi dress.

'Darling, you look divine,' she cried, spotting Isabel hovering nervously by the entrance, achingly glamorous in another one of her dresses. She beckoned her over so that they could work the cameras together.

Isabel tried to shy away. 'I want the event to be famous, not me!'

But Clemency wouldn't give up and clutched her hand. 'Oh, you're so darling to wear me. How are you, sweetheart? You look so well. Are you getting any sex? I've got a great new yoga teacher; you should try him.'

'I'm all sorted, thanks.' Isabel laughed.

'Who?' Clemency looked sideways at her. 'You're so shifty with your boys.' She was still posing as she chatted.

'I think they call it discreet.'

'What. Ever.' Clemency made an exaggerated W sign with her two hands, showcasing a dazzling array of Chopard diamond bracelets that looked as though their weight would cripple her tiny wrists.

'Business going well for you?' Isabel asked. Clemency never seemed to do any work yet she appeared to enjoy a rather fabulous life, hopping from party capital to party capital in a bubble of champagne, exquisite jewels and toy-boy yogis.

'Between you and me, darling, I'm stony broke. The company just about stays afloat because I'm always in the papers and so are all my friends, but it doesn't turn a profit. I just don't have a business brain, for a start. My entire life is a series of exchanges. I get invited on all these glamorous holidays because I have so many connections, and I get free suppers at the best restaurants because I get photographed there and I tell my friends about it. I get loaned jewellery for the same reason, and I pay all my models in dresses, but I don't have a penny in the bank. The Notting Hill house has been re-mortgaged so many times and my whole business is guaranteed against it. Honestly, I have nightmares that it's all about to come crashing down every time my head hits the pillow.' She laughed hollowly and raised a bony finger to smooth back her carefully coiffed hair.

'Can't you go to your family for help?' Isabel had always assumed that some sort of inheritance underwrote her.

'Granny left me the house but that's all that's left. Daddy pissed the rest away on heroin.'

Isabel hugged her. 'There are lots of business brains here. Why don't you team up with someone? You should be the creative side and let somebody else take control.'

'Yes, yes, you're right.' Clemency nodded, cheering up, but Isabel suspected the woman would take the easier route of carrying on as she always had. At least she was able to smile through the tears.

Isabel clasped Clemency's hand as they made their way inside, looking around her. She was delighted to see that as well as all the paparazzi from the newspapers and weekly magazines, top celebrity paparazzo, Dino Larrsson, had also arrived. Commissioned for royal weddings and only the most upscale events, he had worked before on some of Chloe's family's grander parties and had agreed to take this on for her when he'd seen the guest list.

'Can I get the two of you ladies together?' he asked when Isabel and Clemency swept by.

'Certainly.' Clemency smiled. Then Isabel spotted Angus and Fergus, identical from their twinkly eyes to their hippy-style beaded bracelets, belying their advanced ages and the fact that they'd been stupendously successful brewing entrepreneurs in their day. They had brought with them the retail billionaire Phillip Green and a boy dressed casually in jeans, who didn't look old enough to enjoy the cocktails.

'Thought you might like to meet Vikram; he's tomorrow's Mark Zuckerberg,' said Fergus, the fractionally taller of the brothers. 'We're backing him. Oh, and this is Phillip.'

Isabel thrilled a stammering young Vikram with her warmest handshake and then rushed to introduce the fashion retail star to Clemency.

Meanwhile, Ol and his father had also arrived, having spent the entire day together for the first time in years, if Ol remembered correctly.

'Not for me, thanks,' Ol said as a waiter circulated with a tray topped with flutes of Krug champagne. Despite normally drinking like a fish, his father's presence still had the effect of bringing out his best behaviour.

'I'll have one,' said the Chief, beckoning to his son to get him a glass, not the first of the day for him by any means. He watched Isabel working the crowd and chuckled as she almost rugby-tackled a departing waitress to prevent her from taking away the drinks before Phillip Green had had one.

'She's a smart girl. She'll do well.' He nodded approvingly, smoothing down his light blue tie. Ol fixated on the tie, instantly nervous. He knew that this manoeuvre of his father's always preceded a humiliating dressing down. His father began to speak.

'My son. Let me tell you something. I've watched you growing up over the past twenty years. And I must admit I had my doubts. Not about you, but about myself. I wondered whether your mother and I had brought you up wrongly all these years. Spoiled you a bit too much. Let you enjoy the accumulated fruits of your family's labour without learning how to labour yourself. I wondered whether a foreign playground might end up being the ruin of you, so far from your responsibilities and the glare of the Nigerian press. All these …available girls of yours. This …sushi and champagne. But you exercised those very special things you have. A generous heart and brilliant mind. You managed your time and your assets well. You're on track to get a degree that fills me with pride. And you have found wonderful, loyal friends. Friends who will really change the world. I feel blessed to have you for a son. I think you will soon be ready. Ready to come back home and take your part in the business.'

There was a long silence.

'Thank you, Dad.'

Chief Osaloni removed his glasses and rubbed his eyes. Then he put them back on and patted his son stiffly on the back.

It was the happiest day of Ol's life.

When Ol's father spotted Archie Arden arrive, he headed away in the politician's direction and Isabel stepped in, closely followed by Will.

'Have you just met the woman of your dreams or something, Ol? Why are you mooning around like that?'

'Dream woman? No, I met her nearly two years ago at The Club in Oxford but she wasn't interested in mere students. No, this is even better than the love of a good woman – it's a career and the love of a good man.' He winked.

'Another one bites the dust,' joked Isabel. 'We heterosexual women already lost Will years ago, and now you.'

'Excuse me, just because I'm not a tart does not mean I don't like women. I might just be secure enough to wait for girls I love instead of stealing a fumble with every woman who comes my way.' Will pushed back his fringe and looked pointedly at Ol.

'Opportunity makes the thief,' snorted Ol. 'Anyway, buddy, I'm going to be spending a lot more time in Nigeria in the holidays, helping out with things at home, so you might find you finally get a bit of action.'

They laughed.

'So Isabel, where are you going to live after this place is sold?' Ol asked.

'Good question!' She'd been spending her time between the house and Archie's but this was her last weekend at Archie's now that mission 'find a PM's wife' was underway. 'I'll think of something.'

'Well, you know what, as I'm going to be in London less and less, why don't you keep an eye on my house if you like?'

'Seriously?'

'Of course. I don't like leaving it empty for security reasons. You can stay there; keep the staff under control. And there's a great office you can use till you get your own. You'll need somewhere smart to hold meetings.'

'That would be amazing. Thank you, Ol.'

'So where's our artiste?' Will interrupted.

'What?' Isabel said.

'Where's Sam?'

'What? I assumed you'd seen him?'

'No. I thought he was with you.'

'I've only seen Chloe and she said he was on his way back.' Her voice became shriller and began to rise. 'We—'

'Calm down,' said Will, placing a firm hand on her shoulder and maintaining command of the situation. 'I'll sort it.'

The room had filled up and Isabel noticed a few serious players and critics in the art world, people whom she and Will had chatted up at other events and private views over the last six months. One or two had already heard of Sam, and one lady, Divia, the statuesque Indian-born wife of a hedge-fund tycoon who had set up her own gallery and was now serious in the art world in her own right, had pinpointed him as one to watch at the Ruskin summer show, when he was still plain old Sam Smith.

But where was Sam now, and where were the three main surprise exhibits that he was supposed to be bringing with him?

Isabel's heart sunk as she saw Divia looking at her watch and heading towards the exit. Her despair turned to shock when just at that moment a red-faced Chloe appeared, followed by Sam, who'd come dressed in costume. As a giant turd.

He swept into the room in his brown all-in-one outfit and proceeded to position three oversized squidgy brown sculptures in the middle of the room. Silence descended on the space. Horror could be discerned on every face except Sam's, whose eyes were all that were visible from the costume.

It took him twenty minutes to assemble the sculptures, carefully pushing bits into place here and smoothing out edges there. Gradually the initial shock subsided and people began to look on with curiosity. A circle formed around him and the cameras were in overdrive. When he had finished, Sam straightened up and unzipped the top of his costume to reveal his paint-splattered face.

Solemn and unsmiling, he declared: 'When all is said and done and we've taken in everything around us, when everything has entered into our system and penetrated deep inside us, then what we are left with is this. Faeces, my friends, is the glorious summation of our existence.'

The silence was broken by Divia. 'What an incredibly brave and simple way of summing up the eternal truth of humanity's very existence.'

Another critic, not to be outdone, started murmuring about conceptual links with Duchamp, and before long, like the rousing finale of *Spartacus*, the whole room was declaring the same and there were red 'sold' stickers by almost every work of art.

Will and Isabel jumped on the emotion and feeling of revolution. They began their full-throttle assault on potential investors.

'Divia,' Isabel said. 'Thank you so much for coming. Excellent interview on Radio 4, by the way. I quite agree with your views on the increasing inaccessibility of the contemporary art world, and agree that the perception of it can be alienating. It's exacerbating the problem. If we're thinking in terms of perception, then surely that's largely a PR issue?'

As Isabel began her opening gambit with Divia, Will began working the room in the other direction and froze when he spotted an uninvited attendee. Matthias, his jilted ex-boss, and one of the fattest cats at the bank.

'Vill, you leetle sheet,' he said with his German accent, striding over to confront him.

Will steeled himself for an embarrassing showdown. 'Look, it was you who said that success is about recognizing opportunities and jumping on them. I'm setting up a business with a friend. This is my opportunity.'

'I know. You hev bin talking to our clients for yourself. Zat is illegal.'

Will said nothing.

'Zey like you. Everyone likes you, you leetle smarm, and ze ones who don't, zey don't count.'

Will relaxed and allowed himself to smile.

'I vant you back.'

'Not for the world.'

'Double your zalary.'

'Never.' An idea began to form in Will's head. 'We have big plans, but we need to start with a phenomenal bang. Luckily we have people clamouring to invest in us. I've been approached by someone I know from Brinkly Bank but as they were your competitors, out of loyalty, I said no—'

'If I can't hev you, zen I vant a piece of you. Send me your business plan.'

Will beckoned a waiter carrying a tray of martinis. He reached for two and handed one to his old boss.

Matthias picked the olive stick from his martini, popped the olive into his mouth and jabbed Will's chest with the stick. 'Better get me zat plan tonight.'

Will finished his drink and smiled at Isabel also working her magic. He watched her trying to dodge the advances of a chubby trader called Mark and wondered whether he ought to rescue her.

'Miss Bolivia, Miss Bolivia, this is alright, isn't it? Bit of a bash, isn't it?' The oaf kept repeating the same sentiment in slightly different ways.

As Will readied himself for intervention, however, he overheard him asking about ISO's plans, so he left them to it.

Gradually the crowd began to thin as attendees headed on home or to late dinners but, to Will's slight embarrassment, there remained a large enough crowd to witness Matthias' dramatic exit, which involved him turning at the door and pointing at Will on the other side of the room with the parting words, 'Remember Vill, I vant you!'

It was midnight by the time the house emptied, leaving Isabel, Will, Chloe and Sam surveying the wreckage of a very successful first night.

'Come 'ere, darlin',' Sam said to Isabel, swinging an arm around her. He lifted the only two paintings without red dots beside them from the wall and carried them upstairs to the table he'd graffitied.

'Look underneath,' he told Isabel.

She got on her hands and knees and crawled under the table. 'Woohoo!' she shouted.

'It's for you. And the paintings too.' He left them on the table and walked out, barely glancing at a white-faced Chloe, bottom lip trembling, seeing Isabel with fresh eyes.

Chapter 26

Piper Kenton climbed into the driver's seat of her small hired convertible and relished the Miami sunshine and the warm air as she drove along Collins Avenue, praising the legendarily long Oxford summer vacations. She swerved to avoid a driver zooming past and wondered whether she was brave enough to drive here where the roads were like the Wild West. She loved being back in the States but Miami might as well be a different country to San Francisco, where she came from. Slowing down, she gawped at the amazing art deco buildings and shining high rises that formed the Strip. Beyond them she could see Pine Tree Drive, better known as Millionaires Row. Along it, spectacular pastel-coloured mansions overlooked the water. Each house had its own dock for a yacht, and through the front gates she could see bespoke outdoor pools shimmering invitingly in lush, manicured gardens.

Soon she approached South Beach and the Shore Club, the oceanside hotel were she would be staying. A pleasing army of staff helped her out of the vehicle with her luggage and she handed her key to the valet. Her bags were taken to her room while she explored the building.

She took in the height and scale of the calming, white art deco lobby. The smooth surfaces and clean lines of the furniture were softened by the floor to ceiling drapes of rippling white material, tall green plants and lanterns emitting a subtle golden light. Walking through the spacious lobby to the garden, she emerged into the first of a series of outdoor 'rooms'. Flourishing greenery lined the intense blue walls of the Moroccan-inspired space. Comfy cushions in the deepest oranges and reds adorned low recliners, and tables artfully dotted around and a large double bed clad in sumptuous orange silks held court in the centre of the space, incongruous and beautiful under the direct beat of the afternoon sun. In the corner, a barman was serving guests rum.

Piper heard upbeat music close by and couldn't help but feel unburdened by the sun and the music. She followed the sound of revelry into the next area. Here was an olympic-size outdoor pool, surrounded on every side by sunbeds. Perfect for checking people out.

Piper gasped as a drunken topless girl tried to pour the contents of a champagne bottle down her boyfriend's throat, missing his mouth completely and nearly knocking him out with the heavy glass bottle. Behind the sunbeds, in little alcoves that could be sealed off with a white curtain, were rows of beds where yet more bronzed revellers were frolicking. At the far side of the pool was the DJ booth. The Panama hat-wearing DJ bounced as he spun his loud, fast tunes, concentrating on the decks, oblivious to the circus around him.

Piper's stomach rumbled as she watched a baked sea bass being delivered to a table in the shaded restaurant area next to the pool. She'd have to eat soon but she wanted to finish exploring first. She strolled through, passing another, calmer pool area that led directly on to the beach itself and the famous Miami boardwalk. She grinned at the scores of unnaturally endowed men and women zooming past on rollerblades. There was clearly some serious steroid and silicone abuse going on here.

She looked at her watch. No time for food; she was due at bitch school.

'Bitch schools' had first been brought to Piper's attention by an article in *The Telegraph* in England. They had featured one of the first ones set up in a post-communist society where a number of the women, after years of ploughing the fields and working in factories alongside the men, had realized that going shopping was a hell of a lot more fun. The key to a life of shopping was to become a 'bitch'. Piper had read that, according to the school's founder, 'Bitchology is the theory, practice and technique of being successful in a man's world'.

A successful 'bitch', rather than being aggressive and overbearing, gets what she wants by pretending to be weak. 'A bitch should be inwardly strong and self-confident but should remember to use feminine wiles, such as her attractiveness, and, whenever useful, should try to come across as a helpless creature.' That, Piper had read with amusement, was the key to gaining a competitive edge in the hunt for the best men.

The schools had flourished and proliferated and could now be found on every corner of the globe. Piper had decided that the recently opened Miami branch was of particular interest, and eventually convinced the commissioning paper, the prestigious *San Francisco Eye*, that this had nothing to do with her lacklustre sun tan and the fabulous trip the assignment would necessitate.

She made her way to the colossal high-rise that housed the school. It had been built at a time of great optimism but now, post-credit crunch, the apartments inside lay mostly empty. Though Piper was going for a comic angle with her article, the sight of those empty recession casualty properties made her feel sad.

Piper stepped into the glass elevator on the outside of the building and pressed the gold 'P' button. As the elevator rose she enjoyed the increasingly jaw-dropping view of the bay and the different Miami islands.

Beep. 'Penthouse,' said the automated voice.

She took a deep breath and stepped into the room. It immediately felt like she was part of the landscape. Floor to ceiling glass on all sides embraced the ocean and the outdoors. The dark, sheltered quality of the buildings in England, designed to protect inhabitants from the weather rather than to embrace it, had been the most depressing aspect of her time studying there.

She stood at the edge of the room and assessed the girls, seated in groups, chatting animatedly. Nobody looked like the ruthless femme fatale of her imagination. Piercing through the American twangs and heated Spanish, she heard two clipped, cut-glass accents. Wondering why two English girls travelled all the way to the US to attend this school, she went over and introduced herself.

'Hi,' she said. 'I'm Piper Kenton. This is my first class and I don't really know what to expect.'

'Don't worry, it's fun,' the first girl said.

The second had startling eyes, one brown and one blue, in a freckled face framed by flyaway ginger hair. 'Why are you here?' she asked Piper.

'I'm …' Piper thought about telling the truth but decided against it in case the girls became inhibited. 'I'm here to learn.' She gave a cheeky grin. 'What about you?'

The redhead gave her a hard stare. 'I want to seduce Sweet. Then, I want to destroy him.'

'Yikes.' Piper laughed nervously. 'And who is the unfortunate Sweet?'

'The meanest man in the world.'

Thinking that these girls might have a couple of screws loose, Piper made her excuses and moved on to the next group. A smiley girl with waist-length raven hair and olive skin smiled at her. She was in super tight jeans that showed off a large bottom and she wore a ton of make-up, but underneath it Piper could see that she was pretty and had a cute, girlish face. Perhaps she'd make an interesting case study.

'Hi, I'm Piper.'

'Hi! I'm Luminosa.'

'So, Luminosa, is this a course for women who don't like men?' Piper thought of the redhead.

'Not at all,' Luminosa replied with a bubbly Mexican accent. 'It's for women who love being women.' She slipped her arm through Piper's. 'Stick with me.'

'OK ladies, can I have everybody's attention please?' Mrs Bilson, the headteacher, strode to the middle of the room. To Piper's disappointment she was a normal-looking middle-aged lady. 'OK, can I have everybody in first position.'

Immediately the chatter stopped and each girl struck a pose. 'Hooters out, stomach in, back arched,' Luminosa whispered to Piper. 'That's first position.'

Piper stared in amazement as the seemingly innocuous teacher suddenly transformed herself into something to rival any Victoria's Secret Angel.

Next they rehearsed a few manoeuvres. First was 'heavy'. Piper watched open-mouthed while twenty women pretended to struggle as they bent down to pick up their luggage in a way that best emphasized their curves, moaning softly with the exertion. Then there was 'confused', which you needed a map or a gadget for. This was followed by 'cold', a simple stroking of one's own bare arms, surreptitiously squeezing the breasts together just so in the process. The especially skilled could extend this manoeuvre by combining it with 'the princess'. Piper looked into the mirror and burst out laughing as she tried and failed to complete 'the princess,' which was essentially a perfect pout of displeasure without looking like a cross goldfish in the process.

By the end of the first lesson Piper was surprised to find herself exhausted. With all the seductive stretching, her body felt the way it did after an intense yoga workout, and she'd had as much fun as at any parkour session in the most built up urban area. But she hoped it was just that – fun. She was incredulous and did not want to believe these tricks actually worked.

She exited the building with Luminosa just as a Ferrari pulled up to the curb and a handsome, dark haired man in a black T-shirt, which showcased a gym-honed body, jumped out to use the ATM. As he passed them, Luminosa dropped her bag on the ground and pulled a 'heavy', bending down with back arched, round bottom in the air and hair tumbling over her shoulder as she gasped and moaned, struggling to pick it up again.

The man stopped in his tracks and ran to relieve her.

'Here, let me get that for you. Hey, where are you going? Can I give you guys a lift?'

'Oh, thank you.' Luminosa smiled shyly, allowing him to rest a hand on her waist and lead her to his Ferrari, leaving Piper to climb in afterwards carrying her own bag.

'Luminosa, why don't you come over for a poolside drink at the Shore Club where I'm staying? It's quite a scene.' Piper leaned forward to be heard above the sound of the wind whooshing past as the sports car sped along.

'Forget it,' said the guy who'd introduced himself as Fernando. 'I'm taking you both for dinner. Hakkasan at the Fountainbleu.' He bit his lip and glanced at Luminosa, looking very at home in the dazzling white interior of his custom-designed sports car. 'You'll love it.'

'Si, I don't doubt that,' she whispered. 'I've been to both the London ones, and the one in New York.'

He began murmuring to her in Spanish but she replied in English, thinking of Piper sitting in the back.

'So where do you live?' she asked him.

'Little Havana,' he deadpanned.

'Oh.' Luminosa struggled to conceal her disappointment. 'How long have you lived there?'

'I was kidding. I've got a crib in every city where there's a Hakkasan. And that's just for starters. But in Miami I live on Star Island.' Luminosa's eyes lit up. 'How would you like to live there, baby?' He smirked. Luminosa played with her hair, teasing it with her fingers.

He revved the engine extra loudly for effect.

'Aaay Papi, you got a biiiiiig engine.' Luminosa gave a playful shiver.

She heard Piper laughing in the back and turned around and winked at her. 'You OK?'

'Sure.' Piper smiled. It was all part of the experience.

'Oh. My. God,' Piper said as they arrived at Fountainbleu. New, ultra-shiny and Vegas-style gaudy, the hotel was made up of three interlinked buildings and looked as though it went on for miles. Piper decided she didn't like it but she didn't have much choice as Fernando gave over his car to the valet and steered both girls into a cavernous lobby where crowds of loud teenage girls, dolled up in high heels and the shortest, tightest dresses, were milling about making eyes at the men. They fought their way through the crowds and into the lift where, with more than twelve different restaurants in the hotel for starters, there seemed to be a button for anything anyone could conceive of.

The elevator doors shut out the din of the lobby and deposited them on a quieter floor. They walked down a long corridor, at the end of which was Hakkasan. They headed for the bar while their table was prepared and took in the surrounds of the dark and sultry restaurant. The carved teak walls were lit by a dim, turquoise-hued light, and many tables were in their own little alcoves, creating an air of intimacy. The atmosphere of the place was clearly designed so diners had to lean in close to their companions and whisper rather than shout.

Fernando's friends arrived. Unlike slick and groomed Fernando, they were two brutish-looking men, thickset with matching goatees and wearing too much gold jewellery. They took a seat at the table, which was now ready, and looked menacingly at the girls. Luminosa didn't seem to notice. She was too busy whispering something into a smiling Fernando's ear. Piper thought she heard her murmuring, *'Mi amore'*.

Piper watched her, making mental notes and assimilating juicy material for her article. Then she gazed around the restaurant to avoid the stares of the two heavies and the embarrassing drools of Fernando as he watched Luminosa suck the tail off an extra large lobster that had just arrived.

At that moment an extraordinarily tall skinny man with a pallid complexion, ice white hair, piercing blue eyes and a long pointed nose glided into the building. Piper shivered. She knew him from somewhere. As he moved, his strides were so fluid that he didn't appear to lift his feet off the ground. Everything about him seemed strange and exaggerated. Behind him strode what looked like an entourage of seven incredibly striking women. Tall and athletic in matching black mini-dresses and with their hair tied in a single plait down their backs, they 'looked like they would crush you at Wimbledon and then give you the best sex you ever had', joked a group of jocks at the neighbouring table.

By now the entire restaurant was staring. Luminosa had even stopped performing oral sex on the lobster and Fernando had torn his eyes away from her. Piper took a closer look at the seven women and noticed that they weren't wearing heels but flat black pointed shoes with their mini-dresses. They really were tall. Each must have been between six-two and six-five. She took in the surprisingly muscled thighs of each; they possessed levels of fitness she could only dream of. Then, one by one, she looked at their faces. They were all very different – some blonde, some brunette, an angular-featured black woman and a handsome Iranian-looking girl. Her journalist's quick brain noticed straight away that what was uniform about their faces was a strange alertness to their eyes. These women seemed to be watching and monitoring everything. Could they be bodyguards?

'I don't believe this!' Fernando said quietly, his voice choked with hate.

'You know him?' Piper asked, ever inquisitive.

'Sweet? I despise him.'

Sweet …Sweet? Shit. Piper thought back to the terrifying look on the redhead's face when she had described him as the meanest man in the world.

The hairs on the back of Piper's neck stood on end. By now she knew how to sense a story, and if the tingling in her spine was anything to go by, there was a far bigger exposé to be done here than bitch school. This, she knew, was how she would finally make her name in the world of investigative journalism. She had to find out – just who was this Sweet?

Fernando's face had turned beetroot red and he became eerily quiet.

'Who is Sweet?' Piper asked.

Silence.

'I said,' Piper persisted, 'who is this guy?'

'You can see the man does not want to talk about him,' grunted one of the heavies.

They ate the rest of their meal in sombre silence. Once, Sweet turned to gaze at Luminosa. Fernando put an arm around her possessively and immediately topped up her champagne glass with Laurent Perrier.

'Some rosé for my rose,' he murmured, looking not at her but at Sweet. When Sweet looked away, Fernando barked something in Spanish to the others.

'What did he say?' Piper whispered to Luminosa.

'A woman is the way?' Luminosa shrugged, as clueless to what he meant by that as Piper.

Eventually Sweet stood up to leave the restaurant, flanked by his seven wonder women, but Piper was sure he turned to sneer at Fernando before leaving.

As soon as he left, Fernando became agitated. He clicked his fingers for the bill.

'Oh, didn't you know?' announced the beaming waiter. 'Mr Sweet has already settled your bill.'

Fernando went purple, jumped to his feet and for a moment stood in frozen silence. Then, with one sweep of his hand, he knocked all the glasses and crockery off the table so that they fell crashing to the ground, shattering into millions of tiny pieces.

There was a shocked silence.

'Come on, we're leaving,' he commanded.

He stormed out of the restaurant, followed by his two henchmen, while the girls lingered behind.

'I'm so sorry,' pleaded a mortified Luminosa to the waiter. 'Can we pay for the damage?'

'Come with me!' roared Fernando, promptly returning to claim his women.

Piper saw him reach for a steak knife from the table and slip it into his pocket.

'Run!' she shouted to Luminosa, who didn't have to be told twice. They made a dash for it in the opposite direction, unable to head squarely for the exit as the three men were blocking their way. Immediately Fernando gave chase but as he lunged after them he stepped into the mounting pool of oil on the floor, which had escaped from the smashed crockery. His right leg slid sideways, landing him with a thud in an awkward-looking split, just in time for his two henchmen to trip over him, resulting in a bizarre scrum on the restaurant floor.

The incident lasted only a matter of seconds but it gave the girls valuable time to distance themselves a little.

'This way!' Piper shouted, disappearing into the kitchen in the hope they'd lose Fernando, but he'd already spotted them and was now back on his feet and angrier than ever. The three men had caught up them within seconds. Piper regretted her route gravely when she turned her head to see the burliest of them seize a shiny silver meat cleaver from the counter. The chefs milling about had no idea what was happening. They blocked the girls' way through to the other exit more from confusion than intention so that it wasn't long before their pursuers were upon them.

'Look out!' screamed Luminosa as Piper turned to see the meat cleaver slicing through the air in her direction. Its tip just missed the side of her face but it caught a section of her hair, leaving a lock of it on the kitchen floor. She opened her mouth to scream but before she could utter a word she felt a felt a meaty hand around her neck and then a searing pain as a thumb pressed down on her larynx, almost suffocating her as she and Luminosa were both dragged backwards out of the kitchen and towards the restaurant exit. She again tried to scream for help but her breathing was so restricted all she could manage was a rasping gurgle.

Once outside of Fountainbleu hotel, the grip on Piper's neck loosened somewhat but she was still shaking and perspiring with fear. Fernando was circling the girls, looking them up and down hungrily like a huntsman surveying his game and wondering whether to roast or poach it. Piper thought about the steak knife in his pocket. The other two were silent, as though awaiting orders. There were plenty of people milling around outside and she was desperate for somebody to intervene but, with the meat cleaver subtly discarded, it was not clear that the girls were being held against their will. For all anybody knew, this thug was just massaging the sides of their necks.

Fernando motioned to his car and Piper knew they must avoid that at all costs. She didn't dare imagine where they would be driven, or what would be done to them when they got there. Then she had an idea.

'It's getting surprisingly chilly for Miami,' she said with a pout, rubbing her arms. Luminosa caught their captor glancing down Piper's top and joined in.

'Si,' she groaned, looking down. 'I look like I've been smuggling edamame beans out of Hakkasan in my bra!' That was all it took for their captor to lose concentration for a second and release his grip on their necks.

'Come on!' Piper shouted, grabbing Luminosa's arm as they raced off towards the beach. Once again, all three men gave chase but Piper's sporting prowess enabled her to dodge passing cars and people, pulling Luminosa with her, until the men had lost sight of them. They sprinted further, gasping, until finally the bright lights of Fountainbleau had receded, and they collapsed on the beach in the pitch dark, ears straining for the sound of Fernando and his men. Though they could hear nothing, Piper wasn't taking any chances.

'Dig!' she whispered. They scrambled in the sand frantically until they had dug themselves into little caves to hide themselves, leaving just their terrified faces peering out into the darkness.

Chapter 27

Piper surveyed the menu at the Canyon Ranch Hotel and Spa and opted for the whole grain pasta with rapini and Italian chicken sausage, ignoring the warning notes beside each dish telling her the exact proportion of carbs, protein, fat and fibre. She chose a Californian pinot noir to go with it for a taste of home.

'Thank you so much.' Piper beamed at the waiter, leaning back in her chair and grinning across at Luminosa. The two girls sat outside at the tranquil oceanfront restaurant amid the other guests relaxing mid-treatment. Despite the laidback setting, Luminosa was spilling out of a tight bejewelled mini-dress and high wedges that wouldn't have looked out of place in a glitzy nightclub.

'You don't even need to watch your weight, do you?' asked Luminosa, eyeing Piper's athletic figure as the food arrived at their table.

'I just do a lot of sport. I'll never be delicate and skinny, nor sexy and curvy like you, but I'm pretty happy looking healthy.' Piper lifted a fork to her mouth then nearly choked on its contents.

'Don't look now, but it's Fernando.'

'Where?' Luminosa's eyes widened in terror and she swivelled around just in time to see him walking past into the spa behind a uniformed therapist. He looked straight ahead, interested in no one else, so the girls escaped detection.

'Shall we leave?'

'No,' Piper said, pulse quickening. 'Let's follow him.'

'No way, you're crazy. You follow him, but I'm gonna stay here and keep our wine company.'

'OK. I'll be back soon.' Piper slid off her seat, adjusted her shorts and slipped her bare feet back into her raffia sandals before padding off in the direction of the treatment rooms. They were sealed off but she struck gold when she heard a loud, agonized male scream. She quickly checked she was unobserved before inching open the door as another scream was issued, masking the sound of her sliding inside behind Fernando's and the therapist's backs.

She crept behind a filmy, floor-length curtain and hardly dared breathe lest she make a sound. From there she could eavesdrop on the conversation. Through the curtain she could fuzzily see what was taking place and tried not to giggle as she watched Fernando on the bed, half of his chest covered in thick hairs and the other half smooth and bronzed.

'Nearly finished,' soothed the therapist as she slowly spread the hot brown wax over his tensed and well-defined pectoral muscles.

'So what are your plans for tonight?' she asked, making small talk while they waited for the wax to solidify.

'Party at Vita,' snapped Fernando. 'Now shut up. I need to concentrate. This is really hard for me'. He was sweating profusely and he started to whimper as she brought her manicured hand to his chest to feel the stiffness of the wax.

'It's ready,' she said.

'Oh my god,' Fernando wailed, crying slightly. 'Please do it gently.'

The therapist swiftly removed the wax, and with it the rest of Fernando's chest hair, as the room vibrated with the strength of his scream.

'All done now. That wasn't so bad, was it? Now you're all ready for your facial and massage,' she said softly, as he lay shaking on the bed.

He was led to an adjoining room and Piper took the opportunity to make her way back outside to Luminosa and what was left of the sun and her wine.

'So?' asked Luminosa as she sat down.

'So ...we're going to a party at Vita tonight. Something's up and it's a hell of a lot stranger than bitch school!'

'Do you want to get us killed?' asked Luminosa. 'Have you not had enough adventure for one weekend? Those guys are not nice people.'

'Yeah, I figured that. Don't worry, we'll keep out of sight.' Piper took another sip of wine and began plotting. She knew she was taking more and more liberties with her work. But then again, why should she always do things by the book? She thought of Isabel Suarez-Octavio; a shady character if ever there was one. And yet people were always falling all over her. Yes, perhaps it was time she started taking more liberties.

'Are you on the list?' asked a reed-thin, six-foot black girl with a huge Afro. She looked down at the list of names attached to her clipboard.

'Fernando,' Luminosa and Piper said quickly, standing tall and trying to look cool and confident.

'Oh OK, come in,' said the door girl with a wide smile, not even checking her clipboard. She muttered something to a colleague that sounded like 'see to it these guys are looked after'.

With bolstered confidence, the girls sauntered into the club. They moved quickly through the indoor area and into a vast garden. Purple lights illuminated tall palm trees and the many faces of the men and women, some milling around, flirting and chatting, others seated around tables tucking into late dinners while there was a little bit of space, before the club filled completely with revellers.

Spotting Fernando at the centre table with his two thugs, the three of them surrounded by women, Piper grabbed Luminosa's arm and pulled her into a thicket of cosmetically enhanced Pussycat Doll lookalikes who towered above them both in sparkly platform heels, their big bouncy hair adding further inches.

Piper had put on her shortest, slinkiest dress for the occasion but these girls' dresses were so tight that you could make out their belly buttons. Piper watched one girl begin to gyrate sexily, perilously close to an unnecessary outdoor heater.

'Whoa, is silicone flammable?' asked Luminosa, wincing.

As the chilled lounge music gave way to pumping bass, the dancing doll began to pick up speed, flicking her long dark hair dramatically and swaying back and forth before climbing onto a table from where she could really work it.

Piper laughed. 'Come on, let's slip around the back away from Fernando so we can relax. Besides, I think she's about to draw some very unwanted attention to us.'

'Too late, Piper – I think he's spotted us.' Luminosa glanced at Fernando striding in their direction and broke into a run. Piper followed suit.

Immediately Fernando also began running, followed by his two men. The gap between them and the girls closed quickly and within seconds Piper could sense him right behind her. She held her breath, stricken with fear. Fernando pushed her aside, not even registering who she was, and carried on running. His two men had caught up and where now charging ahead, pushing more people out of the way to clear a path. Fear had now turned to confusion. She had to know where they were going. She followed the trio straight out of the club, keeping a distance but certain that she was no longer on their radar. They ran down the sidewalk until they came to a corner where they were met with about eight other men, not dissimilar in look to Fernando's bejewelled henchmen.

There was obviously some sort of problem but Piper couldn't make out what it was. She saw some pushing and shoving until Fernando raised his hand and silenced everybody. They were clearly some kind of gang, and from what Piper could tell, Fernando's word was the law. He now seemed to have settled whatever the issue was. Piper hid behind a tree as the group dispersed, jumping into various jewel-coloured sports cars. The sound of five or so Lamborghinis and Ferraris revving their engines before zooming off at speed made Piper jump.

When the cars had all left, only Fernando remained on the sidewalk. His hands were jammed in his pocket and his brow furrowed, deep in thought. Then he turned and sauntered back in the direction of the club, towards Piper. Suddenly a shrill whine pierced the air. Fernando stopped and listened. There it was again; it sounded like an animal in pain. Something shot out of the darkness, limping uncertainly in Fernando's direction. It looked like a puppy and Piper was surprised and touched to see Fernando bend and put out a hand, softly beckoning the animal towards him. The wounded creature wavered for a few seconds then hobbled to meet his fingers. Fernando grabbed hold of the puppy, lifting it by its neck. He put his two hands firmly around it and squeezed. As Piper saw the puppy's body go limp, she threw up all over the sidewalk. Fernando tossed the dead puppy aside and walked away out of sight.

Chapter 28

Will sank into the butter-soft leather of his chair in the private jet. Isabel had kept loosely in touch with gazillionaire Warren Buffett from his turn at the Union, so they'd decided to charter a plane, a Hawker 400 XP, using his company, NetJets. It would be a great excuse to drop him an email afterwards. Will began rereading some of the clippings from the Sam Fire event early last month. The reviews were unanimous in hailing Sam as the artistic genius of his generation. On the cover of *ART* magazine there was a picture of him glowering moodily into the camera and looking as deadly as any man dressed as a turd possibly could.

Automatically he turned to the seat beside him on the plane and remembered with fury that it was still empty. Where in God's name could she be? Biting his lip to stop him swearing out loud, he thought back to their heated exchange on the telephone just one hour earlier.

'I'm so sorry but something has happened. I won't be able to come with you to Cap Ferret. I need you to trust me. To not ask me questions, but to take me at my word when I say this can't be helped. I can join you soon. The day after tomorrow, even, but I need you to do this without me. I know you can secure the investment on your own, Will, but I swear to you I will get to France for D-day, for our big pitch lunch. We'll wow them all and we'll have the contracts ready and waiting to be signed.'

'Don't be stupid, Isabel. I don't have time for your games, for Christ's sake. Where are you?'

Silence.

'I said, WHERE THE FUCK ARE YOU?' The vein at the side of Will's tensed, reddened neck was enlarged and throbbing. His hand shook with anger and he struggled to keep it still.

'You have to trust me,' she said.

'What the hell am I going to tell them? What if this falls through, Isabel? I left my fucking job for you! What if we don't get the investment we need? You know we can't go through to phase two without it, and we've already spent so much money on ISO. All of this will be for nothing! We'll be finished, our reputations in tatters before we've even built them, and we'd sure as hell never get hired again. You bi—' Will checked himself; he'd never called a woman a name before. But then, he'd never been so angry. 'And why did you insist on all this bloody extravagance? This reckless spending? I mean, a fucking private jet?' he continued.

'Will, we've talked about this. They need to know we're serious. That we operate in the highest circles and are already successful. That we've got skin in the game and that I'm prepared to risk my own money in the venture too.'

'They don't care about money,' Will spat. 'Money is no object for them. At this stage, what they want to get involved in is something that's young and energetic and going to be fun to work on, and you were meant to be here with me to give them the time of their lives!'

'Will, I want this more than you know.'

'Then why aren't you here?'

'I'll be there for the pitch, Will.' There was a click and then the line went dead.

Will buried his dark thoughts and turned his attention back to the present.

'Come on in.' He stood and confidently ushered Divia into the aircraft. It was a tiny streamlined plane, which they'd chosen for its high speed and ability to access even the smallest and most awkward of private airports. Inside, its beige leather upholstered cabin could seat up to eight passengers.

Admiring Divia's glossy raven hair, casual-chic cream jeans and cashmere sweater, and the regal way she carried herself, Will could hardly believe she was nearly fifty. He could happily keep her entertained on this trip, but he desperately wished Isabel were here to keep Matthias, his old boss, in high spirits and help him with the other three. Matthias ascended the stairs behind Divia and had barely sat down before getting stuck into a beer and devouring a copy of *Spears Wealth Management* magazine.

Will turned to welcome the final passengers.

'This is grrrrreat!' said Mark, an overweight trader who never stopped making wisecracks. 'Glad you chose Cap Ferret and not Cap Ferrat. Much more low-key and classier. So, where's Miss Bolivia?'

'Oh, she's meeting us there.' Will tried to be polite, but he wasn't entirely sure about Mark. He'd expressed more interest in ISO than anyone else at the Sam Fire exhibition and still maintained he was 100 per cent behind it, and yet he clearly hadn't even read the business plan. Will had a sneaking suspicion he was a timewaster – less well off than the others and more interested in having a crack at Isabel and a free luxury weekend away. When it came to the crunch, Will doubted he'd put his money where his overzealous mouth was. Still, he couldn't be sure. He couldn't be sure of anything. He and Isabel could walk away from this trip with their wildest dreams realized, or they could leave with nothing.

Bringing up the rear were brothers Angus and Fergus. Recently retired, they had been serial entrepreneurs and had made a fortune in the eighties. Now they spent their time investing in promising young people, like Vikram, the tech wiz they bought along to Sam's exhibition. That night he'd enjoyed their stories of their tough early days when they'd had trouble getting funded. He'd learnt that, consequently, they tended to invest from a philanthropic standpoint more than a financial one and had a particular interest in technology and the arts.

'Now, Divia, did we meet at Damien's party last year?' asked Angus.

'Yes, what a hoot! How about Tracey Emin and that giraffe!' She threw her head back in delight at the memory.

Matthias looked quizzically at Angus. 'And didn't vee meet at ze World Economic Forum in Davos?'

'Ha! We did indeed!' his brother Fergus answered for him, cracking open a can of ice cold coke from the selection of hard and soft drinks at his side. 'You were the brilliant guy who was doing the moonwalk on the table with Bill Clinton. Gotta say, that made my trip!'

'Oh yeah, Davos,' cut in Mark through a mouthful of handcrafted liqueur chocolates. 'Yeah, I didn't bother to go this year.'

Will had been watching the easy banter with relief and now

suppressed a snort at Mark's desperate interjection. He was about as likely to have been invited to that gathering of world leaders as Chloe Constance. Actually, Chloe had more chance of an invite than Mark, if only through her father. He thought of Chloe's sweet, trusting face and smiled, relaxed for the first time since Isabel's phone call.

Chapter 29

By the time the plane touched down on French soil, the party had bonded and everybody's spirits were lifted by the sunshine.

Will had organized a convoy of chauffeur-driven cars, all with air con and well stocked with beverages to transport them in comfort to the big white waterfront villa where they would be staying. They'd chosen the villa for its understated luxury. On first impression it had a rustic charm, with simple wooden furniture and fresh white cotton furnishings and upholstery. There was nothing in sight that required a remote control. The view out to sea was one of extraordinary tranquillity, with its charming little fishing boats instead of the great big honking yachts they were no doubt used to. Of course there was state of the art security, a world-class personal chef and all the technological mod cons that every strata of modern society had become addicted to, but these were all neatly hidden away to be uncovered only when needed. Will hoped it would delight his guests, provide a rare environment of calm and relaxation, and leave them not quite knowing why a weekend working on ISO had felt like a therapy. He'd even hired a masseuse, who was staying at the villa next door with the chef and housekeeper.

Will left everybody to freshen up in their rooms while he sat outside on the terrace, reading through the revisions he'd made to the financial side of Isabel's business plan. He heard Divia springing down the hand carved wooden steps and into the living room, with its sun-bleached wooden floorboards. It led out onto the front, beachside terrace; the one at the back looked onto the private pool.

Will turned to beckon Divia out, where a chilled, freshly squeezed juice awaited her, brought discreetly by the house-keeper who had been pre-warned by a perfectly prepared Will that Divia didn't drink. She was glowing, and clutching a single purple flower.

'My goodness, I've just had a shower outside. My shower is just a hosepipe on my balcony – are you sure the bedrooms aren't overlooked? Oh, it's so revitalising to be naked outside. And Will, my room is the most exquisite thing. It's just a big white bed and bursting with fresh flowers. And what are these?' she said, holding up the flower. 'I've never seen one like this before.' She paused to catch her breath. This barefoot and radiant lady was a different Divia to the calm, assured art guru he'd met in London.

'That,' Will said, glad he'd done his research, 'is a very special type of flower indigenous to France. It's particularly famous for its smell and unique colour.'

When the entire party had reconvened downstairs, Francois the chef prepared the fresh oysters, which they had with a dry white wine local to the region.

'Oh, this is great stuff,' said Mark, studying the label on the bottle. 'I'd like to take a couple back to Blighty with me. Any spares I can take?'

'Certainly.' Will asked the housekeeper where the wine cellar was located and disappeared into the cavernous, perfectly dark and dank basement with many hundreds of bottles of carefully ordered wines. He soon re-emerged with three for Mark.

'Actually, I've arranged wine tasting on Sunday morning for those who want to,' he said.

'Oh, I want to alright!' exclaimed Mark.

I'll bet you do, thought Will, *especially if it's free*. But it suited him to get everyone a bit merry before they talked contracts and he got the signatures he needed, so he grinned happily. He saw children tearing across the beach in the distance, so impish and fast that at times they seemed to fly. They were weightless. Unburdened, and with everything in life still to play for. He felt a pang of nostalgia. When he had the money he needed from these people, he would have more responsibility on his shoulders than ever before. This was the end of his weightlessness. The thought excited him.

'Let's play a game,' he said abruptly.

Mark spluttered on his wine.

'Vot?' Matthias asked. The guests looked at each other in horror.

'Come on,' Will said encouragingly. He ran to his room and returned with sheets of paper and coloured pens, which he began handing out to all five of them.

'I am sceptical, but intrigued,' said Matthias with a smile.

'It will be fun. After these games we'll know each other very well indeed!'

Divia, being massively outnumbered by men, looked alarmed.

'Oh don't worry, they're nothing naughty; just quiz-style games. Now, for the first one. Lotto. Pick six numbers between one and thirty, please.'

When everybody had picked their numbers, Will reached into a hat and began calling out numbers. Despite initial reservations, the room became extremely animated.

'Yes!' Angus shouted as he matched up one more number, giving him four out of six. He stood up and did a jig as Mark sulked in his chair.

'What you win,' Will announced, 'is a forfeit. You all get a forfeit for every number you got correct.' The room erupted into friendly jeers and cheering and before long, Will had Fergus and Angus, both long eligible for free bus passes, doing headstands in tandem, while Will himself was dressing up in the 1940's women's clothing he'd asked the housekeeper to supply. He tried it all on with a full face of make-up applied by Divia. Then the two put on an impromptu cabaret show for the others.

'Vot iz it about you boarding school boys and dressing up in drag?' laughed his old boss.

'What on earth are you trying to say?' asked Will, puckering his rouged lips and feigning offence in as camp a voice as he could manage. He was enjoying the acting, which in a weird way was providing a distraction from fretting over Isabel's lack of contact. Eventually his guests drifted off happily to bed.

By the time Saturday evening had come and gone with no word from Isabel, Will had to take himself off to the pool and hold his head underwater just to keep himself sane.

The first thing he did on Sunday morning was check his phone for a message from Isabel, but there was nothing. He'd never felt so angry, so humiliated. He'd dropped everything as soon as she'd come to him with her proposal and now she didn't even have the courtesy to let him know where she was. He had to remain calm. He wasn't going to lose everything. Not when they were this far along. He got up and prepared to join the others for brunch, followed by the wine tasting he'd organized. He was desperate to begin drinking. Despite having planned to go easy on it himself, the desire to abstain and keep his wits about him was trumped by the need for a very stiff drink to steady his nerves and calm his rage.

The men left Divia relaxing happily by the pool with a novel while they donned their walking shoes and embarked on their tour of the local chateau and its sweeping vineyards, before settling down to the serious business of consumption.

'You know you might want to save some room for lunch, buddy!' Will slapped Mark companionably on the back as he chewed on a massive portion of strong cheese, meant for the entire group, and washed it down with a slurp of the light-bodied red they were now on.

'Oh, I'm insatiable,' retorted Mark with his mouth full.

'Down boy!' Will joked. In actual fact he was feeling anything but amused, what with the terrifying prospect of the final late lunch to follow. Decision time loomed.

When they arrived back at the villa, they found that lunch was served and Divia was by the pool enjoying a massage. It became clear that, although Isabel's whereabouts were still a mystery, Will could stall for no longer. So, when everybody was seated and relaxed, he began with his ISO presentation.

He'd rehearsed it so many times he knew it backwards. He began with a slight falter but as he saw the interest etched on every face his confidence grew, even digressing slightly to enhance the presentation with anecdotes and asides. 'So what we envisage with ISO operating at full scale is a highly profitable vehicle through which we can change the world. Politics will become more transparent, the arts more accessible, businesses more innovative, more adaptable ...'

Eventually he realized he had talked non-stop for twenty minutes and had better wind up. 'And so now, it's over to you,' he concluded, waiting hopefully.

'I hate to say this, my friend, but I don't think you're specialized enough,' Mark wheezed, piling a mountain of foie gras on his blini. 'So I'm out. I didn't know you were working across sectors.'

Will grimaced. *Yes you did, because it was on the bloody business plan you said you'd read before we flew you out here and you drank half the vineyards of western France dry,* he thought to himself, but he just nodded, kept his poker face.

Fergus and Angus looked at each other and then Angus said, 'I'm afraid we're out. I think you are very focused on financial gain. And although we like that – we know that anything for the good of society, even charitable enterprises, should be financially self-sustainable – we don't think that should be the whole picture.'

Will's heart started to thump.

'I don't think that *is* the whole picture,' Divia said, turning to Will. 'I think you're getting behind some campaigns which are seminal. I know you're thinking about doing something with the Lib-Cons and you've shown real gumption in backing a shockingly talented but more or less unknown artist. I'm going to wait until Isabel gets here before signing, but I'm in. I'll invest the full amount. But for a forty per cent stake, not the thirty you're offering.'

Not one to be outdone, Matthias stood up and shouted, 'Jawohl! I'm in too. Divia, let's split ze risk. Do half ze investment each at twenty per cent?'

'Good,' Divia said. 'And that way we can bring in different expertise and contacts, which, let's face it, these two brilliant but irritatingly young people are still going to need.'

Will hardly dared to breathe lest they change their minds.

'Will, what do you say?'

'I say I can't think of two people I'd rather work with. Divia, your contribution to the art world has been revolutionary. You're perhaps the most important cultural figure in our country. And Matthias, my time working for you at the bank, well, I've never known a more inspirational teacher.'

'God, hiz good, isn't he?' Matthias grinned at Divia.

'So I guess it's just a case of waiting for Isabel and then we'll get everything signed.' Will excused himself and went into the next room to try Isabel's phone for the hundredth time that trip. As he held the handset to his ear he realized his hand was trembling. He had never been violent towards a woman before but he was so angry he felt as though he could take her in his hands and physically shake her if he were to see her now. Her phone was still dead. He groaned loudly in despair and hit the wall with the side of his balled fist as hard as he could. He hit it again and again, needing a release for his frustration. Finally collapsing against the wall, he slid down it.

He closed his eyes and tried to calm himself. For some strange reason he thought of Chloe again. Of how she would never act in such a selfish, inconsiderate way. He wondered how she was and resolved to meet up with her as soon as he got back to England. The thought succeeded in calming him somewhat.

After twenty minutes he returned to the other room and forced a bright smile while they waited for Isabel. But Isabel never came.

Chapter 30

'They didn't fucking sign.' Will almost never swore. Isabel blanched.

'I'm so sorry. I'm so truly sorry. I know, I know you gave up your job. You dropped everything for this.' Isabel's usually radiant skin was sallow and she had come out with a rash around her neck. Her eyes were bloodshot and she knew she looked dreadful. But not as dreadful as she felt.

'And now you won't bloody tell me where you were when you damn well ruined everything for both of us!' Will's face was red with a deep anger Isabel had never seen in all the time she'd known him.

'One day I will tell you. But just believe me, it was something … something I had to do.'

'I'm never trusting you again.'

Will turned on his heel and left Ol's palatial Hampstead house. The heavy front door slammed so hard behind him that Isabel felt tremors underfoot.

She ran to a locked cupboard in her bedroom and reached for its contents. A small safety deposit box. She unlocked it and took out two photographs. She stared first at one and then the other. Carefully, she wiped a speck of dust off with a tissue.

Chapter 31

Sam Fire had moved out of his squat and into a 2500–square–feet loft apartment he was renting in Shoreditch. He was back East where he belonged. It made him feel more like the artist he was, being back in his gritty motherland where creativity was king. He chose to ignore the fact that half of West London had moved East with him and the areas were now virtually indistinguishable in their rising house prices, joint love of trendy bars and cafés, and inhabitants who cared very much about appearances.

He lay back against the headboard of his vast new bed and beckoned the two girls to come closer. They were both naked, like him.

'Kiss each other,' he ordered. He tried to get off on it but his thoughts kept straying back to Chloe. How she'd been last night, begging and whimpering for him to pay her some attention, to make love to her the way he used to. Damn. Nothing made his bone drop faster than a needy woman. Even these two hotties couldn't resurrect it.

'Relax, let me get you hard,' purred one of the girls, humming as she took his cock in her mouth, but he brushed her aside and got off the bed. The girls stared after him as he reached for his phone and ordered another three girls to join them.

If he was to snap himself out of this mood, he needed to go all out.

He checked he had enough condoms left for the rest of the afternoon then he reached for his digital camera and started snapping the girls. They jumped up in outrage and grabbed their clothes, horrified at the idea of being identified, so Sam found two black balaclavas he'd worn for a self-portrait and put one on each girl. Then he picked up his camera again and started taking more photos.

'Just move anyhow,' he said. The shapes their bodies made were filling his head with ideas …watercolours, sculptures, drawings, entire exhibitions.

'You're beautiful, beautiful women.' Suddenly he felt alive.

A wave of relief washed over him because, although he had only become celebrated a few months ago, he knew he was slowly losing his creativity and had not felt alive for a while. It bothered him, but not enough for him to do much about it. He thought about last Sunday. Sacred Sunday for his aesthetic assimilation work. Everyone thought he was out communicating with nature, but nowadays the reality was that he didn't leave bed on a Sunday. He would sleep in late, until the afternoon. Then he would lie in bed until the evening smoking and drinking. While there, he would read the celebrity shags sections of the tabloid press and have a quick read of the culture sections in the broadsheets too. Then he'd order a large pizza and eat it in bed watching telly or surfing the net. On that particular Sunday he had logged on to youporn.com and had a quick tug. Then he'd gone back to sleep.

Sam's phone rang, reminding him he had company and was expecting more. Damn. It wasn't the new girls – it was Chloe. Sinking resignedly into a chair, he pressed the green answer button, wedged his phone between his cheek and shoulder and began a sketch of the two nymphs in front of him.

'What's up, baby?'

'Hey you,' Chloe said quietly. 'Watcha doin'?'

'Baby, is this one of those chats where you don't really have anything you want to say to me?' Sam's tone was direct but not unkind.

'Meanie poo! I just wanted to hear your voice.'

Nobody spoke.

'What is it, baby?' Sam said finally.

'Oh nothing really, I was just calling about that *Paintbrush* mag piece. Amazing, isn't it? These people all think you're some kind of overnight genius.'

'Hardly overnight,' scoffed Sam. 'I've been working my ass off at this since I was sixteen – you know that. But I guess it just needed that breakthrough exhibition. Hey, sweetie, I'm just kind of in the middle of something. Can I bell you back in a sec?'

'That's what you said last time. Then you didn't.'

'Didn't I? Sorry, you know how absent-minded I am. You should have rung me back.'

'But I always ring you. Why don't you ever call me? Why do I always have to be the one to call you?'

'Look, I'm sorry, honey, I've just been so busy lately with—'

'No, you look. I'm sorry but nobody is that busy that they can't spare ten seconds to send a sweet text message or something. Five minutes for a quick chat of an evening.'

There was a long silence.

Sam sighed. 'Baby, maybe you've just answered your own question. I didn't want it to have to end like this, but I can't be in this relationship anymore. I can't give you what you need. What you crave.'

When Chloe had put down the phone with a trembling hand, she stroked Sam's photograph in the magazine, staring at it with unseeing eyes. She could hardly believe she still found him so handsome after all he had done.

Chloe pulled the duvet up over her and sank deeper into her bed. She hadn't left it for two days and it was the only place she felt safe. She reached out a hand for the packet of cookies at her bedside table and swallowed the last one in two bites. The cheap chocolate stuck to her tongue. The additives and chemicals left an acidic aftertaste that would linger long past the artificial high from the surge in her blood sugar level. Just like Sam. The biggest, most artificial high ever.

In all the time they were together, she had felt like nothing the world could throw at her would be too great for her to withstand because she had him. She'd felt amazing. Now she didn't know what to believe. What was real and what was artificial. She heaved herself up to grab the TV remote control and switch it on, the lethargic manoeuvre the only bit of exercise she'd done in days. To her horror a painfully familiar figure was being interviewed.

'Are you surprised at how successful you've become, Sam?' The interviewer, all perky and glossy, accompanied her question with a coquettish tilt of the head.

'Who is truly surprised at his own success?' Sam shot back pompously. 'Don't we all think we deserve it? Don't little girls think they will be princesses and prima ballerinas? Boys hope to play football for their country. To be rich and famous when they grow up. Don't we all believe we are born to be great? It is those sad souls who reach the late afternoon of their lives and realize that they are still unremarkable who truly find themselves surprised. Flabbergasted by their own mediocrity.'

The interviewer's mouth hung open for a moment and then she swiftly changed tack.

'You've been the subject of some pretty intense media coverage lately, particularly after that infamous kimono affair.'

'What kimono affair?' Sam asked, clearly knowing full well what she meant by the shifty look in his eye.

'We have the footage here, if you need reminding.' Before he could say anything she motioned for a recording to be played and they both watched a video of an intoxicated Sam trashing a hotel room while dressed in a customized kimono. He was throwing toiletries and tubes of suncream at the wall while screaming at the top of his lungs: 'Rock and roll, rock and roll ...ROCK AND ROLL!'

When the video came to an end, the interviewer turned to Sam with a titter but he did not share in her mirth.

Sitting up, Chloe reached for her phone and thought of who she could call. Isabel had betrayed her, happily walking off with those extraordinary gifts that her own boyfriend hadn't even considered her worthy of. It still stung too much.

She would call Will. She remembered all the times he'd looked out for her in the past. The way he'd attacked that lecherous old singer for upsetting her. He always made her feel safe.

Chapter 32

It was election night and Isabel couldn't sleep. She got out of bed and switched on her laptop. The TV was on, showing constant election coverage. She browsed the blogs of her favourite political commentators.

'With more than five hundred seats counted,' reported one, 'the BBC is predicting that the Lib-Cons will end up with 398 seats, the Workers 180 seats, and the Democrats fifty-six seats. The Lib-Cons are currently on fifty-six per cent of the vote.' Before she knew it, Isabel had read over twenty different accounts of the election and her tired eyes were now glued to the television screen.

Ol's big house felt cold and lonely. Finally, as the morning birds chirped outside the window and the sun shone on her sleep-deprived face, all the results were in. Isabel gripped the arm of her chair.

The camera zoomed in on Archie. His face set first in an unreadable expression and then exploding into one of wild ecstasy. Archie had done it. He turned and pulled his new wife close to him, burying his face in her shoulder. Perhaps he was crying. Seconds later, more composed now, he looked up and smiled into the camera. His wife whispered something in his ear and he turned to kiss her.

She didn't take in his acceptance speech but somewhere in the patter she heard him thank ISO for their work on the Prime Minister for a Day campaign for underprivileged children. There was now little left of ISO, except Isabel herself, a couple of unpaid interns, a small fortune in wasted money and a set of broken friendships. His thanks was no comfort.

Chapter 33

Days later, Isabel was preparing to lunch with Charlie, or Sweet as he was also known, according to her research on him. She knew he owned one of the world's largest yacht broking businesses, but there was strangely limited official information available about him and, worryingly, a fair few rumours and past accusations of criminality which had never amounted to anything because nobody had been willing to testify against him when it came down to it.

From what Isabel gathered, he was now looking to expand his influence from the business world into the cultural and political life of the countries in which he operated. In other words, almost all the countries in the world. Isabel had thought long and hard before agreeing to lunch, but the eye-watering size of this account, should she get it, would make him a bigger client than she had ever imagined possible at this stage. What's more, he was her only client.

They were lunching at Scotts at her suggestion. She slipped on a smart knee-length red dress, tan patent leather heels and put on red lipstick. It had become her armour. Glancing at her reflection in the mirror, a sexy, pulled-together powerful woman stared back at her. The Oxford student seemed a distant memory. She placed her tiny laptop into her bag and hailed a cab to take her to the Mayfair restaurant where she was to meet Sweet.

The taxi pulled up outside the exclusive restaurant and a uniformed doorman approached to open her door. She made her way into the sleek and glamorous main room, a mirrored, oak-panelled hall dominated by a marble mosaic oyster bar at its centre.

Her table was beyond the bar, in a corner that overlooked the entire restaurant, and she was ushered to her seat on a plush leather banquette opposite Sweet. He rose to greet her as she arrived and she gasped at his astonishing height and appearance. She didn't notice the two tall, muscular women in tight black dresses dining three tables down from their boss. From there they were out of the way and less conspicuous but could see all that was going on, just as Sweet wanted. The first woman's clutch bag contained a gun that was fully loaded. The second was highly trained in unarmed combat. She raised a square of shrimp-topped toast to her lips as she appraised her boss's stunning lunch companion, and sensed trouble.

'So, Mr Sweet, I must say I was surprised to get your call. Surely you can hire whoever you choose, and we're relatively new.' Isabel knew she should appear confident but she couldn't help but ask. She watched him carefully while he processed her question, trying to gauge his personality, but he was oddly inexpressive.

He took a long slug of the red wine he had already begun drinking prior to her arrival. The liquid stained his lips and pooled at the corners of his mouth. He wiped them with the starched white napkin that lay across his lap and then replaced it, but the wine had already left his lips a deep burgundy colour, like congealed blood. Now they were set into a thin smile. Isabel thought he looked like a vampire. He opened his mouth to speak.

'Because you are discreet and connected, that much is clear from your little mention in the Prime Minister's acceptance speech. But most of all, you are young and hungry. You will do anything it takes to achieve success.' His accent, like his emotions, was completely unplaceable. He could be from anywhere, but Isabel's due diligence had already informed her he was a British tax exile who liked to work in Miami, rest in Monaco, and party on his yacht along the Italian Riviera.

'I'm not sure I like the sound of that.'

'Perhaps you'll like the sound of this.' He leaned forward. 'The last man I hired to take care of my public profile came to his initial pitch meeting by train. A year later he came to his twelve-month appraisal on his own Gulfstream. People who work for me get rich.'

'So why aren't you still with him?' She wasn't entirely convinced by his reasoning for wanting her and she guessed the big firms had refused to take him on. For the first time, she detected emotion in his expression; a flicker of annoyance.

'You ask a lot of questions, little girl.'

Isabel said nothing, so Sweet grudgingly answered, 'He died. There was an incident.'

Isabel swallowed. 'How terrible.'

'Quite.'

'Are you ready to order?' a waiter cut in.

Another waiter arrived to set the table with a tray filled with the many additional utensils they would need to best eat their platter of assorted seafoods. Isabel had to stop herself from laughing out loud. The gleaming silver contraptions with their sharp spikes and terrifying angles looked like instruments of torture. When the food arrived she discarded them all, preferring to remove any shells with her hands.

She licked the tips of her fingers afterwards and felt Sweet's stare as she did so, but by the time she glanced up to meet his gaze he had assumed his passionless regard.

'Isabel, what you will do for me is make me some nice friends. That's what you're good at, isn't it? You will make me all sorts of *lovely* friends. Very soon, my name will start to *pop* up in a number of widely read articles about philanthropic causes. My face will miraculously begin to appear at all sorts of upmarket charitable and political functions. I have a great face for photographs, don't you think? And the more my delightful face *pops* up in these delightful places, the more money will *pop* into your bank account.' Each time he said the word 'pop', he opened his eyes wide and splayed his long fingers, wiggling them either side of his face like a demonic clown.

Isabel dabbed the sides of her mouth with her napkin. 'What sort of budget do you have in mind for this? We're not cheap, but we do things properly.'

'Fifteen in your first year, provided you perform. and then … and then we'll see.'

'Fifteen thousand?' *What a disappointment.*

'Fifteen million. Plus unlimited use of my yachts.'

Isabel tried to remain composed. They talked shop a little more.

When the bill came, Isabel paid it. She was entertaining a prospective client, after all. Sweet smirked, allowing her to make the token gesture.

They made their way back outside.

'Think about what I said,' he told her. His eyes bore into hers and he took her hand for a second. It made her feel uneasy.

'Thank you, Mr Sweet.'

'My staff call me Mr Sweet. For playmates and partners in crime, I'm known only as Sweet.' He sneered.

'Thank you, er, Sweet. I'll be in touch.' The doorman hailed her a taxi and she jumped in.

Seconds later Sweet's female bodyguards caught up with him. His driver rolled up in a Bentley and they slid inside.

The following week, an email arrived from Sweet inviting Isabel to spend some time on his yacht where he would be hosting a party of special friends for a long weekend sailing along the Amalfi Coast. She couldn't think of anything more enticing than the thought of sailing along the southern Italian coastline: a natural, rugged beauty to contrast with the grey metropolis that was London. The problem was Sweet. The more she thought about him, the uneasier she felt. But she had gone ahead anyway and signed the contract the day after their lunch. Now he owned her. Now his invitations were orders.

Part Three

Chapter 34

The boat's captain climbed up from below deck and set about inspecting the table layout for brunch.

'Carrrrrrlo!' slurred the already drunk blonde in his direction.

Carlo was a serious looking middle-aged man with salt and pepper hair and a moustache. He wore a crisp white aertex shirt with red lettering: *Sweet Smell of Success*. He enjoyed having the name of the boat he ran emblazoned across his chest. He was proud of it. He had been working for Mr Sweet since 2001 and he had a crew of staff under him to help ensure that everything ran smoothly for Mr Sweet and his guests, whenever they made use of it. Of course his boss also had many other yachts but these were not Carlo's concern.

He smiled politely at the blonde, one of the latest party of sea-borne revellers. And now who was this embarking? He waved at another of his crew to assist the two already clutching her luggage and helping her aboard the vessel.

'Oh, who are you?' shouted the blonde from where she lay on a recliner on the front deck, facing the gleaming oval brunch table. She wore only a pair of miniscule black bikini bottoms.

'I'm Isabel.' Isabel extended her hand, squinting in the sun and grinning as she clocked the glass of champagne in the woman's left hand. She avoided gawping at her breasts, which were so huge Isabel was getting backache just looking at them.

The woman didn't reply, already having lost interest.

She couldn't believe how incredible the yacht was. From the outside, the smooth, streamlined silvery vessel looked like something that had fallen from outer space and was now floating on the rippling water. There seemed to be tons of different deck areas where she'd be able to lounge around in the sun. She'd even spotted two big swimming pools on a lower deck, which seemed excessive with the sea all around. She couldn't wait to get into her bikini and soak up some rays before diving into the iridescent greeny blue water for a swim before the others emerged from their cabins. And she was even more intrigued to find out who the rest of her travel companions would be.

The captain appeared at her side. He bowed down low and spoke with a lilting Italian accent.

''Ello, I am Captain Carrrlo,' he said, rolling his 'r's. 'Brunch will be ready in one hour. Just a light meal as we will be sailing to Nerano for a late lunch en route to Ravello, where we will spend the evening. Then it's on to Positano where you can explore, do a leetle shopping, and then we will finish the trip in Capri, where you will 'ave more fun than you even dreamed possible.' He stroked his moustache and eyed her pensively.

'That sounds like heaven, thank you!'

'Do you like Italian food?'

'It's my favourite.'

'Good, because everything we will prepare for you 'ere on the boat will be the best of the seasonal, local produce. You know, the Costiera Amalfitana is a source of the most outstanding food. 'Ere you will taste the freshest fish known to mankind, the most flavoursome buffalo mozzarella in the world, the most intense olive oil you will ever find, and of course a limoncello, which will make you wish every tree in the world bear nothing but sweet, sweet lemon. Everything 'ere is so simple, and so perfect. You will see.' He returned to his fussing over the brunch table, slowly smoothing the white table linen with the utmost concentration.

Everything here *was* perfect, so why did Isabel feel uneasy? She watched Carlo pick up a sharp knife and run a finger along its gleaming side and shivered as he turned his head and stared down at the entrance to the cabins, where, Isabel presumed, Sweet was still sleeping. The captain of the boat was not smiling.

Isabel was escorted to her cabin. Inside the boat there were semi-circular glass walls, which could slide back to create one spectacular entertaining area, wraparound windows, recessed LED lighting around the many skylights and portholes, and the smoothest polished teak floors.

She reached her cabin suite, where unusually large portholes let in plenty of sunshine, so the room had a feeling of light despite the low ceilings that nautical design necessitated and despite being decorated in dark mahogany wood. The padded leather walls were sumptuous, as was the huge golden bed piled high with pillows. To the side, Isabel could see a door left ajar to reveal a compact but spotless en suite bathroom, complete with mother of pearl panelling and what looked like a Picasso on the wall. She went over to admire it, momentarily lost in the poetic shapes and lines. Then she set about opening cupboards and drawers, marvelling at both the quality of all the finishes and the way that every inch of space in the boat was maximized.

She hung up her clothes. She had not brought high heels, thinking of the ancient cobbled Southern Italian streets that would make walking in stilettos a virtual impossibility. Instead she'd bought flat leather sandals, which she'd wear with jewel-coloured sundresses set off by her tan. Once unpacked, she changed into bright orange bikini bottoms and a white halter-neck top and headed back outside.

She walked to the end of the deck and looked around for the half-naked morning drinker but could not see her, or any of the crew. She stared out to sea and contemplated the colour of the water. It was miraculously clear. Green and then blue, shifting to turquoise and then a darker emerald. It winked and twinkled, beckoning her in. She jumped. As she fell through the air, she screamed at the top of her voice.

She was free. She would never go back.

By the time Isabel had swum, showered outside under the sun – stripping completely naked in the belief she was unwatched – and quickly changed into a short white cotton dress and a wide-brimmed sunhat, it was time for brunch. The table was set for ten and there was a welcoming selection of exotic cold meats and fabulously pungent cheeses already on the table. Gradually the guests gathered around.

'Hi, I'm Natalya,' said a gorgeous whippet-thin girl with short peroxide blonde hair, who was followed closely by her small but handsome boyfriend. Isabel already knew who they were – the Latvian supermodel Natalya Ozolin, who'd dazzled on the catwalk in Oxford, and the movie star, Jake Jendar.

The next to arrive was a loud English man with pink cheeks, a cheerful smile and an excitable demeanour; greatly in contrast to the laidback cool of Jake and Natalya.

'How do you do?' he exclaimed, pumping Isabel's hand with alarming enthusiasm. It turned out he was a minor royal called Prince Peregrine, and he took a seat between Natalya and Isabel.

Next, a suave, silver-haired man named Jeffrey appeared with the topless woman from earlier and her smug-looking boyfriend. Jeffrey introduced himself warmly but did not flirt and Isabel noticed a wedding ring below his expensive Swiss watch. The woman, who did not proffer her name, was completely transformed. She wore a jewelled black Cavalli kaftan, her hair was pulled into a topknot, and she had an immaculately and far too made-up face with lashings of mascara, dark eyeliner, bronzer and shimmery lip gloss. She looked completely different from the dishevelled thing lolling on the recliner earlier and she was really only recognizable by the size of her chest.

'Hi there, I'm Gareth,' said her boyfriend. He leered at Isabel and Natalya, then turned to Prince Peregrine and offered him some bread in a braying voice not dissimilar to the Prince's but lacking the relaxed confidence. Appraising the three latest arrivals, Isabel guessed that Jeffrey was a wealthy businessman, probably playing more than he was working these days, but still dabbling in investments and enjoying the spoils of his labour. But she wondered what this younger couple's story was.

They should both have been attractive but were somehow slightly repellent. The woman's clothes were a bit too tight and her hair a bit too blonde for her complexion. Her eyebrows were plucked too thin and her loud, drunken laugh verged on jarring, with the effect that what should have come off as sexy and confident seemed hard and brash. She gave the effect of a seasoned hooker who'd managed to bag one of her clients, scrubbed up and made some respectable friends, but still couldn't quite shake off a lingering air of grubbiness.

As for her boyfriend, Gareth, he was too well-spoken, too dandyish. Too keen to fit in and be liked. Isabel sensed it immediately. He was not who he said he was.

Finally, Sweet glided towards the table, flanked by two pretty girls. One small and raven-haired, the other a redhead. The redhead slid her retro shades up from the bridge of her nose to rest on top of her head, pushing back the long locks of hair falling about her face. Isabel did a double take to realize she had different coloured eyes. One was brown and one was blue.

'Hi, I'm Ginger,' the redhead said, with little interest. She pointed to the other girl. 'That's Candi.'

Isabel thought Candi could be South American too; perhaps it was short for Candelaria. Ginger sounded American. She smiled at the two but they were already cosying up to Sweet, pouting up at him and doing their best to look alluring. But, while Candi seemed natural and cute, there was something forced about Ginger's performance.

'So you made it on your own.' Sweet smirked, ignoring the girls at his side and leaning over close to whisper to Isabel. 'Rather rude of you to spurn the use of my plane. I'll make you *pay* for that later.' He extended a cold tongue and let it snake deep into her ear.

Isabel gritted her teeth and thought of ISO, and of the challenges and indignities that Branson, Buffett, Gates and all her other heroes must have overcome to get to where they were today.

She turned to Natalya and smiled.

'Are you a model?' Natalya asked.

'No.' Isabel sat up straighter. 'I'm CEO of a communications agency.' The sentence still made her feel giddy.

Natalya seemed to relax then.

A second conversation was starting up between the men and Isabel overheard Prince Peregrine discussing appearance fees with Jeffrey and Sweet while Gareth, Ms Porn Star's boyfriend, kept nodding, as if he was part of the conversation, although none of the men were taking any notice of him. Conversation was loud, forced and sprinkled with too much laughter. There was an underlying air of tension, competition even. Isabel guessed that each and every one of them, with the possible exception of a couple of the girls, had some kind of work agenda with Sweet. This was not a bunch of friends relaxing on vacation.

Chapter 35

As Piper jogged towards the harbour in the sun-kissed Amalfi village of Nerano, she marvelled at the expanse of jagged Italian coastline unravelling before her. She was due to meet her mysterious accomplice at the harbour in precisely two minutes.

She scrolled down on her phone, faltering on a wayward piece of rock as she averted her eyes from her path to begin re-reading the email that had arrived earlier. It was from her editor at the *San Francisco Eye*. It read:

> *For this, your most perilous assignment yet, we feel it necessary to provide you with an accomplice, Bryan, who will serve not only as your assistant, but also as your protection. We hope you will not need the latter, but should you find, regretfully, that you do, Bryan is more than capable of fulfilling both of those roles. Indeed, we have employed his services for other investigations in the past.*
>
> *Now, a few things you ought to know about Bryan. Bryan has been in and out of juvenile detention centres and state penitentiaries from the age of twelve, when he was first detained for the manslaughter of the man who raped him.*

Subsequent offences range from the relatively minor, such as petty shoplifting, to more serious cases, including kidnap and armed robbery.

Wow. This was heavy stuff. Piper slid her phone back into her pocket and started running again. Moments later she had reached the harbour. She could see two figures by a row of compact white speedboats that, to Piper's untrained eye, looked new and ultra high-spec. Her bosses had clearly felt this mission was worth spending on. She walked briskly towards the men, one short and stocky, the other slim, sullen and awkward, refusing to meet her gaze. She hoped he wasn't Bryan.

'Hi, I'm Piper.'

The stocky guy took her outstretched hand. '*Ciao bella,* I'm Guido.'

Piper's heart sank. So the other must be Bryan.

Still avoiding eye contact, Bryan made a rough grab for her hand before dropping it quickly as if it were a burning hot ember.

'So, how much do you know about this investigation?' Piper asked him, keen to get a handle on the situation as quickly as possible.

'Come with me,' he muttered, jerking his head towards a little cove.

Piper followed him. A faded tattoo of a ladder made up of chains snaked along the side of his neck.

'Can't talk in front of Guido. You mustn't underestimate Sweet's reach. He has spies everywhere.' He looked darkly at the ground in front of him.

'So you've done a little research on him already – that's great. You think we're up to the task? That we can track him for the duration of this trip and gather all we need for a groundbreaking exposé?'

'We'll gather all the dirt we need to put his arse in jail for the rest of his goddamn life.' Bryan met Piper's eyes for the first time and in them she saw nothing but hatred.

'You've come across him before?'

'I've spent my life in and out of jail. Let's just say that Sweet is to a criminal what Justin Bieber is to a fourteen-year-old girl. He's infamous.'

Piper sensed there was more to it than that, so she said nothing in the hope he'd elaborate.

'And there is nobody I despise more than a sexual deviant.'

No sooner than the words left his mouth, a huge missing piece of the puzzle seemed to fall into place. She had been wondering why Sweet's face had seemed so familiar to her that very first time she saw him in Miami. Now she knew. She thought back to that grainy photo of the suspect with the evil eyes in the article on Laurelie Fairlie's murder. It was him! It had been many years ago, but it was him alright. They hadn't named him in the article and he had been mysteriously cleared, just as he had in a number of other cases. And then there had been that prostitute in King's Cross. She had surprised Piper by calling her sweet for asking about the Laurelie Fairlie murder, but Piper now realized that was not what she'd meant. She knew Sweet had done it. Everybody seemed to know. Yet the man seemed to avoid incarceration. He was more powerful and more dangerous than she'd thought.

They walked back towards Guido, who was chatting away happily on his phone and didn't seemed to have missed them. He carried on laughing and shouting into the mouthpiece for another few minutes, illustrating every sentiment with elaborate gestures and operatic facial contortions until finally he wound up his phone call and turned to Piper and Bryan.

'*Allora!* Which is it to be?' Guido asked.

'She's the boss,' said Bryan

Piper turned to him. 'Do you know anything about boats?'

'Sure. And I spent the morning testing the different ones. There was a clear winner.' He kicked the side of the smallest vessel. 'We should take this one. For its high speed and robustness.'

Piper shrugged. 'Fine by me!'

Once the payment was settled, Bryan helped Piper onto the boat and then steered it out to sea.

'So we know they have a booking at Nerano, right? That much I worked out from my preliminary research back home, but other than saying where he wants his boat delivered for the start of his trips, he never leaves instructions regarding the route, so it's impossible to track.'

'So we don't know where they plan on going after that?'

'No. All we know is we can't lose them!'

Before long, their target was in sight. Piper looked at her troubled assistant, staring focused and single-mindedly ahead. This was one hell of a frightening assignment, but if anyone could help her get it done, she was sure that person was Bryan.

Chapter 36

When brunch was over, Isabel picked up her BlackBerry and headed to the front deck. Her plan was to fire off some work emails and have a quick online research of her fellow sailors to see what collaborations might be possible with ISO, but she didn't get as far as entering her password into the device, so mesmerized was she by the beauty of the Amalfi Coast. She lost track of how long she'd been there for, but they were now approaching the village of Nerano, a picturesque cluster of gleaming white houses and villas embedded in the tree-studded coastal cliffs.

'This is the only way to do it, you know,' a lightly accented Eastern European voice said behind her. Isabel turned to see the model, Natalya, standing there. 'I did it as a road trip with my girlfriends after I escaped a horrible affair. But it's useless by car; all we saw was the back of dirty coaches and all we smelled was petrol. But by boat, you really get to take it all in. There is really little else so beautiful.'

Isabel decided she liked Natalya. They stood side by side, looking out to sea.

'What do you want?' Natalya said quietly.

Isabel stiffened. Did Natalya know something of her past? She chose not to reply and was stunned when the model then turned and hugged her. She lowered her lips to Isabel's ear and whispered, 'Hungry child, you remind me of myself. Be careful, huh?'

The boat was moored some way away from the Marina del Cantone, a small pebble beach in Nerano. The village folk relaxing on the beach all stared as they made their way across to the Ristorante Maria Grazia; so many comely women and the astonishing-looking Sweet towering above the men. Nut-brown children stopped playing to point and giggle, watched over by mothers and grandmothers, plump and dark from long days lying in the sun.

Isabel was surprised at how basic the restaurant was, seemingly just an average low-key beach shack. Fresh from the old world glamour of London's Mayfair, she wondered why this place was so high on Sweet's list. She started to look around and check out the other customers but was distracted by an anguished wail from a waiter.

'Ho visto la Madonna!' he cried, dropping to his knees, hands clasped together above his head. The sight of Isabel and Natalya together was obviously too much for him, but it was not clear which one he had decided was the Madonna herself. The girls couldn't help but be charmed by his theatrics and they took their seats in the corner table of the restaurant. Isabel was surprised to spot the tennis player Roger Federer on the next table and realized that, for whatever reason, this was a place to stop by.

She soon learnt why when the restaurant's signature dish, *spaghetti con zucchini,* arrived. She recalled Captain Carlo's words: 'simple but perfect'. The shabby unpretentiousness of the restaurant, the hospitality of its waiting staff, and the many bottles of Piedmontese wine the group consumed connived to create an atmosphere that was far more relaxed than that at brunch, and by now everybody was loosening their guard and enjoying themselves. Prince Peregrine even broke into a rap, reaching for Captain Carlo's white baseball cap and putting it on his head backwards, shouting:

I'm in Amalfi with a bunch of pretty ladieeeees,
Well I'd say that's rather better than having rabieeees,
I've lived a life of luxureee,
Of Corgis and high teeeea,
Yeah, too right, there ain't no fucking stopping me!

He grinned, flushed and panting after the energetic outburst, while the table collapsed into laughter.

'Jay-Z better watch that back of his!' said Jeffrey.

'Yeah, Peregrine from the Projects!' shouted Jake. 'Hey, I see a movie coming on.'

Isabel finished the last of her pasta with a satisfied lick of her lips.

'*Saluté*,' she cried, raising her fennel-infused limoncello at Sweet. He didn't respond, only looked at her. Again, she felt a sudden chill. She felt the need to look away and smiled gaily around the restaurant, though she took in nothing.

She certainly didn't notice Piper Kenton sitting just three tables behind her in a sporty swimsuit and denim cut-offs, her face covered by large glasses and a baseball cap. In fact, nobody in the restaurant had really noticed her quietly filming the group with her camera phone.

Chapter 37

Piper Kenton waited five minutes for Mr Sweet and Isabel to return to their yacht before quickly settling her bill and beckoning to Bryan to follow. She had shared the *San Francisco Eye*'s keenness to hire an ex-convict because she believed that prisoners needed to be rehabilitated and given another chance in society after they got out of jail, but his past experience pursuing victims and dodging police was proving more than useful. She watched him run his eyes over the restaurant as though he was casing the joint, his intense eyes taking everything in.

'Wait, what's that?' He swooped under Mr Sweet's vacated table and picked up a small gold petal-shaped earring. 'Must belong to one of his girls.'

'My god, you have eyes like a hawk.' Piper took the earring and studied it. It looked precious. She'd find a way to return it after the investigation. 'Let's get out of here.' They rushed over to their glinting white speedboat and followed in the wake of *Sweet Smell of Success*.

'Where do you think they're headed?' Piper asked nervously.

'Only one way to find out. Do you want me to get a bugging device on there?'

'Really? Can you do that? If he catches you, well, god knows what he might do.' She shuddered, thought of poor Laurelie Fairlie and of all the other unsolved murders.

'I'll find a way.'

Piper held her breath and grabbed onto the handle at the side of the boat as it suddenly picked up speed, bouncing and jerking violently on the water, which was becoming choppier the further out to sea they rode. As she opened her mouth to speak, a high spray of water rose and smacked her across her face so that she was temporarily blinded and choking on the salty liquid. Then the boat lurched higher than ever and her sunglasses and hat were blown clear off her head into the water. Clinging to the handle, her body briefly suspended in mid air, she only narrowly escaped being thrown overboard with them.

'Whoa, don't you think you should slow down a bit? What if they spot us?'

Bryan slowed down fractionally and Piper exhaled, hoping he wouldn't see how terrified she was.

'Uh-oh,' Bryan muttered. 'It might be too late for that!'

Piper gasped as the humongous yacht completed a sharp and unexpected 180° turn and surged back in the direction it had come. It was coming right at them.

Through her binoculars Piper could make out Isabel on the front deck. *Oh hell.* She too held a pair of binoculars in her hand and was about to raise them to her eyes. Minus her disguise, Piper was vulnerable. In a split second decision, she threw herself overboard.

'What the fuck!' shouted Bryan, his head oscillating wildly between the splash in the sea into which Piper had disappeared and the approaching super-yacht. He swerved out of the way and navigated the boat in a large circle near where Piper must be and out of the way of the yacht. Thankfully, the big boat was not on his tail; it was heading back to the marina from where they had come.

One crisis averted, Bryan now needed to rescue Piper. But she was nowhere to be found. Bryan kicked the side of the boat. Its engine was now off and it was just floating in the water. 'Ruined. Ruined. Ruined,' he muttered to himself.

'What's ruined?' Piper emerged, treading water at his side.

'What was that about?' asked Bryan, briefly meeting her eyes. 'If anything happens to you, I'm going right back to jail. Do you know how hard it has been for me to find work? And then I got hooked up with the *Eye* and I've finally found a way I can be helpful instead of just some hated delinquent, and you go and do this. Nearly get me framed for your murder!'

He extended the ladder into the water for Piper to climb aboard and she did so, hanging her head in shame.

'I'm sorry, I – I didn't even think about that. I guess I was scared, and that girl I told you about, Isabel, she might have recognized me.'

'Well, you're the boss,' Bryan said quietly, as though he realized he'd overstepped the mark.

'You don't have to keep saying that. We're in this together.' Piper glanced at the fading outline of Mr Sweet's yacht. 'And they weren't even coming for us! They must want that earring back. I guess we wait here for them to return once they decide it isn't there.'

The wait took half an hour, during which time Piper filled Bryan in on her backstory with Isabel and of her subsequent accomplishments with ISO.

'Tricksy girl.' Bryan nodded. 'Look, here they come on their way back.' He let the boat sail past then kick-started his own engine and, once more, set off on the tail of *Sweet Smell of Success*.

After fifteen minutes it became clear where the spectacular yacht was heading. They were en route to Ravello. Bryan hung back a little more, widening the gap between the two boats. Piper picked up her binoculars and tried to keep her hands steady. She should have known that Isabel Suarez-Octavio would be mixed up with these sorts of people.

She thought back to that awful evening at *Cherwell* when she'd seen Isabel and her puppet, Will, sneaking out of the offices. And then the subsequent failure of the paper to come out. That girl had ruined the two goals Piper had spent all year working to achieve. Her biggest ever story in *Cherwell* and the dreams she had of transforming the Union, giving automatic access to every student by abolishing the joining fee which meant that not all the students could afford to become members. And then she thought of the way Isabel had always made her feel humiliated when Professor Crayson had made one of his disdainful remarks at her expense. Piper hated to hate, but she did. She hated Isabel.

Chapter 38

'Ravello is the most beautiful place I've ever seen!'

'I defy you not to fall in love here, Isabel.' Jake threw an arm around his girlfriend, Natalya, as he led the two girls away from the central piazza and the great white duomo with its bell tower and mullioned windows.

They strolled along winding cobbled streets, flanked by medieval stone cottages and walls. A proliferation of vines and flowers snaked up the sides of the ancient stone. The greens, purples, lilacs and reds of the petals were so vibrant that it seemed to Isabel as though she was hallucinating. They turned into a secluded, winding path and strolled uphill where the views of the coast under the setting sun left them momentarily speechless.

'Let's take a look in here,' suggested Natalya, heading towards the magnificent hotel ahead of them. Dramatically styled, the interior was all white marble, high ceilings and arches, with gilt-framed Renaissance paintings on the wall and statuettes in the vast atriums. It was classically and unapologetically opulent. They explored the hotel grounds, peering over a balcony to see that each suite had its own private landscaped garden, impressive enough to win top prize at any world-class horticultural show.

'Let's get a room,' Jake murmured in Natalya's ear.

'What about Isabel? We can't leave her.' Natalya turned to look at Isabel but she had disappeared.

Wanting to be alone, Isabel had slipped unnoticed down a winding path, with no aim except to see where it led her. At the bottom of the path was a view over the entire Amalfi coast, so spectacular that, if she were not looking at it now, she would be unable to believe it existed. She sat down and stared out, intoxicated by the intensity of the colours and the scope of the beauty spread before her.

When Isabel made it back to the boat for dinner, she found that the others had not ventured out all day and, with the exception of Sweet, who was presumably amusing himself or sleeping in his cabin suite, the men were all sitting on deck drinking ice-cold champagne under the stars. She decided to enjoy the beautiful night by herself and not let anybody know she was back, so she climbed up onto a sumptuous deck area directly above them where they could not see her. She could hear them, though, and listened to them chat, amused at the descent into feral territory the moment they thought there were no women around. She heard a voice she didn't recognize and, poking her head over the side, she looked silently down on the group and spotted the newcomer, who was sliding a cigarette packet across the table to Jeffrey. She could only see the top of his dark head.

'OK gentlemen, I'm off now, but that should keep you going for a while yet.' He winked.

'Who are you doing now, then?' asked Gareth, a teasing inflection to his voice.

'A children's party next; kids of those pharmaceutical billionaires in Capri. I'll be keeping the adults entertained there.' Another wink. 'And then it's on to Rockerboy's concert where I'll be looking after him backstage.'

'Get out of here, you awful name-dropper, and keep my name off the list!' Jeffrey smiled at him as he made his way to exit the boat and ride to shore in a tender waiting for him.

'You know I've always looked after you,' the mysterious newcomer said as he left the party.

Isabel relaxed back into her soft recliner and looked up at the stars. The nonsensical chat now going on below her milled about her ears, though she wasn't really listening anymore. She was dreaming, making plans. After a while she noticed their excessive long sniffs punctuating their conversation. She sat up and listened properly, having to restrain herself from running down to confront them.

'I'm only young,' Gareth was now saying, 'but I've done a lot.' He sniffed. 'I've done a lot. You know I never stopped going, back in the day. You know about that pitch. I went to Coca Cola and I just said: "the man's the mirror". That's how good I was. Yeah, that's how fucking good I was.'

But now the men were all talking over each other.

'Yes, yes, but you can never stop; if you stop you'll keel over and die,' said Jeffrey. 'I've done everything I can do and you're only just beginning. Life is rich and I've lived it. You know, I used to be famous.'

'Yeah, I've shagged loads of famous women,' Gareth cut in. 'I mean, I'm not gonna tell you how many women I've slept with, I'm not gonna tell you that. I've slept with a lot of famous women. I mean, you wouldn't believe my celebrity shag list but I'm not gonna tell you. I'm not gonna tell you who I've banged.'

'Yeah,' Jeffrey said, not really listening, just waiting to tell his story. 'I've been honoured by twelve countries. Who can say that? But I want more because it's just silly—'

'Peregrine's cousin,' Gareth announced as soon as Peregrine had got up to go to the bathroom.

'What?!' exclaimed Jeffrey.

'Yeah, I slept with Annunziata.'

'What happened?'

'Well …' He paused, drawing out the tale. 'The question is, what didn't happen? But you know what really turned me on? For all her elegance and assuredness and all that, when you took her clothes off – it was one word. Vulnerable. She became vulnerable when I took her clothes off …'

When Peregrine returned, talk briefly turned back to business. 'I've got a groundbreaking plan which you should come in on,' Gareth bragged. 'Do you know about Coca Cola? I went in there and said, "the man's the mirror". "The man's the mirror", that's all I said.'

'Let's talk about women. You know, they all look like they're on the make nowadays.'

'How did they look before? We're not as ancient as you, Jeffrey.'

'Different.' Jeffrey sniffed again. 'Like they'd made it.'

As Isabel listened to their intoxicated banter, her head began to throb painfully and her jaw ached from an involuntary clenching of her teeth. The next thing she knew, she was somewhere entirely different. An even darker place than here …

The bush was prickly and uncomfortable. But it was the best place to hide, right? In all those books she'd read, people always hid in bushes and they never got caught. From here she could wait for her to arrive and watch her in secret. See what she really got up to.

And, right on cue, here she came. And with a boy. A boy who was small and hunched.

Evita crouched even lower in the bush and widened the small parting in the leaves from which she could see the couple approach. She had expected the man, not this boy. She strained her ears to try to make out what they were saying but to no avail.

Then Evita frowned as she saw the girl begin to push the boy. She was pushing him repeatedly. Shouting. Crying. Why didn't the boy respond? He just stood there, until she had stopped pushing him. The last push sent him flying backwards to the ground where he lay. Evita resisted the urge to intervene. Was he wounded?

Slowly he got up. Then he stood on the tips of his toes and kissed her lips. The girl and the boy kissed for a very long time. Evita couldn't look away. She caught her breath as they removed their clothes. They thought they were alone in the woods. Evita wondered where the man was.

'Isabel, honey? Wake up!' Natalya crashed into the side of Isabel's lounger in tipsy high spirits, followed closely by Jake. 'What are you up to, hiding out here on your own?' Natalya eyed her suspiciously. 'Come on, let's go down for dinner.'

Isabel shook herself out of her reverie and banished all thoughts of the past from her mind. Grateful for the distraction, she followed them to the main dining table.

Carlo went about summoning the other passengers. 'Mr Sweet asked not to be disturbed, so you will dine without him this evening,' announced Carlo, depositing a perfectly arranged plate of buffalo mozzarella balls and juicy tomatoes with fresh basil and olive oil on the gleaming surface.

Isabel sank her knife into some mozzarella and found it was soft as a cloud. Next came the spaghetti alla vongole. Afterwards they had fresh peaches in wine. The boat rocked gently and Isabel felt a pang of longing when she saw the way that Jake and Natalya looked at each other.

'Have you ever done it on a boat?' whispered Natalya to Isabel. 'There's something about the swaying and the sound of the sea all around that makes it even more intense. Otherworldly …' They giggled.

Isabel noticed that now that Sweet was not around, his two lady friends were becoming a lot more animated. She'd been trying to work out the relationship between Candi and Ginger, who were chatting away happily together. There didn't seem to be a rivalry between them. Candi had seemed genuinely into Sweet whereas Ginger, who'd apparently known him for much longer, was robotic in her dealings with him.

Beside them, she overheard Jeffrey on the phone to his wife. 'I'll bring you something from Capri,' he was saying, silver hair glinting in the moonlight. He had talked about his wife a lot on the trip and hadn't flirted with any of the girls. Despite his bravado with the boys, Isabel guessed he was a devoted husband and a kind man. She felt a pull at her heart and wondered whether she'd ever end up with anybody of her own.

The next day they decided to lunch in Positano, where they could do a spot of shopping before heading to Capri, the glitziest part of Amalfi, for dinner.

In Positano they separated into small groups, with the men staying on the boat to swim and relax while the girls headed off to shop, bringing Jake and Sweet with them. Isabel preferred to browse the quaint tourist shops and the rustic stalls alone, stocking up on little white cotton dresses and woven fedoras, so she left Natalya, Jake and Sweet to lead the remaining three girls through ivy canopied walkways to the Missoni store.

'This is heaven!' Candi cried, shooting straight over to the crocheted bikinis and knitted floor-length gowns. She reached for a dress and held it against her, standing on the tips of her toes. Even then, she was so tiny that the hem of the garment pooled and dragged on the floor.

Meanwhile Jake treated Natalya to a bikini and Natalya treated herself to a dress and then casually picked out a pair of €600 high heels as a present to Isabel. The rest of the group looked on enviously, and Candi reached out a manicured little hand to inspect the shoes, stroking the sharp heel.

Not wanting to be outdone, Sweet patted Candi on the butt and announced, 'You can choose anything you like.'

'Ooh, I was hoping you'd say that,' she squealed. 'I know just the place – next door.' She took Sweet's hand with a delighted smile and Ginger followed eagerly, wanting to get in on the act herself.

'We'll catch you later, then. We're not done here yet.' Jake put his arm around Natalya, who was carrying almost half her weight in dresses and shoes.

'Amazing how Candi makes him seem almost human,' Jake whispered as they left the shop.

'Yes, he's definitely fond of her. But Ginger told me that once his hot passion runs cold, he becomes a demon. One of her girlfriends found out the hard way.'

'What's she doing with him, then?'

Natalya shrugged. 'She says she's obsessed, despite herself. I think a certain type of girl is seduced by the power.'

Natalya thought darkly of the girl she used to be, of how an ill-fated affair with a monster she met in Saint-Tropez nearly ruined her life. 'But that never ends well,' she added.

Chapter 39

'Phew! That was close!' breathed Piper as Sweet pushed past her outside the entrance of Missoni and stalked into the neighbouring store followed by Candi and Ginger. She kept her face buried in her guidebook. The shades that had disappeared into the ocean had been replaced by an even bigger pair, obscuring her face.

'They don't suspect a thing,' observed Bryan. 'This way, they went next door.'

Through the window of the neighbouring clothing store they were able to observe the eye-catching trio inside with ease. Bryan wolf-whistled quietly as Candi stripped down to her bikini on the shop floor and pulled on an indecently tiny dress, modelling it for Sweet while Ginger looked on.

Piper was not interested in Candi. She was watching Ginger closely, remembering the girl's words back at bitch school in Miami. 'I want to seduce Sweet, and then I want to destroy him.' Her contrasting eye colours were still extraordinary but the look in them told Piper nothing. She was oddly inexpressive. After a while, Candi disappeared back into the changing room, emerging again with the dress in hand, which Sweet then took to the counter along with a metallic clutch bag that Ginger had picked out. Other than a moment of awkwardness where the shop assistant dropped the papers she was holding and had to scrabble on her knees to collate them before giving them to Sweet to sign, there was nothing unusual to report.

As the satisfied shoppers stepped outside into the balmy air, Piper pulled Bryan into a clinch, burying her head in his neck as though they were lovers. Afterwards he looked at her in surprise, his face bright red. They hung back for a while longer and watched the trio depart in silence.

'Where do we go from here?' Bryan finally asked.

Before Piper could answer they were interrupted by four dapper Italian police in gleaming uniforms running towards them and then straight past into the shop.

The policemen searched the empty store, emerging with a shop assistant who had been out back. The one who had served Sweet was nowhere to be seen.

Chapter 40

Back on the boat, which was by now fast approaching Capri, Isabel looked out at the rugged terrain. She could see ancient ruins and caves embedded high in the cliff tops. From the sea emerged three stand-alone stacks of rock. Isolated from the great mass of cliff, these were the Bay of Naples' world-famous Faraglioni. Gazing at them, Isabel felt an inexplicable sense of foreboding.

'Tonight's gonna be a big one!' squealed Ms Pornstar, tottering through the boat in a short skirt and ludicrously high heels but, as usual, no top. 'We're all dressing up tonight,' she said, finally throwing on a sequinned black blouse.

Isabel kicked off her leather sandals and slid on her new heels. 'Thank you, Natalya, I love them.' She grinned.

Natalya was wearing wide-legged silk palazzo pants, a Prada bra top and a sheer white blouse over the top. Anybody else would have looked ridiculous but Natalya was ravishing.

Isabel pulled on a simple long white shirt and belted it tightly around her waist. She piled her hair on top of her head and painted on her signature red lipstick, which always made her feel polished.

'Gosh!' exclaimed Prince Peregrine when the girls emerged en masse in the main lounging area above deck. The men had made an effort too in crisp, light-coloured shirts and smart cream trousers. Peregrine and Gareth were both wearing navy blazers.

'Where's Sweet?' Isabel asked nobody in particular.

There was an awkward silence.

'He is like this sometimes,' offered Captain Carlo, appearing out of nowhere in his *Sweet Smell of Success* T-shirt. 'Sometimes 'e go for days with no contact with anybody and just don't want to be disturbed.' He raised his hands skywards to show that he was as baffled as everybody else.

The redhead felt the need to steady herself against a table as the boat swayed.

Carlo eyed her peculiarly. 'Choppier waters in Capri,' he said. It came out more like a threat than a reassurance.

Suddenly a chill descended over the boat despite the balmy evening.

'I will dine with you tonight.'

Mr Sweet had appeared. Tonight he seemed even taller than Isabel remembered. And what on earth was he wearing? A white cape was thrown around his shoulders over his shirt. This he wore tucked into white slacks.

Once the party reached solid ground they travelled in a convoy of cars to the highest part of Capri, walking only once they reached the centre. As they approached Capri's Villa Verde restaurant, overtaking hoards of pretty girls dressed up in skin-tight sparkly dresses and even sparklier make-up, Isabel realized this was definitely not going to be a low-key evening. The men were just as tarted up and, with the number of perfectly toned and tight male buns encased in the tightest of jeans, you'd be forgiven for thinking they were heading to the Italian offshoot of London's G-A-Y club. As if to stick two fingers up to that, a young boy with slicked back hair and a bright handkerchief folded jauntily in the breast pocked of his blazer turned to ogle Isabel slowly from head to toe. Just as she was wondering whether the precocious thing could even get it up yet, his cigar-smoking father turned to do exactly the same. Isabel was amused. She was pretty damn sure that she was too hot for either of them to handle.

'Eyes bigger than their dicks,' whispered Natalya in her ear.

The entrance to the Villa Verde ristorante was deceptively unassuming, enticing in visitors with a cheery colourful sign that looked as though it had been hand-painted. The charming, personal touch continued in the form of a hospitable welcome from one of the owners. He quickly commandeered the party's attention, rushing to greet the group. The restaurant was expansive and made up of open adjoining rooms increasing in size. The walls were decorated with hundreds of photographs of famous faces who'd dined there. John Malkovich, Mariah Carey and countless performers past and present beamed down at Isabel from their frames.

The group was led through the loud, packed restaurant to the largest space of all, the patio at the back in the exquisite garden. It was lined with greenery that took on a golden hue in the sultry lantern light. White-linen-clad tables, squeezed in close together to meet enormous demand, supported the weight of mountains of fragrant food and copious bottles of fine Italian wines. The place was buzzing, with diners flitting around the garden greeting friends and waving at acquaintances, or checking out an attractive unknown across the patio.

Fish was laid out and displayed on ice to one side and Isabel quickly pinpointed her lobster, jumping when she realized it was still moving, so fresh was the fare.

Dessert was lemon cake made from the zingy local lemon the region was famed for.

After a leisurely dinner they decided to walk off their excess and take in the surrounds before heading back to the yacht. Sweet settled the bill while they ventured out into the night for a long stroll.

'Let's play hide and seek,' said Ginger. Her brown eye glistened, but the blue one was curiously dull.

They climbed up a winding path for half an hour, and, having already travelled a number of miles on the drive up the steep passage to the restaurant, were now many hundreds of metres above sea level.

It was the dead of night. The sky was lit only by the full moon, the lights of the scores of yachts moored down below in the vast expanse of sea and the orange glow of fireflies. There was a sense of magic; of time standing still. Perhaps it was the light, or the dusky views. They pressed on along the path in spellbound silence, not knowing what lay ahead. Eventually they discovered a cave embedded within the cliff side and huddled inside giggling.

'I'm it,' said Sweet. 'Run and hide. You have five minutes. And then you're dead meat. The last person to be found alive will … get a million dollars.' There was a collective gasp.

'Er, but if anyone hasn't been found within half an hour we'd better all reconvene here so we can make our way back to the boat together,' said Gareth at once.

'You're scared, aren't you?' laughed his girlfriend.

'No I'm not.'

'Yes you are!'

'Boo!' shouted Peregrine from behind. Gareth jumped and let out a high-pitched scream.

Chapter 41

Inside the cave, Bryan held his breath. He'd been waiting there for the group, having quietly overtaken them earlier. He'd needed somewhere to assemble his bugging device and had spotted the cave. He knew they would pass it a few minutes later as they were heading in that direction and his plan was to plant it in Sweet's pocket as he passed. Reverse pick-pocketing. What he'd not reckoned on, though, is that they would all actually enter the cave rather than just pass it by.

He inched further back into the darkness. They had not spotted him yet. He'd been working on this investigation long enough to know what Sweet was capable of. He fingered the knife in his pocket and contemplated the best course of action. He decided to wait it out and hope for the best. Finally, the group dispersed, running in separate directions to hide.

Only Sweet was left in the cave with him.

Sweet's telephone rang.

'Yeah?' His lips twitched in the gloom. It could have been a grimace or a smile. 'Mmmmn. She'll die in my arms tonight.'

He ended the call and then started walking towards the mouth of the cave. Bryan crept forward in the soundless way he'd learnt over the years and slipped the device in Sweet's back pocket. He slipped back into the shadows, waiting for Sweet to put some distance between them, and then he slinked out of the cave to follow him.

Bryan tailed Sweet as he strode purposefully down a winding path. Being tall and dressed in white, he was easy to keep track of in the dark. Bryan, dressed all in black and lagging some way behind, was more effectively concealed. He was thankful that Sweet had left his gang of female bodyguards behind on this trip. Evidently he had decided that there were fewer threats at large in this sleepy part of Italy.

Now they were nearing the bottom of the path, getting closer and closer to the cliff edge that overlooked the inky water. Sweet began to whistle. Softly at first, and then it rose to a shrill high-pitch.

'Isssssabel.' Sweet began laughing to himself. 'Isaaaabel ... You can't escape me ... I'm coming for you ...'

The hairs on the back of Bryan's neck stood on end. He'd come across his fair share of nut-jobs in prison but there was something especially strange about Sweet. Again, Bryan felt in his pocket for his knife. Just as he did so, he heard an almighty rumble as a giant boulder broke loose from the cliffside above and dropped down with an ear-splitting crash just inches from Sweet's head. Jumping out of the way, Sweet lost his footing and plunged headlong into the water.

'Oh god. What's going on? Is he OK?' Ginger's voice called out, seemingly from nowhere.

Bryan looked up and realized she was standing higher up, looking down from the place where the boulder had fallen. Did it fall, or had she pushed it? Unwilling to be detected, he pressed himself back against the cliffside into a shadowy crevice as Ginger made her way hurriedly down to the spot where Sweet had fallen from.

Suddenly Jake and Natalya appeared, followed immediately by the rest of the group. It seemed none of them had got very far. Candi collapsed to the floor and began crying. Gareth wasted no time in gathering her up in his arms to console her. Immediately Gareth's girlfriend started wailing even more loudly herself. Her epic chest bobbed up and down dramatically until Gareth was forced back to her side. Candi's crying then shot to a crescendo and reached hysteria, while Jeffrey, the eldest of the group, stood white as a sheet and tried to take control.

'Stay calm. We need to ascertain exactly what has happened. He may still be alive.'

From what Bryan could see, the shock of the event had forced Isabel into some sort of frenzied psychosis and she was wandering about like a phantom, talking to herself in Spanish. Natalya held her hand helplessly. Now Ginger had also started shouting alongside all the crying and gibbering. Pandemonium had broken out.

'Oh god, he's drowned! He's dead! He's dead! He's drowned, someone help!' Ginger cried out at the top of her lungs.

'Wait a minute.' Jake put up a hand, straining his eyes as he surveyed the water. 'No he's not, he's alive,' he announced, somewhat despondently, spotting the ghostly white figure of Sweet being hauled from the sea to safety by a small boat.

'What?' rang out the shrill collective response, followed by a stunned silence that was more piercing than the almighty noise that preceded it.

Finally, after an interminable wait while Sweet had insisted on being checked out by a doctor, the party was back on his boat. Following the accident, the mood had darkened and everybody had gone straight to bed in an uneasy reluctance to talk about what had happened.

Isabel, however, was still out on the deck. She loved the view of the sea so late at night, when nobody was around. Or at least she'd thought nobody was around. She turned at the sound of soft footsteps behind her. It was Sweet.

'Sorry, I've been a bit preoccupied on this trip. We haven't had a chance to talk yet. About our …arrangement.' He had changed into fresh white slacks and a blue shirt and was perfectly composed, as though his near death experience had never happened.

Surprised, Isabel flashed him a bright smile. 'Not at all. I've been having a wonderful time and I think the arrangement we came to in London works very well for both of us, no? I'm looking forward to working with the Sweet Corporation and doing for you what I did for the Prime Minister.' She edged away from him as he came towards her.

'I'm not interested in the Prime Minister,' he leered. 'I'm interested in you.'

Isabel gave a nervous cough. 'Well, thank you. And I must say I, er, find you interesting. But let's not complicate things for now. There's so much we can do together with—'

'I think you made it pretty clear what services you were offering.' He raised an eyebrow. 'Compliance being a key part of our … agreement.'

'Yes, I certainly promised to make sure that every UK transaction that bore your name would *comply* with legal stipulations and that your profile would be significantly raised in a way that does not encompass any element of sleaze and scandal. That's an undertaking I am very serious about.' She looked him in the eye. 'You understand, this is hard for me too,' she lied. 'But it's better for us both if we keep things professional.'

He lurched forward and made a grab for her, thrusting his tongue into her mouth. Isabel bit down hard on it. 'Don't you dare!' she hissed. She shot him a murderous look and ran past him back into her cabin.

Sweet slammed his fist on the shimmering gunwale of the boat. 'Bitch,' he muttered. He whipped out his new phone – his old one was now languishing at the bottom of the sea. Fortunately Carlo had the foresight to keep spares. He made a call.

'Yes. Cancel all payments to ISO Communications,' he ordered before hanging up.

He felt his tongue where Isabel had bitten down on it. The bitch had drawn blood. He put his finger in his mouth and sucked on it, enjoying the pain.

Meanwhile, Isabel had thrown herself on her bed and tried to sleep. After an hour of tossing and turning she got up and began packing her things.

That was odd. Where were her new shoes? She packed the rest of her things and thought again of Sweet. Surely no one else would touch him with his reputation. She kicked her suitcase as hard as she could.

'The bastard,' she muttered. The door to her cabin suddenly closed with a soft click. She'd definitely shut it when she'd come in. She shivered. She couldn't get off this floating hell hole soon enough.

The 5 a.m. air was cool. She slipped on a thick jersey dress in an effort to get warm and crept barefoot towards the door. She would enlist Carlo's help to get her off, and in the morning she'd calm Sweet down from somewhere safe and far away. For all his 'I don't care about the Prime Minister', she knew that when the blood had drained from his loins, he cared far more about the Prime Minister than he did about copping off with her.

She picked up her case and handbag and slipped down the corridor. She thought she heard movement and froze, unsure of what to do, then she moved swiftly on towards Sweet's door. She held her breath and slowed down to check the coast was clear.

Chapter 42

Piper put down the printout of the files Bryan had scanned over to her. He had made the quickest of trips back to the UK while she had remained in Italy to keep a close eye on Sweet. She didn't know how Bryan's source had obtained the files from Isabel's office, or whether Bryan himself was actually the source he spoke of. She didn't want to know. All sources remained anonymous and she didn't have to ask them how they operated. That was how the system worked.

The more she read, the more astounded she became. Isabel did not pay a single employee to run her agency. She used an array of what she called 'interns' but what the law would call slaves. These people worked for far longer than they were allowed to work without pay. Piper didn't know what Isabel had promised them in return. Perhaps the name of the agency on their CV and the experience they gained would pay dividends in the end. Or perhaps not. One thing was strangely clear, though – the interns seemed to love working for her. They all wanted to stay with her, willing to work for free. Strange but ultimately irrelevant; what mattered in the eyes of the law was that what Isabel was doing was illegal.

Piper placed the files in a separate cabinet, beside the one labelled Mr Sweet, that was full to bursting. She had gathered a ton of information on Mr Sweet, from the relatively harmless – like his penchant for sadomasochistic sex with obliging girlfriends – to the terrifyingly violent, like the sexual assaults he'd been accused of and the manslaughter – or murder, depending on whether you believed the car incident with a business rival had been an 'accident'. There were similar 'accidents' involving dozens of his employees, colleagues and competitors. There were outright murder accusations he'd managed to get himself acquitted of again and again – Laurelie Fairlie was just the tip of the iceberg!

Then there was the organized crime. The years of international people and drug-trafficking and money laundering. The man was a monster. He hid all of this behind a yacht broking business, which was the front for his criminal activity and actually did make a fair bit of money in its own right. This was the company he registered and kept clean books for.

She knew that his main residences were in Monaco and Miami, and while he pretended to be a glamorous international mover and shaker from a mysterious and powerful dynasty, he was actually the son of a modest couple from Slough, in England. Now he was a tax exile and was only in England for the ninety days he was legally allowed to be there before he'd be expected to pay tax. It was in that ninety days that he was hoping to work with Isabel Suarez-Octavio to grow his 'legitimate' front and ingratiate himself with the establishment. If he could merge the two worlds – the underworld and the only marginally less dubious 'establishment' – his power would know no limits.

Piper's phone began to ring and she saw that it was Bryan, who was now back in Italy and supposed to be out watching Mr Sweet. Not now; she wanted to think about these files. She'd call him back. A few seconds later he rang again. She realized it must be something important.

'Hi Bryan,' she said, standing up with a stretch. She bent down and touched her toes.

'It's Isabel,' he said breathlessly.

'What?' Piper straightened up. 'What is it?'

'She's been arrested on suspicion of murder.'

Piper felt her knees give way and she collapsed onto the floor. 'Tell me everything.'

'Well …' Bryan began, overly controlled, as though trying to contain his elation at the news of Sweet's death. 'Sweet's body was discovered by Italian police at five this morning, with a barefoot Isabel standing over it. He was lying in a pool of blood and had been stabbed in the neck. All guests were evacuated from the boat and Isabel has been taken into police custody in Naples. Her body has been examined by experts and traces of Sweet's blood were found on her. The boat has been cordoned off with police tape and forensic scientists are now going through the yacht collecting evidence with tweezers, blushes, luminal, cameras, the works. They're gathering some pretty damning evidence against her. I didn't get to find out what the murder weapon was but the talk is that Isabel's DNA was all over it. Piper? Piper are you still with me?'

'Yes, yes I am. Oh my god. Oh my god. I – I can't … Wait.' She had a thought. 'What about the bugging device?'

'There was another accident, or an attempted murder, just hours before Sweet died. I watched as a rock fell from high above and nearly landed on Sweet's head. He fell into the sea as he tried to escape it. The device was drenched and completely destroyed. It can't help us now.'

The room was spinning and Piper struggled to think straight.

'Get back to London now and go through everything in Isabel's offices,' Piper instructed. 'As soon as you can. Before the police get there. And don't leave a trace.'

As soon as she hung up, her phone rang again. It was her step-brother, Tyler. Piper quickly filled him in on what had happened.

'I'll do some research,' he said straightaway, the lawyer in him picking up the scent of a good case like a bloodhound.

Piper started to protest but he cut her off. 'I can help you, sis. And then you can write about it.'

Oh, he was clever.

'Well, I am already writing about the man she supposedly murdered. I guess I could use a little extra help. I've got a feeling this could be the biggest exclusive this paper's ever seen.'

'Are you still in Italy?'

'Yes.'

'I'm flying over from New York tonight', Tyler said, promptly hanging up so Piper couldn't say no.

Piper needed to let off some steam. And she needed to think. She put on her running shoes and sprinted along the craggy Capri terrain. Nothing got her thinking juices bubbling better than an alfresco run.

Chapter 43

Piper ran for a good hour. Not really thinking about where she was going, she had arrived near to where Sweet's yacht was moored for police examination. When she reached the shore she stripped down to the simple bikini she wore under her clothes and dived headfirst into the waves. The monstrous boat was anchored way out ahead and it would take her a while to swim there, but she relished the challenge.

When Piper finally arrived, she stopped short of swimming right up to the boat and surveyed the scene first. The police tape was fluttering in the sea breeze. She could see there was no way she could access it in any conventional manner. In the near distance she saw a boat carrying the forensics team away from *Sweet Smell of Success*, obviously having got their material.

Tiring now, she had to work hard to stop herself from swallowing the seawater as she gasped for breath, working out her plan of action. It seemed she had got there at just the right time and there was nobody left on the yacht, though it was impossible to tell for sure. She waited another twenty minutes, slowly treading water. Then she swam up to it and grabbed a hold of the boat's mooring line, hoisting herself up onto its side. She then scaled it, as carefully as she could. She should have been exhausted to the point of collapse but her heart was racing, adrenaline kicking in.

The open deck areas and doors had all been sealed off, so Piper needed to make her way to the very top of the covered area of the yacht, which had been ignored by police, who probably hadn't imagined someone would be doing their own little investigation from that angle. She realized she would leave prints on the boat but she hoped that as they'd already taken note of any prints in the immediate aftermath, they'd be unlikely to do that again.

Piper inched forward to peer over onto the main deck. She gasped. They had taken away Sweet's body but the teak floor was stained with a horrifying amount of blood. Forcing herself to keep calm, Piper shimmied along the top of the boat, not wanting to risk stepping inside.

When she had taken in as much as she could from that angle, Piper crawled along the top, slowly lowering herself over the boat, catching its tip with her hands, clinging on for dear life. From this position she could see in clearly through the window of what must be one of the bedroom suites. It had been cleared out so there was little to see. She moved further along the side of the boat, inching her hands little by little, still in her hanging position. Each window she passed revealed nothing. Just empty rooms. There was just one more room at the end that she hadn't checked. By now Piper's arm muscles were straining. Even worse than the pain was the prospect of being seen, which became more real with every passing second. She decided to risk checking the final room before dismounting to safety.

This room was also packed up, but they had left one item on the floor – a discarded magazine. Obviously it had not been of enough interest to be taken for further examination. It was face down with only the page of advertising on the back, so Piper couldn't make out a title. But she didn't need to; newspapers were her passion. From the shape, size and texture of the paper, she knew instantly that it was *How To Spend It,* the fashion and arts magazine that came with the *Financial Times* weekend paper. The same magazine she had spotted Isabel flipping through on deck through her binoculars, and, incidentally, the very same issue which had interviewed her step-brother Tyler about the unusual court cases he had been involved in. The magazine was jogging a memory. Telling her something, but she couldn't think what.

She loosened her grip on the side of the boat and let herself fall into the water. It wasn't until she was fully submerged that she remembered. All the while Isabel had been reading that magazine, Ginger had been watching her. Her odd eyes had not shown any signs of warmth, just a scheming hostility. Piper surfaced and began her long swim back to the shore. She warned herself not to jump to conclusions, but the last time she had sensed murder in somebody's eyes was looking at the photo of Sweet in the Laurelie Fairlie newspaper article, and look how right she'd been there. Ginger had not been exaggerating when she'd first set out her plan for Sweet back at bitch school. Piper had a suspicion that Isabel was not the murderer.

Part Four

Chapter 44

Isabel's temporary prison cell was barely bigger than her outstretched arms in each direction, with two stone benches lining the walls, a toilet and basin in the corner and a mattress on the floor. It was dark, dank and smelled of the thousands of people who'd been there before, all sweating, retching and defecating in fear. She had no idea how long she'd been in there but it already felt like days, and although she'd demanded again and again to speak with a lawyer, nobody had been sent.

'Oh great, what a fucking cliché,' she snapped, when a young Richard Gere lookalike walked into her tiny cell and announced he wanted to represent her. It was ridiculous he was so absurdly young. What the hell would he know? 'Next you're—'

'Enough,' he said. 'You need to listen. I'm here to help you and you're going to co-operate.'

'I've got Warren Buffett on speed dial. I *know* people. Why should I choose you?'

He cursed his sister for not telling him what Isabel was really like. One minute in and she was already acting impossible. He threw her a contemptuous look.

'Why should you choose me? Because I'll fight to the death if I believe someone's been wronged.'

'OK, let me rephrase the question: why would *you* choose *me*?'

'I'm not choosing you. I'm choosing justice. Mr Sweet has enemies. Serious enemies. Enemies who are much more powerful than you. There are at least six contracts out on him in Miami alone, and you couldn't dream of the depravity he is capable of. My sister thinks you could have killed him, but my gut says you didn't. And you don't get to survive in this game without having instincts that deliver.'

'Well, you can't be surviving very well from what I'm seeing. Young, inexperienced, too compassionate, too unprofessional.' She stared at him, goading him on, but he said nothing, just stood there.

'And who the hell is your sister, anyway?' Isabel asked.

'Piper Kenton. You may remember her from university. She's my stepsister.'

Isabel frowned. 'Piper? No, I don't think I . . . Oh, yes, wait, she was involved in the Union, right? Oh God. Just leave. I don't believe this.'

'You might want to give one of your contacts a ring and do your research. Because I'm good. Believe me. The cases I lost were bought. It's as simple as that.'

They stared angrily at each other, not moving or speaking. Then Isabel slumped against the wall, the fight gone from her.

'I'm not like this. I'm not normally this aggressive but I'm so scared,' she whispered. 'And I'm angry at myself.'

'Why?' Tyler's stance softened.

'I put myself here. It was my greed that put me here.' She turned her face away, too ashamed for him to look at her.

'You didn't kill Mr Sweet, so you shouldn't be here. Greed or no greed.'

She didn't meet his gaze. 'I'm no angel,' she said, thinking of her past. She closed her eyes and then stiffened and let out a gasp.

'Are you OK?' Tyler asked.

But she didn't hear him. She was a young girl again, sizing up the security guard at Heathrow airport. He was armed, dangerous …and into her enough to deliver her safely over the border.

She opened her eyes and scrutinized Tyler. She too had instincts that had served her well in the past. They may even have saved her life.

Chapter 45

Ol led the way onto his father's plane, followed by Chloe. Will brought up the rear.

'I guess this isn't what any of us had in mind for our summer holiday.' Ol's attempt to diffuse the tension was not successful.

Chloe collapsed into one of the spacious white leather seats. Will sat beside her and Ol sat opposite them.

'Can I have some?' asked Chloe, reaching for the bottle of Evian water among the selection of drinks in the transparent mini fridge by her chair.

'Of course, take whatever you like. Sorry there's no stewardess on board but it was such short notice and as it's only us three—'

'Don't be silly,' Chloe said, unscrewing the lid. She could barely summon the strength to open it. She reached into her bag and pulled out a packet of extra strong paracetamol. Selecting two, she popped the painkillers in her mouth and swigged some water straight from the large bottle.

'Hey, go easy on those,' Will said with a frown.

'I can't shake this headache. It began when I heard about Isabel's arrest and it hasn't gone away since.' She pressed the button to recline her seat, holding it down until it was a completely flat bed. 'I'm sorry guys, I know we have so much to talk about, but I can't right now. I just feel so terrible. Do you mind if I sleep?'

Ol stood up and grabbed a cashmere blanket from an overhead locker, handing it to Chloe.

'Thanks.' She draped it over herself.

Will immediately took the blanket and spread it more evenly over her body, smoothing it down. His eyes were red and far away.

'Isabel must feel so frightened and alone.' He punched his seat. 'I would take her place if I could.'

'You really care about her, don't you?' Ol said.

Will shrugged. 'Always have done. Haven't we all?'

They glanced at Chloe. She was sleeping.

'Neither Chloe nor I have spoken to her in in far too long,' Will confessed.

'I know you haven't and she's missed you both, badly. But what's the use going over all that now? None of that matters now.' Ol picked up the file of papers he'd brought with him. 'Here's some more research I've done on Tyler. He's good. Goes the extra mile.'

Will clutched the file without a word, immediately consumed in its contents.

'Does Archie know you're here?' Ol asked.

'No. I didn't want to worry him any more. He'd have probably jumped on the plane with us, but he's got a country to run now.'

'I wonder what Isabel will think when she finds out you landed a job as the Prime Minister's spin guy!'

'I know, I wanted to call and tell her. The strange thing is this Lib-Con communications job is ideal for me. I'm happier in politics than I ever would have been being Isabel's bitch.' He cracked a fond smile.

'Let's have some food.' Ol got out some slices of smoked salmon, prepared just minutes before take off, a baked salmon salad and some fresh sushi, laying it all out on the fold-out perspex table between them. 'Shall we have something to drink?'

'Please.' Will's response came quickly.

A couple of precious Pétrus bottles beckoned invitingly but Ol reached behind for something more modest. It seemed wrong to be indulging in the light of Isabel's plight but they sure as hell both needed a drink. Before they knew it, the bottle was empty and the captain had landed them safely in Naples, where Isabel was being held.

As prearranged, a car was waiting to take the three of them to the holding cell. When they got there, Isabel was led out by two stout female wardens to a small, windowless visitor's room.

When she saw who it was who'd come to see her, Isabel burst into tears. Eventually she began to speak. 'I'm sorry,' she said. 'I've let you all down. Will I—'

'Half our time's already up.' Will stopped her mid flow. 'First things first, we've found out all we can about Tyler and he's good. Not conventionally so, but you're not conventional. We think he's the best fit for you.' Will tried to keep his voice neutral, to hide just how shaken he was by Isabel's unkempt and malnourished appearance.

It seemed they were barely able to get out the basics they needed to impart to Isabel before their time was up and so much was left unsaid. Chloe, still in a daze, had not uttered a word, but just before she left she held up the wad of magazines she'd brought over from England. Everything from *Vogue* to *OK!*.

'I thought you might need some distractions,' she said quietly.

Isabel nodded gratefully, tears in her eyes, before once again she was led back to her cell.

Chapter 46

Tyler had marginally better luck with Isabel the next time he paid her a visit. She grudgingly allowed him to question her. But that didn't mean he would get any easy answers.

'Siblings?' Tyler asked.

'I don't have any. I've told you everything there is to know about my family, but you keep at it. And now, of course, my parents want nothing to do with me. Who wants to be associated with a murderer?'

Tyler gave a long sigh. 'Isabel, I know you're hiding things from me. I cannot help you if you don't adequately equip me to do so. We'll leave your family for now but we will have to return to them again later. Now, with regard to ISO Communications. Your company undertook to represent a number of clients in the spheres of politics, business and the arts, including, but not limited to, the Sweet Corporation, which at the time was under the ownership of one Mr Charles Sweet. The very same Mr Sweet with whom you are alleged to have—'

'"Including but not limited to"?' asked Isabel. 'What's with all this stiff lawyer speak? I thought you said I could be free with you.'

Tyler stared coldly at her. 'I speak in the formal way in which

I have been trained because it enables me to remain in control of myself. Right now I'm angry. I'm very angry. Isabel, I'm asking you once more to tell me the truth. Where were you on the night of 15 June last year? You were supposed to be in Cap Ferret at an important investment meeting and yet you were nowhere to be found.'

She folded her arms, glowering at him.

'If you don't give me evidence to the contrary, they'll say you were in bed with Sweet. Is that what you want?'

'Tyler, I'm tired. Please, just give it a rest. Where I was is not relevant. It wouldn't help you.'

'Try me.'

Isabel pointedly crossed her arms and turned away. After a few minutes of silence, Tyler realized she had fallen asleep.

He watched her, thinking. Then he stood up to go just as she began to speak. Spinning on his heels he turned back, but she was still fast asleep.

'Ques ejbp'jbj.' Gibberish. Talking in her sleep. But he took out his dictaphone and recorded her utterances for twenty minutes before eventually leaving.

He jumped into a taxi to his hotel. It was basic, but it had a comfy bed, a clean bathroom and great Italian coffee. That was all he needed. As soon as he arrived he called for an espresso and then sat heavily on his bed, leaning forward on his elbows, head between his hands. When his coffee arrived he tipped and thanked the young man who brought it up, drank it quickly then got out his phone and called a Spanish translator. He played the recorded nonsensical mumbling down the phone to him.

'Nothing,' the translator said. 'It doesn't mean anything. I'm sorry I can't help you.'

He hung up and tried another number.

'Can you replay the message?' asked the Spanish lady.

'No, I'm sorry,' she said after the second listening.

He got the same answer again and again.

'OK, thanks anyway.' Tyler sighed to the final translator he tried. He was just about to delete the recordings when something stopped him. Maybe he'd enjoyed *Inception* a little too much at the movies, but something told him dreams were always a big clue to our waking lives. He saved them instead.

He threw himself down on the bed and rubbed his eyes. He was exhausted. He set an alarm for forty minutes' time. He would take a short power nap before getting back to work. He was studying every spare minute he could to gain his PhD in criminal law. On top of that he somehow had to earn a living. He could easily adjust his legal career to make it more commercial – he already had a number of qualifications after all – but he didn't want to do that. He liked working for the overlooked and the mistreated. But these people were usually the ones who had no money. So his pay was essentially a pittance and he kept it low on principle or often waived his fee completely, which meant he had to work nights to subsidize his fees and pay his bills. Hardly anyone knew this, but in the evenings he often sang and played the guitar in Manhattan jazz bars. He must be the only guy in New York who played the guitar to support a career in law.

OK. Nap time, he thought to himself, but for some reason he couldn't sleep. He picked up a law book and started reading. Maybe it was the heat, but he found he couldn't concentrate either. He stood and paced the room, a bundle of energy. He went over his meeting with Isabel in his head. He was unsure if he'd made the right move offering to represent her. She was hard work. And if he was honest, he was not now entirely convinced she was innocent.

Chapter 47

The sole criteria for the hotel at which Chloe, Ol and Will would stay in Italy was that it be the nearest to wherever Isabel was held. The outcome of that decision was a simple but perfectly comfortable family-run hotel with small and pristine ensuite rooms and a small friendly restaurant. In the mornings the mother cooked a breakfast of freshly baked bread and croissants. Lunch and dinner was whatever she felt like making with the seasonal vegetables, meat and fish her husband had fetched from the local market earlier. In the evenings, the eldest son played the aged piano in the corner of the room during dinner and afterwards the younger son and daughter cleaned up ready for the following day.

The evening after their first visit to see Isabel, Ol finished the last of his lasagne and went through to the kitchen where he insisted on helping Alessia, the daughter, with the washing up. She was happy to accept.

'How can he think about girls at a time like this?' Chloe asked Will, as the soft tinkle of the piano started up.

'It was wonderful seeing Isabel today, even in such miserable circumstances,' sighed Will. He slung an arm around the back of Chloe's chair. She leaned her head on his shoulder.

'After all this time, even now, we're so dazzled by her, so in her thrall.' Chloe mused. 'When she helped me make president of the Union, she gave me a sense of purpose. For the first time ever. Now I have no idea who I am – no man, no aim in life, no direction.'

With Chloe's term as president over, Ol less bothered about spending time at uni now he had his job in the family firm secured, Will and Isabel having long since left Oxford, and Sam having dumped her a while back, Chloe had been able to hide from everyone the undeniable fact that she'd been sinking ever deeper into despair.

'I've known it since our first day at uni. Standing there during matriculation, knowing I was a fraud. Just not good enough.'

'Nonsense!' Will said sharply.

'What then? What? What am I good for? What are my talents?'

'You're the kindest, truest, most loving person I've ever met.' He looked as if he had almost startled himself. Chloe went red. Will turned towards her and cupped her face in his hands. 'And that's not spin.'

'What have we here?' cut in a smiling Ol. 'I knew I'd made the right decision making myself scarce. I'm off to bed. Alone. Let's regroup in the morning and work out what more we can do for Isabel. I just hope she's innocent.' They all laughed a little too hard at that last comment as Ol headed up to bed.

'Seriously, though. What do we really know about her?' Will shook his head. 'What the hell does she do all those times when we can't contact her? Who is she? She'll always be our friend, but I live and breathe a world where bullshit, bitching, and backstabbing is the currency. I want something more real when I'm not at work.' He paused and held Chloe's hand. 'Thank you for helping me to realize that.' He was still looking at her, as though only now seeing her properly for the very first time.

Chloe spent the next couple of hours talking with Will, about everything and nothing. It dawned on her that conversation had been so unnaturally stilted with Sam, even after all their time together. She used to need to store up talking points in her head before she saw him to cover up those long awkward silences that he hadn't seemed to mind himself. Yet being with Will was as effortless as it had always been, except now it was charged with an electric tension which she supposed must have always been there but, both of them so occupied with other people, they had suppressed it.

The last two diners retired to bed and Chloe realized they were completely alone. Suddenly she was scared. Mental images of all the men she'd never been able to please in her past sneered down at her, dredging up awful memories of years of rejection and insecurity.

Will tucked a flyaway strand of hair behind her ear and tilted her chin to lift her face to his. He looked into her eyes and she could barely bring herself to meet his gaze. So bloody tender! But why set herself up for another fall.

'What are you thinking about? Please don't be worried.' He leant over to gently kiss her but she pushed him aside.

'Don't,' Chole warned.

Will recoiled in horror. 'God, that was so stupid of me. I'm sorry I shouldn't have. This is probably the last thing you…' His voice tailed off and he slumped forward in his chair burying his head in hands, his splayed fingers combing through his hair. 'I'm such an idiot when I fall in love,' he muttered.

Chloe gasped.

'I'm so sorry,' Will continued, 'I should have known you wouldn't feel the same way. But I can't help how I feel.' He looked up. 'I love you Chloe. I've never felt emotions like these before. Never needed anybody the way I need you now. Never found a person as beautiful and as inspiring and as life-affirming as I find you. Never felt like I could happily give up everything I own if it meant I would always have you by my side. I'm a rational man, but you make me feel like I could take off all my clothes and dance naked through the central piazza if you only asked for it!'

'Don't say these things to me, Will,' Chloe pleaded.

'Oh Chloe, I accept that you don't feel the same way. That's too much to hope but I think I've achieved something just voicing how I feel about you – even if it's just getting my own head around it. I just hope we can still be friends.'

'Who says I don't feel the same way?' Chloe whispered.

Will held his breath.

'I'm just scared.' Chloe continued. 'So scared. Whenever I love a man, well, he runs a mile in the opposite direction.'

Will took her hand and brought it to his cheek. He pressed himself against it, sliding his face back and forth against her soft skin, eyes closed as he savoured her touch and her smell. Then he kissed her, and for a moment time stood still.

When their lips eventually parted, Will took a deep breath. 'I've known you too long to run from your love. I want you. All of you. And I want to spoil you. I'm going to give you all the love you deserve. All that I have.' He embraced her, moaning as their bodies pressed together.

Chloe felt disgusted with herself for feeling so happy when Isabel was in prison. She broke away to try to get a grip on herself.

'Just think about yourself for once,' Will whispered, pulling her back to him and brushing his lips against hers. She kissed him back and they embraced again, tightly. Chloe could feel a strong heartbeat but she couldn't tell whether it was his or hers. 'Oh I love you too, Will. So, so much.'

Chapter 48

At the next visiting slot it was decided that Chloe ought to see Isabel alone.

'I wish I could break through that bloody glass and hug you. Oh Isabel.' Chloe could feel herself tearing up. She gave herself a mental shake. 'How are you getting on with Tyler? How is the case coming along? As soon as they get you in front of a jury they'll see they've made a huge mistake and then we'll sue the hell out of everyone!'

Chloe had so many questions she wanted to ask and they all tumbled out on top of each other, but Isabel seemed determined to avoid all talk of her situation. Instead she simply replied, 'I've missed you, Chloe.'

'Not as much as I've missed you.'

'How have you been? Tell me about life outside here. It'll keep me sane.'

They stared at each other through the partition glass. Chloe thought she saw a hint of a smile. A hint of the girl she'd so adored and admired at Oxford. The time felt right for a confession.

'I'm desperate to know what I can do for you but if you want to talk about me, I know you can be stubborn.' Chloe smiled. 'Look, I know I was horribly jealous about Sam. It was wrong of me. You didn't accept his work out of malice. It's just that his art meant so much to him and when he gave it to you, it was as if he'd … as if he'd slept with you. No, worse. It felt like an even more intimate exchange had taken place because the value he places on art is a million times more to him than sex.'

'It was insensitive of me not to see that. I guess I shared an understanding with him in a way. With his struggle.' Isabel averted her eyes. 'But you were always the greatest friend to me.'

'Well, it's all water under the bridge now. Basically, Will and I have realized that, well, that we're in love.'

Another smile flickered across Isabel's face. 'I was wondering when you would.'

'Really? Wow, it seems I'm always the last to work things out. And he's so happy working for Archie, you know. It was your "PM for a day" idea that led to him getting the job. He and Archie got on so well during it and Archie was so impressed with his crisis management during that press conference that when the previous guy resigned, he was straight on the phone.' But she'd already lost Isabel. Chloe could see that her mind was elsewhere.

'We'll get you out of here, hon. Don't you worry.'

'Have you been following it in the press?' Isabel asked.

'Yes,' said Chloe grimly. 'You're pretty famous!'

'I've been getting mail. Fan mail, hate mail, you name it. This world frightens me. I'm not sure I want to be in it anymore.'

'Don't say that, Isabel. Everything will work out. I promise. Let me read one of the letters. What have they been saying to you?' Chloe clenched her fists, angry on her friend's behalf. Isabel slid a letter through the slit in the glass. A guard eyed her but let them continue.

'"Hi Iza-bale?"' Chloe read. 'Wow, this person can't even spell. "Hi Izabale, I looked at the news and saw you and your preety face. I would lik to meet you. I keeled peeeple too. I lik you Izabale. If you want I can tell you about the peeeple I keeled because I think you are preety and funny. I keeled my —" Oh god I can't go on.' Chloe put the letter down and stared open-mouthed through the glass. Isabel slid another letter through.

'Try this.'

Chloe silently read the letter.

Dear Ms Suarez-Octavio,

I wept when I heard of your plight on the news. With such poise and intelligence, it was patently obvious that you are incapable of any crime, let alone a murder. I've been following this story very closely and it is clear that the murderer was that taxi driver who drove you to Naples. Time was when taxi drivers were charming young things who had good dispositions and who spoke English. Now I don't know what went wrong. Actually, yes I do. It was the last administration in this country and whoever the equivalents are over there, I suppose, but anyway, I digress. It became evident to me that after the taxi driver had committed the murder, he made the opportunistic calculation—

'Oh wow, I can't finish this one either!' Chloe put the letter down.

Isabel's face was expressionless. 'They still haven't confirmed a date for my trial yet but it's a matter of months not weeks, so it seems I'll be here for a while. I might even start to appreciate reading these just for some company.'

'Months! I feel so useless. I want to help you so much, I really do.'

Poking out from beneath another letter Chloe thought she could make out a photograph of a much younger Isabel. But as she opened her mouth to speak Isabel pushed it aside, obscuring it from view.

Isabel did not tell Chloe that the photograph had been sent to her with the head decapitated from the body and that she had stuck it painstakingly back together with an old lipgloss. Nor did she tell her that she knew who'd sent it.

'No one can help me now,' she replied.

Chapter 49

By now, after six months of incarceration while she awaited trial, Isabel was used to the rough way they grabbed her. Pushing her here and there. They had stripped her naked, searched her intimately, interrogated her. She was used to it and no longer felt violated by it.

She entered the courtroom. The fear clutched her heart and made her stomach turn. She registered the shocked silence and then the murmurs. Shame prevented her from looking around to see who had come. Desperation made her change her mind. She saw Chloe instantly and their eyes met. Isabel turned away and shivered despite the intense southern Italian heat and suffocating lack of air in the courtroom.

The first judge stood and spoke. Isabel didn't need the translator to understand what he was saying. All she had done in the past months was read. She'd read books, magazines, fan letters, and most of it in Italian, as that was what she had access to. All her life reading had been the only way she could escape. And she had escaped, once. Really escaped. But now it seemed she had come full circle. She could never get back what she had built, and now lost.

Piper rushed into the courtroom and up to the press gallery. She surveyed the room and gasped to see so many of her old Oxford contemporaries sitting to the side of the public gallery closest to the defence table, in support of Isabel. There was Olu Osaloni, flown in from Lagos with a man she presumed was his father, looking nothing less than heartbroken. Beside him sat a red-eyed Chloe, fingers intertwined with Will, both of their knuckles white. Even Sam, the celebrity artist, had managed to pull himself together and get to the courtroom. They would not be allowed to be present for the entire time but they had come to support their friend while they could. But something seemed odd. It took a while for Piper to pinpoint what it was and then it clicked. Where was Isabel's family?

The courtroom quickly filled up. There had been massive press coverage of the arrest in Italy, England and in America, where Mr Sweet mostly operated. The attention showed no signs of abating, not least because every paper delighted in printing full page photographs of Isabel, whose unforgettable looks had inspired endless conspiracy theories both in her favour and against her. Fan clubs and sites had sprung up and proliferated online and the prison where she'd been awaiting trial had received unprecedented amounts of fan and hate mail.

Piper studied the prosecution. The attorney looked respectable enough; a woman in her early forties with neat, highlighted hair and a dark suit. The two burly men sitting beside her, their chunky frames squeezed into slim-cut suits, seemed slightly incongruous and they looked sullen and uncomfortable to be in a court of law. They claimed to be Sweet's close family friends, as the man had no living relatives at the time of his death. There was a third guy in the row behind them who leant forward and whispered into one of the men's ear, but his face was obstructed from Piper's view.

The other passengers, the captain and the entire crew who had served on the yacht trip were all waiting on the witness benches, tense and nervous. Of the guests, Jeffrey the eldest was the most pulled together. Jake and Natalya sat cuddled together while Candi stared straight ahead, talking to nobody. Gareth and his girlfriend appeared to have split up and sat on either ends of the stand, both sets of eyes darting around the courtroom. Prince Peregrine was sweating profusely, mortified by all the extra press his involvement had brought to the case, no doubt desperately sorry he'd ever got involved with the likes of Sweet in the first place. Then there was Ginger. Although she too looked tense, she also appeared triumphant.

The courtroom quietened as the judges walked in. There were two of them, as was customary in a murder case in the Italian court of law. Judge Donato was a white-haired man in his fifties and wore a plain black robe. The measured, confident way in which he walked to the bench marked him out as the senior judge and seemed to reassure the crowd. The air of panic subsided, replaced by one of intense suspense. Piper began scribbling in her notebook, only looking up again when a loud murmur reverberated through the room.

Dressed soberly in black trousers, a shirt and black heels, Isabel was escorted in by two female officials with blue berets perched on their heads. Her trousers were too baggy and had to be held up by a belt. Her eyes were dull, sunken hollows and she looked as though she hadn't eaten for days. Piper was surprised to feel some sympathy for her. Isabel took a seat beside Tyler and they locked eyes. This would not have caught anybody else's attention but Piper could read her stepbrother like a book. He stared at his client and raised both eyebrows just a fraction. He was pleading with her for something. But whatever it was she didn't give it to him. She turned to face the front and gazed down at her bony knees. She said nothing.

Piper let out a small gasp and quickly suppressed the noise with her hand as her neighbours turned to look at her in surprise. She ran her eyes over the prosecution as it dawned on her why they had so captured her attention. Her neck burned as she remembered the way it had been squeezed by a meaty, gold-ringed hand in Miami. She mentally added goatees and jewellery to the men at the plaintiff's table and swapped their suits for black jeans and tight black T-shirts. It was them alright. Ferrari Fernando's henchmen. One of them rose to stretch his legs, stomping petulantly as he shifted position. Piper got a perfect sighting of the man behind who had until now been hidden from view. Fernando himself.

Before long Judge Donato struck his gavel and called the court to order. After the initial official court procedures had been completed, the prosecution attorney was called upon to come forward and give her introductory presentation of the case.

'Ladies and gentlemen of the jury,' she began.

Piper leaned forward. She thought her seat might rock with the vigour of her pounding heartbeat.

'Today I will show you a woman who has built her relationships, her business, and her life on a web of deceit and lies. I will show you a delusional and dangerous narcissist, a calculating seductress, an unrelenting perpetrator of evil. And, worst of all, I will show you a murderer.' She gestured at the projector screen. 'Give me exhibit A, please.'

Three photographs appeared on the screen. All three featured Isabel and one also featured Chloe, Will and Ol. In each one, Isabel was dressed up in a latex catsuit with fishnet stockings and studded black stilettos. She stared wildly into the camera, baring her glistening teeth like a vampire waiting to pounce. Chloe was in a similar get up but with a gag through her mouth and droplets of blood painted around it. The two young men were both naked apart from a pair of rubber underpants. They had silver chains around their necks attached to short leashes, the ends of which Isabel was holding as she posed for the camera.

There was a gasp in the courtroom. Isabel whispered something into Tyler's ear.

'Even at university, Isabel was already indulging in unutterable depravity and sexual violence,' stated the prosecutor with a smirk.

'Objection. That was a university fancy dress party. It happens every year at Oxford.' Tyler stood, furious.

'Sit down please, Mr Kenton. Let her present her case.'

'But this has no bearing on the case.'

'Oh yes it does,' snarled the prosecutor. 'It's an indication of the sort of character we're dealing with. Exhibit B, please.'

Exhibit B was a series of ten photographs. A compilation of clippings from various magazine social diaries showing Isabel and Archie sitting or standing suspiciously close together and chatting very intimately.

The prosecutor took a long sip of her water to give the court time to appreciate who the man was.

'Yes,' she said. 'That is the British Prime Minister. For those of you who do not know, he was ISO Communications' first client of note. Ms Suarez-Octavio, our "star businesswoman", takes credit for masterminding his ascent to power. Claims she put together key, talented members of his team. Raised funding for him. Got him involved in the arts. Helped to raise and improve his profile among young voters.'

Tyler stood. 'All of that is entirely correct. Call the man in for questioning if you dispute that!'

'But looking at these photographs,' the prosecutor continued, piercing Isabel with her hateful stare, 'all you did for him was assist his torrid penchant for affairs.'

'Objection! This is completely uncalled for. These photographs do not prove my client and the Prime Minister were involved sexually and even if that had been the case, all of these were taken before he got married. There would have been nothing amiss. Irrespective of any prior romantic status, Isabel and her company did indeed perform all of those aforementioned services, and played an invaluable part in the Prime Minister's communication strategy.'

'Objection upheld.' The judge nodded. 'Can we make this presentation more relevant to the case of Mr Sweet?' He looked sternly at the prosecutor, who was still eyeing Isabel.

'Fine. Exhibit C.' There were two short videos of Isabel and Mr Sweet, seemingly obtained from restaurant security cameras. The first showed her slipping him her business card, and, as she wiggled off to the toilet, he turned to obviously check out her rear. In the second they were inside a restaurant. Isabel was in a fetching red dress that showed off her figure. She was laughing and running a hand through her long hair as she leaned in to listen to Mr Sweet, who was gazing at her with a rapt expression.

'Think about what I said,' was all that could be discerned from his conversation before the video came to a standstill.

The prosecutor sighed as if truly saddened by the immorality of the videos. 'A number of intimate meetings with men for money? I thought a woman who did that was called an escort.'

Isabel started up off the bench in anger but Tyler held her down then stood up himself.

'If my client were a man, you would call that meeting a business lunch.' He was astounded that a woman herself could be so sexist and crude. And then he got it.

He realized that part of her plan was to get the notoriously volatile Isabel worked up so that she would do something stupid in court. An own goal. He realized then that the prosecution was not 100 per cent confident that the forensic evidence would put her away. There was still a chance for her. He leant in and communicated this to her but frustratingly she didn't react.

It was not long before Isabel was called to the stand for cross-examination.

'Ms Suarez-Octavio, can you kindly tell the court how long you were having a sexual relationship with Mr Sweet?'

'I have never had any kind of sexual relationship with him.'

'The court would like to remind you that you are under oath. Now, I'll ask you again, when did you and he first have sex and then we'll work it out from there because the evidence shows that you were kissing violently shortly before you killed—'

'Oh for goodness sake! I have never done anything with him!' Isabel screamed out, banging her fist against her leg. She was completely at her wits end from lack of food and sleep.

The prosecutor looked smugly around the courtroom as if to say, *Well, there's a murderer if ever I saw one.*

'OK, let me put it this way. Where were you on the period commencing 14 to 16 of June last year, when Mr Sweet was also untraceable? You were supposed to be at a meeting to secure the successful launch of the first incarnation of your business but you did not turn up there and you would not let anybody know where you were, as witness statements will soon testify. Was this because you were with Mr Sweet? Have you in fact been having a sexual relationship with Mr Sweet since that period? Were you then rendered so angry at being rejected by him when he flaunted not one but *two* women in front of you as his dates on your *luxury* yacht trip along the Amalfi Coast?'

'No!' Isabel screamed but the woman would not stop.

'Did you then argue with him on the boat? Try to seduce him again but to no avail so that in your evilness and newfound hatred towards him you bit down on his tongue? When he then decided to terminate his contract with your agency, was that not the final straw for you? The reason you then crept out of your cabin in the dead of night, lured him out of his, and murdered him in cold blood?'

The prosecutor had shouted the last five words so hard that they had come at Isabel like a physical punch. She felt winded and could not answer. All she could do was shake. She willed herself not to cry but she couldn't control the hot tears pricking her eyes.

The prosecutor watched Isabel sob. Saw that she didn't deny the accusations made against her.

'That will be all.'

The court broke up for lunch and in a private chamber Tyler begged one last time for Isabel's co-operation.

'You are about this close to being locked up for life,' he said, his thumb and forefinger almost touching as he illustrated the precariousness of her situation. 'Are you going to help me? Help yourself? Do you recognize any of the prosecution at all? They say they're estranged family friends of Sweet. Love him like a brother but haven't had contact with him in years. Somehow I don't see it!'

'Never seen or heard of any of them in my life.'

'OK. What about the payments? Why didn't you tell me before that he'd stopped the payments to your company?'

'I didn't even know. If he did do it, he must have done so just before I was arrested. Do you really think I've had access to anything so luxurious as my bank account since then?'

'They've got copies of all your business bank accounts. It's been verified. But if we can prove you weren't involved sexually with him, they have less of a motive. Isabel, you have to stop hiding things from me. Where were you on that weekend?'

She covered her face with her hands.

'Isabel, next they're going to come down hard on us with the forensic evidence. Give me something.'

She thought for a minute and shrugged. The fight had gone out of her.

'What about Sweet?' she sighed. 'Do you have anything on him?'

'He's the world's greatest criminal with enemies in every country but none of them want to talk to a lawyer or get near a court. And the legit business of your client, or rather ex-client, is squeaky clean. Fuck!' He kicked the wall. 'Don't be an idiot, Isabel. Come on, I don't have time for this. We don't have time. You need to tell me.'

She looked up at him and shook her head. 'It's all my fault,' she whispered.

Chapter 50

When the court reconvened, Piper was first back to her seat. She had so much she needed to tell her brother and yet no way of communicating with him now that the trial had started.

The first witness to be questioned was Natalya.

The prosecutor eyed her for a few seconds and then began to speak. 'Tell me, what was your impression of the defendant during the time you spent together on the boat?'

Natalya did not hesitate. 'I found her interesting and interested. Charming and pleasant. I liked her. Very much.'

'Was she not distant from the rest of you?'

'Objection – that's a leading question.' Tyler shook his head in anger.

'No, of course not,' replied Natalya.

'But were there any times where the defendant would just wander off? Demand some time to herself? Seem to tire of the company of her fellow holidaymakers?'

Natalya wrinkled her nose in confusion. 'Not really. I mean, well yes, at times she wanted to go off and explore, but don't we all want some time alone every now and then?'

Isabel thought of the many times when she would sit alone on deck, enjoying the scenery, or strolling through the bustling coastal resorts unaccompanied. How could they know that? She wondered whether one of the other guests on the yacht was now acting as an informant to the prosecutors. They must be.

The prosecutor changed her line of questioning. 'What were you doing, Ms Ozolin, while Charles Sweet was being killed just metres from your door?'

'It was night time. I was in bed with Jake. Sleeping.'

'And you heard no screams?'

'Not a thing. The boat is huge and I was very, very tired. We had had a busy evening, running all around Capri. I was exhausted.'

The cross-examination continued for what seemed like hours and as Natalya claimed to have heard nothing at the time of the murder, Tyler declined to question her much further when it was his turn.

Gareth was next to testify and he didn't help matters by making entirely clear his jealousy towards his deceased host.

'No,' he told the attorney. 'Isabel did not flirt with me. None of the girls did because they only had eyes for Sweet. It was his yacht, he was the big host, and all the women spent the entire time fussing over him,' he huffed, with a glare at his ex-girlfriend.

'So Isabel Suarez-Octavio was obsessed with Charles Sweet?' the prosecutor nudged.

One by one, the witnesses each testified, shedding little new light on the case and revealing nothing to help Isabel's case, even though most of them were desperate to help.

Finally, Candi was summoned. Isabel had not really spent much time on the trip getting to know Candi but neither she nor Tyler were too worried about her cross-examination. So far everybody on the boat had testified the same thing: that they had been fast asleep and not heard anything. So they were stunned when Candi took to the stand and spoke of her intense fear of Isabel.

'From the start I avoided her because she seemed so full of hate,' she said. Slight and without the make-up she'd plastered on in the boat, the girl looked no older than fifteen. 'I was so afraid of Isabel. Every time we spoke, all she wanted to talk about was how much she hated Mr Sweet. I became so worried for him when I overheard their argument in the middle of the night and I saw how she was jealous of me and Ginger, who I met on the trip, and how, like the attorney said, she tried to seduce him in one last desperate attempt, but grew angry when he turned her down. I didn't know what to do. And she was wild about him firing her. Stopping payments to her. And then I saw her doing …this.'

The screen once more flickered to life and a slightly grainy camera phone video came on. It was clear enough, however, to see instantly that it was Isabel. She was kicking a suitcase again and again, shouting, 'Bastard! I'll kill him!'

When it was Tyler's turn to cross-examine the witness, he got quickly to his feet.

'And why was it that you were creeping around so late at night? Why were you spying on and recording my client? Were you the killer?' The girl was so small it seemed a ridiculous question.

At once the prosecuting attorney was on her feet. 'There is absolutely no forensic evidence linking the witness to Mr Sweet or to the murder weapon. Whereas your client's prints were all over both at the time of his death.'

When all the witnesses had finished testifying, prosecution prepared to interrogate Isabel for the final time.

'Ms Suarez-Octavio, are these your shoes?'

Isabel stared at the Missoni heels Natalya had bought her and that had gone missing from her cabin, now produced and displayed as evidence. They were covered in blood. She glanced at Natalya at the witness stand, who had gone deathly pale.

'Yes.'

'Can you tell me why you inserted a metal corkscrew into the heel?'

'I-I didn't.'

The prosecutor turned to the judge. 'These are the very same shoes, Your Honour, that were used to pierce the neck of Mr Sweet. When Ms Suarez-Octavio emerged from her cabin for the final time on the night of the murder, she stopped outside Mr Sweet's cabin and called to him, luring him out. Once out, she enticed him on deck, where they ended up in a horizontal position. I will not lower the tone even further but I am sure you can all guess how she got him on the floor. Once there, she gagged him with'– her face contorted in utter disgust –'her underwear, no less. And then stepped on his neck in the doctored Missoni heels and killed him instantly, as you have all seen the forensic reports and the description of the murder weapon in the preliminary hearing. Now you have just witnessed Ms Suarez-Octavio's confirmation that the murder weapon is, indeed, her own.'

There was a collective horrified gasp in the courtroom.

'You know my client has already declared that the shoes went missing from her suite prior to the murder.' Tyler looked at Isabel to back him up but all she could give was a listless nod.

'Yes, she would say that, wouldn't she? Very convenient, despite the fact that the only prints on the weapon were hers and the only person with the victim's blood all over her was your client. Now the following image may be disturbing for some of the court,' the prosecutor went on. 'Exhibit D, please.'

Someone screamed. There, blown up extra-large, was the image of Sweet lying in a pool of blood on the front deck of his yacht. Blood had oozed from a hole in his neck and stuffed in his mouth was a blood-splattered ball of cotton. His eyes were open and his legs were splayed.

'Exhibit F,' the attorney ordered. And Isabel could see that the ball of cotton, now extricated from the murder victim's mouth and photographed in isolation, were indeed a pair of her knickers. She hadn't even noticed they'd gone missing. Her face fell.

'Ms Suarez-Octavio, do you have anything to add?'

'No,' she said.

Chapter 51

At over 48°C, it was the hottest summer Italy had ever known, but Isabel shivered in the courtroom dock. Chloe watched her from the gallery, hardly recognizing the thin, dark girl sitting rigidly by her lawyer and translator. Guards in light blue shirts and bright blue berets stood guarding her. Isabel turned her head and, for a brief moment, their eyes met.

Judge Donato cleared his throat and pounded his gavel. He spoke first in Italian and then the translator said, 'Ladies and gentlemen of the jury, on the indictment on the count of murder, how does the jury find the defendant, Isabel Suarez-Octavio? Guilty, or not guilty?'

Chloe closed her eyes. They stung from days of crying. How had it come to this? She wanted to turn back the clock. Go back to that sunny day in Oxford, when the world had been theirs for the taking and the stories of their lives were yet to be written.

The jury took just fifteen minutes to decide on their unanimous verdict.

The spokesman stood. 'Guilty.'

A sad hush descended over the courtroom as Isabel was escorted to a prison cell where she would await sentencing.

Just before she left, she slipped the key to her office into Tyler's hand. 'There are two paintings there. Please look after them for me.'

Isabel wasn't aware of her feet moving as she was led away to prison. In a state of dazed miscomprehension, she allowed the women to take her to wherever she must go. She thought only of *them*. The last time she had seen them. Her new company had been on the verge of launching and Will was in Cap Ferret with the people who would make both of their fortunes, but she had let it crumble. She hadn't needed to think twice. She thought of the flight back to Bolivia. The first time in nine years. She had turned off her phone, lest anybody trace her whereabouts. Nobody could know where she was. It was too dangerous.

Isabel felt a sharp tug on her arm by one of the wardens.

'Get a move on,' she barked in Italian.

Chapter 52

Bryan had done an even better job than Piper could have imagined. It had taken him far longer than she'd hoped to get into Isabel's temporary offices in Ol's house. Partly because his security was second to none, but also because, unbelievably, Isabel's skivvy interns had loyally formed a sort of unofficial, additional security service by keeping an eye on the property and clearing everything out in protest at the various different parties sent to search the office. Their untrained eyes, however, had missed Isabel's hidden safe, so it had been there for the taking when he had finally snuck in. There had also been two paintings on her office wall but he'd left those. She hadn't wanted him to steal anything, just let her know what was there, but he had taken its entire contents and brought them to her.

Piper sat open-mouthed, staring at the photographs he had produced from a safe underneath a slab of marble in the ensuite bathroom floor. Again, Piper did not need to know how he had learnt to search a property so thoroughly. Or how many safes he had cracked before Isabel's. In the safe had been three photographs.

She was thinner and more tanned, but it was Isabel in the photos alright. And in her arms she cuddled a child who was already about eight years old. The spitting image of Isabel, and staring up at her with glee. Piper picked up the phone and rang her stepbrother.

'What are you doing now, Tyler?'

'I'm looking at the Facebook photos of the various people on the boat. Something doesn't quite add up, but I can't think what.'

'I've gotta show you something. Now.' She needed him to help shed some light on her scoop, which was getting more and more confusing by the day. And she wanted to help him too, if she could. Even greater than her dislike for Isabel was her contempt for unwarranted punishment, and she sensed something was gravely amiss.

Chapter 53

The prison where Isabel was to await sentencing was a grey, concrete block, bordered off by tall steel gates. An inexpressive male officer had taken her to the prison reception, a dank cubbyhole of a place, and there she had handed over the property she had on her. Hardly anything, as she had come prepared. They allowed her to keep two shoe boxes worth of books. She had thought about bringing the photos, but decided against it. It was too risky.

'Would you like to have a bath or shower before we take you to be searched and then on to medical?'

Isabel shook her head. Let them get it over with. Her dirty, sweaty body was the only way she now had of making a stand against these people.

'OK, take prisoner Z8889 to room C.'

The officer led her to room C where two female guards waited. Immediately the first guard bolted shut the door, double locking it with her key.

First frisking Isabel, the second guard took a step back and barked, 'Remove your clothes.'

Isabel did so and handed them over. She'd learnt that resistance was futile.

By now the surly guard had donned gloves and proceeded to shake out each item and examine it with painstaking care. The other guard asked Isabel politely, almost apologetically, to stand next to the wall. She flicked a switch and a bright light illuminated Isabel's scrawny body. The guard scrutinized her from head to toe.

'Turn around,' she said, satisfied. Isabel turned.

'Touch your toes.' Isabel barely had the energy but she managed not to fall forwards.

'Good. Put this on.' Isabel was handed a prison jumpsuit, which she quickly changed into.

Immediately her officer reappeared at the door. She was shocked to find that his dispassionate face and permanent frown strangely reassured her. He had been the one source of continuity in the two hours or so since she had first been bundled into the prison van.

He barely looked at her as he led her down two long corridors, past rows of cells with steel doors. Eventually he stopped and pushed her into a cell, no bigger than four by five metres. The fact that the southern Italian sunshine penetrated through the tiny window, making it a bit brighter than she'd imagined, was little consolation. There were four thin steel beds lined up side by side. She was to share the cell with three other inmates, all of whom were now in the concrete courtyard for their one hour of daily exercise.

The basics taken in, Isabel focused her attention on the three beds next to her own, trying to arm herself with as much information on her new roommates as she could. Immediately she noticed that the first two beds were pulled close together. Magazines and notebooks had been dumped on the third bed, suggesting it was currently used as storage, rather than as somewhere to sleep in. She guessed that bed would now be hers. The fourth, nearest to where she stood, had clearly had somebody in it very recently.

What did it all mean? Was the occupant of the fourth bed the outcast? Were the two inmates sleeping close together a couple? The idea of a strong alliance between two of the girls, in whatever form it took, was unsettling. Two were always stronger than one and they would be in a position of power if it turned out relations between the cellmates were hostile. She decided to befriend the other girl.

She moved to the unslept-in bed and lifted the magazines and notebooks off it, putting them in a neat pile on the floor. The magazines, all of them fitness magazines or women's fashion and beauty, were well-thumbed, particularly on the pages where there were glossy pictures of the women or the great outdoors – beaches, mountains, forests. It seemed the inmates wanted to be those women. Looking at a fit and healthy girl running freely through a leafy park carrying dumb-bells, Isabel wanted to be her too.

There were long articles in some of the magazines but these pages had obviously not been looked at much and Isabel also noted an absence of books in the cell. She wondered if any of them could read. Picking up one of the notebooks, her suspicions were bolstered. It was filled with amateurish drawings of exercises and workouts that could be done in a confined space, but not a word in any language. Another notebook was just pages and pages of red stains that looked like blood. She gasped and threw it back onto the floor before picking it up again and arranging it neatly. She couldn't afford to get her cellmates' backs up the moment they came in and found her there.

Tired, she sat on the bed and closed her eyes. And her thoughts took her away from the cell. But somewhere she didn't want to be. It was the 15 June again …

She reached the hospital just in time. She gave the fake name they had agreed: Amy. They would be Amy and Carolina.

'You will have your operations at the same time. Carolina is already in theatre.'

When Isabel was ready and wearing the white hospital robe, the nurse led her to the operating theatre.

She gasped to see Gabrielita lying on the bed. She looked so helpless. Isabel walked over to the bed and ran her hands over her forehead. Along her eyelids which covered her big chocolate eyes. The eyelashes, still thick and long, were the only things on her face that had kept their lustre. The high cheekbones were now so protruding that she could have been ten years older than the twenty-two she was. Born on the same day as Isabel.

'Amy, if you can pop yourself on here for me, sweetheart. In a few moments you'll be asleep and then you won't feel a thing.' The nurse was kindly. Like the mother she'd never known. Isabel resisted the urge to throw herself into her arms as she climbed onto the other bed on the operating theatre. She lay with her head to the side so she could look at Gabrielita and reached out to hold her hand. Then she felt the prick of the needle in her arm, penetrating the vein. She wanted to keep watching Gabrielita but she couldn't because she was falling … falling …falling asleep.

When she woke, Gabrielita was also awake. And the doctors and nurses were crammed in the operating theatre crying. And there was a camera crew filming and a photographer taking pictures.

'Such a beautiful pair and such a miracle that this life-saving liver transplant occurred so quickly and smoothly. We think you are angels come to bless this hospital and you are going to be all over the news and press. You will give hope to all the other angels who have lost their wings.' The nurse sobbed uncontrollably and hugged the two girls to her bosom. They smiled thinly at the camera and then looked at each other, their own fear reflected back.

As soon as they were alone together they panicked. 'We're dead,' Gabrielita said. Isabel stared at her then picked up the hospital phone and called Ol.

'One day I can tell you everything but for now I just need your help. I'm in trouble.'

'You don't have to tell me what you've done,' Ol said. 'I know and trust you.'

Isabel clutched the phone tighter; she might just have a chance.

'Then you'll help me?'

'What do you need? Money? Protection? I can get you some boys from Lagos. Or my father's security, they're trained by the Gurkas.'

'I need to get out of Bolivia and I can't use any commercial flight which can be easily tracked.'

'I'll send the plane for you.' She listened carefully while he gave her details of where to catch it. 'But you will still need your passport, or the pilot won't do it, or not without arousing massive suspicion and getting my father and a whole lot of other people involved. I would do anything for a friend. But my father might not.'

'Understood. Oh Ol, thank you. You may well be saving my life. And Ol?'

'Yes?'

'Tell no one.'

*

They had until 1 a.m. to break out of the hospital, retrieve Gabrielita's son and get mother and child into hiding before getting Isabel back to the spot where she needed to meet Ol's plane.

Isabel spotted the needle used to sedate her before the operation. Beside it was the sedative.

They waited until two nurses came back into the room to take them to rest and Isabel asked if she could first just get something from her handbag. One of the nurses went to get it and return it to Isabel. Then Isabel threw her arms around her while Gabrielita stabbed her with the needle. Before the other could work out what was happening, she too was pricked in the vein. Their legs buckled from under them and they were soon unconscious.

Quickly they stripped the nurses of their uniforms and covered their modesty with their own hospital robes. Then they slipped on the nurses' outfits, pulling the caps low over their heads. They walked quickly out of the room and into the office overlooking the car park, where the nurses had been chatting. They searched the office for car keys and found those of a tiny battered Hyundai on the verge of extinction. Isabel figured the car cost around £500 worth of Boliviano. She reached into her bag and left £4000 in an envelope where the keys had been. Then they rushed out into the car park and jumped into the car.

Gabrielita drove as Isabel no longer remembered the roads. They headed to the local brothel where they had left the boy for the few days they had been in hospital.

'Mama! Mama!' shouted the child happily. Then he spotted Isabel and his eyes lit up even more as he jumped into her open arms. He beckoned them both to come over and play with the two prostitutes who had been looking after him.

'Muchas gracias,' cried Gabrielita, taking the two older women's hands in hers. She had had nowhere else warm, sheltered and discreet to leave her son during the operation and she hadn't dared take him with her.

Isabel reached into her bag and gave the women what money she had left. 'How did you end up in here?' she asked, trying not to show her unease at the sordidness of the place.

The younger of the two looked ashamed. 'I have a young daughter. Your sister has a son. She knows what a desperate mother would do for her child.' Her tone was defensive.

'I'm not here to judge you but to thank you,' Isabel whispered, gratified to see the woman's face soften.

The other prostitute cut in angrily, 'I wouldn't have agreed to watch over this moronic child if I'd known you'd come charging in here to patronize us. How did I get here? Who cares? It's my body, nobody owns it but me, and I can use it as I please!' She lit a cigarette and did a provocative dance, grinding obscenely against Isabel.

Isabel held her still. Now she, as her sister had just done, took the two women's hands in hers. A defiant silence became a sisterly silence. An understanding. They each had their struggles.

The younger prostitute began to speak. 'Every day since I arrived here, I lost a little more of my soul. I lost my fear, and I lost my pride too, until there was nothing left of me. Now I am dead. All there is is my daughter.'

Isabel found she was unable to let go of the woman's hand. 'There is hope,' she said.

'We must go now. Thank you again. You are kind women.'

Gabrielita, who had been hugging her son close to her, squeezing him with such passion that he was in danger of being suffocated, smiled gratefully, with tears in her eyes, as she and Isabel left, holding the young boy between them.

'I wish I could take you with me,' Isabel said when they were back in the ailing car. 'But they will not fly you without a passport.' They were driving to a small, innocuous shack in a secluded area far south of La Paz, used before in times of need. Isabel would then drive to meet the plane and discard the car somewhere nearby.

'I know,' Gabrielita said. 'You have done enough for me. I'll stay in hiding, I'll recover and I'll get out of here eventually.'

'We'll get you to safety,' Isabel promised.

That parting had been the most painful of Isabel's life but it was sweeter than the forever parting that would surely have occurred had she not made the trip.

The cell door flew open and then shut with a loud clang. Isabel collapsed in surprise, looking up to see a black girl with a pretty face but a muscular body.

'It's you,' the girl said, flexing her muscles instinctively.

'I'm—'

'You're Isabel,' finished off the girl. 'I'm Celestina. Nice work.'

'What do you mean?'

'Killing that bastard.'

Isabel didn't know what to say. 'What are they like?' she finally asked, gesturing at the other beds.

Celestina shrugged. 'They don't speak English.'

They heard footsteps approaching the cell and the other two inmates entered. They stared at Isabel and then spoke under their breath to one another in Italian. Isabel had been picking up more and more Italian each day as she'd awaited trial and its close relationship to her native Spanish meant that, despite it being littered with street slang, she could understand most of their conversation, but something told her not to let on. They, like Celestina, already knew who she was.

Isabel smiled, but not too brightly. She hadn't sussed them out yet and didn't want to show weakness. The taller one, similar in look to the other, was slim with a bony face, close-set eyes and cropped dark hair. Isabel wondered for a moment whether they were sisters and felt a pang of wistfulness, but from their body language as they whispered about her and the brutality of the way they'd heard she killed Sweet, she could tell that they were intimate with one another. They both nodded curtly at her and sat on the first bed, from under which the taller one extracted a pack of cards and began dealing for four.

Isabel looked quizzically at Celestina. 'Do they want us to play?'

'That's Luisa and that's Mafalda. Yes, we'll play,' explained Celestina. 'And the loser will give over her belongings to the other three. That's what happens. The new person has to give her belongings.'

'What if I don't lose?'

'You will.'

Luisa had finished dealing the cards. She clicked her fingers and Mafalda came to sit beside her. She beckoned Isabel over to join them. As the taller of the couple, she seemed to be the dominant one, both physically and emotionally. Celestina joined the trio on the bed and they began playing. At first Isabel thought the game was Hearts but as she lost more and more rounds, it appeared the game was whatever Luisa decided it was. Isabel followed each move closely but, just as she was getting the hang of a game, it would suddenly change. Again, Isabel would quickly work out the new rules and then they would change them. Luisa slammed down a queen of diamonds and glared at Isabel.

'Listen,' Celestina warned. 'The new person *always* loses.'

Eventually Isabel stopped even trying. Luisa gestured for Celestina to go and bring Isabel's things over. Celestina looked sheepishly at her but went ahead and reached for her box of belongings in the corner of the room and brought them over to Luisa, who took the box eagerly and tore off the lid. The three stared at the box of books in horror.

Luisa screamed something in Italian and made smoking movements with her fingers.

'Don't you have cigarettes?' asked Celestine, aghast.

'Sorry, I don't smoke.'

'Well, maybe we can still trade them. But they look boring,' grumbled Luisa in Italian.

Mafalda shook her head and put her hand on Luisa's arm. 'Please, let her keep them. We won't get much for them. Let her have them.'

Isabel felt relief and gratitude flood over her. She decided it was time to try out some Italian and thanked them profusely when Luisa grudgingly relented. They looked at her in surprise at her near-perfect Italian but then seemed pleased to have somebody new to chat to.

'They're not boring, they're all love stories,' Isabel lied. They were actually business books she was planning to read on the chance a miracle might one day happen and she'd get out of prison and be able to go back to work as normal. 'Let me read one to you.'

'But are they in Italian?'

'I'll translate.'

Celestina wandered off to one side at the sound of all this unintelligible Italian and began doing furious press-ups.

'So,' began Isabel in Italian, opening a book called *Financial Risks for Greater Gains in Business,* 'There was once a young woman named … Gretchen. She thought she knew everything, but she didn't know quite how lost she was. Then one day someone came into her life. He was a little older than her and his name was …' Isabel paused and tried to come up with a suitable name but couldn't, so she said the first name that came to mind. 'Tyler.' She cleared her throat, warming to her story. 'Now Tyler was hard and tough and persistent …and he was also incredibly intelligent and …handsome and …kind …' She broke off.

'Go on,' pressed Luisa.

Isabel lost any sense of time as she created her story, turning the pages of the textbook at random, so caught up was she in this Tyler character. Before any of them knew it, it was time for bed.

When the lights were off, Isabel lay still in her bed, not daring to close her eyes. She hadn't yet asked what the other girls were in for. To be honest, she'd rather not know. But she was scared and, in the company of these three strangers, had never felt more alone. Her eyes became accustomed to the dark and she saw that Luisa and Mafalda were sleeping, snuggled together for company, and she envied them their companionship. She closed her eyes when she was sure everyone was sound asleep and hugged herself. She imagined she too had a companion. A friend to protect her in this awful darkness.

She barely slept at all and in the morning woke up at 4.30 a.m., before any of the others, so that she could have a shower in relative privacy and some time to herself. She hardly recognized the red-eyed monster in the mirror but she didn't bother to brush her long wild hair. She would ask the prison warden if she could have it cut off.

Over the next few days, Isabel developed a sort of trade-off with the other girls. She would make up stories for Luisa and Mafalda. Then Celestina, who was Jamaican, had asked her if she would teach her to read in English, so she had started to do that too. And though the four girls were not friendly, as such, they had become tolerant of each other.

It was a different matter outside the cell. Isabel dreaded having to eat with the other prisoners in the communal dining hall. Breakfast was always porridge, which tasted as though the oats had been boiled in petrol. As soon as she entered the room, the other prisoners would start heckling her. Shouting obscenities at her. About what she was said to have done, the perverseness of which escalated each day. By now she had killed not only Sweet but various other criminals that everybody seemed to have heard of but her, and most upsettingly of all, she was also accused of killing their children.

'Hey, you bitch dyke,' hissed one woman, tugging at Isabel's now boy-short hair and looking over her body, which was losing its curves by the day as she lost her appetite amid the taunts. 'Don't think you can do that to kids and get away with it. You will die in here.'

'Attention-seeking whore!' shouted another, who Isabel suspected had mental problems that the prison doctor hadn't yet addressed. 'You kill a man and a couple of babies and you come in here acting like you're freaking Lindsay Lohan with all your stupid paparazzi and your retarded fan mail.' The screeching woman, clawed at the table, making scratching sounds with her nails. 'You should take comfort from them letters because we sure as hell aren't your fans. No way, José, I'm a crazy bitch stalker who wants nothing better than to see a bullet in your brain!'

Isabel ran back to her cell, trying to hold in the sick which had risen up in her throat, only to be confronted with Mafalda cutting her wrists with paper from the blood-splattered notebook.

Isabel threw up on the floor. Mafalda didn't even look up.

The next day things did not get better. Each day became worse and worse. Isabel was crying more than she was dry-eyed. She was sick more than she was well. She spiralled into a despair so deep that it she could see no way out. The only prospect offering her a glimmer of hope was the chance of a visit from Tyler. She refused to see Chloe, Ol, Will or anybody else because she felt so ashamed, yet everyday she asked the same question: 'Is there any news from my lawyer?'

'Have you heard from a man named Tyler Kenton?'

'Can I please speak with my lawyer? I need ...'

But the answer was always 'no'.

He had given up on her. One more rejection, one more abandonment. Funny how it never stopped hurting. Sometimes she couldn't believe the human capacity for hurt. It seemed it was limitless. Just when she thought she must surely have reached the threshold, another day would come and the pain would be even more intense.

Eventually she stopped asking for him. But that didn't stop her thinking about him. She remembered the way his face became very serious and he began to speak in extra formal legal language anytime he got worked up. She smiled, despite herself. She thought so hard about him that she could almost smell him. Her stomach felt leaden with the weight of her constant, dull ache for him. But nobody came.

Chapter 54

The dark room smelled of sweat, blood and urine. Gabrielita paced the length of it. Oh god, what was that? That scratching noise again. She stopped pacing and kept very still. Someone was just outside the building, watching her through the draughty holes. They had found her hideaway. She knew it. She crouched down in the darkest corner, holding her son to her, not moving. Her son began to whimper and she clamped his mouth shut. Oh god, she had really blown it now. She knew it was over and whispered a prayer.

'Oh Lord, forgive me for my dreadful sins and please protect my two loves; my strong, kind Evita and my little one who, should he live, will grow to have all those qualities too. Please do not let my cowardice and my vice ruin the lives of those I love. Father forgive me, for I have sinned.'

The scratching outside became louder. And now someone began to bang on the walls. A man shouted. A mad man. She couldn't make out what he was saying. She didn't understand what he was shouting to her. Oh god, it was a mad man they had sent. He kicked at the door, yelling and heaving. He kicked again and the door to the shack flew open.

Chapter 55

Piper barely even stopped to brush her hair, so eager was she to get to the courtroom. The final day of sentencing had arrived. She rushed to the taxi, already sweating from the heat and her nerves as she climbed inside. She had been writing non-stop for weeks, months, taking her own notes on Mr Sweet, Isabel and the case, and yet the more she wrote, the more confused she became. She longed to discuss her recent thoughts with her brother but she hadn't been able to contact him. She assumed he had locked himself away to work on the case, investigating ways out for Isabel. Not that he would have been able to help Piper anyway; he was 100 per cent committed to the confidentiality of each client's case. Even family were not exempted.

The driver pulled up outside the courtroom and she paid him the twenty-five euros he asked for. He made frantic gestures at the court, jaw agape and began jabbering in Italian.

'I'm sorry, I don't speak Italian.' Piper shrugged apologetically, even though she had understood the gist of his questions. He wanted to know whether she was going in to watch.

Piper jumped out of the taxi and had to push her way through a scrum of international paparazzi and camera crews. There must have been at least fifty of them, all jostling, pushing and shouting with excited laughter, as though they were awaiting a royal wedding party, not a murder sentencing. She heard a group of girls waving sheets of paper and calling out 'Samphire! Samphire!' Piper looked about, bewildered, as the paparazzi started snapping frenziedly, then she realized Sam Smith, now known as Sam Fire, was entering the court.

Entering the courthouse herself, Piper headed straight for the press gallery. She took in her surroundings and noted everything down. Once again, Isabel's old friends had turned up for the sentencing, just as they had for the trial, but no family members were present. She wondered where the devoted couple with the glittering diplomatic career Isabel used to talk of had gone. Piper wondered how she herself would react to the news that her daughter, if she had one, was a murderer. With horror, that much was certain. But could she leave her to face a life of imprisonment, without so much as a goodbye? She didn't think she could.

She studied Chloe's body language: both tense and despondent as she clutched Will, her face deathly pale. The two of them stared straight ahead, not talking, though Will had his arm around Chloe in a protective manner and it seemed to be the only thing which stopped her from collapsing. On her other side, Ol was doing his best to help everybody relax. He was constantly looking to his left and right, smiling and nodding at people. From time to time he would reach out and knead Chloe's shoulders, unlocking the tension in them, and then he would reach across and do the same to Will, even cracking a joke or two.

The last person seated on that row, sat at a considerable distance from his Oxford contemporaries, was Sam Fire. He looked like a rock star. But then he'd always looked like one. But where his long hair and stubble had sometimes overwhelmed the eighteen-year-old boy, it now seemed to fit. He looked angrier than he used to; a thick line was already etched across his forehead from a permanent frown. He was just as skinny, and his clothes were still as scruffy, but they were more expensive, now that he'd made it. She wondered if he'd got his clothes here in Italy while he, like everybody else, had waited with frustratingly little information on when Isabel would be sentenced. Finally the date had been announced, but the circumstances and timing of the various stages of the trial had been shrouded in secrecy and chaos.

Piper scribbled all of this in her own form of shorthand, understandable only to her. Beside her a press artist was sketching with practised speed, capturing the interior of the court drama and its key protagonists with an uncanny accuracy. Piper observed the scene growing on the page, gradually turning the paper from white to grey. Then she turned her attention to a row of young people behind the Oxford crew, who had also flown out to Italy in support of Isabel. These must be her 'interns'. The kids who Isabel was exploiting for her own ends and to whom, by the time she had been arrested, she should have paid many thousands of pounds in wages which would now never be seen. They sat quietly, shooting defiant stares at the prosecution. Piper recognized Anna, from Bryan's description. The small, sweet-looking girl was said to have been the one who'd put up the biggest opposition to the police searches of Isabel's office.

The room was completely packed out, as it had been at the trial. Now it was just a matter of waiting for Isabel to be brought into the courtroom. She had already spent months locked up, but today she would find out just how many years she would have to spend in there.

Piper pushed aside a sense of foreboding as she looked for her brother. He should be here already but perhaps he'd chosen to accompany Isabel into the court. She bit her lip, sitting on her hands to stop them from shaking.

The door opened for the final time to let in Isabel. There was no Tyler. Piper felt sick, unable to take her eyes off her old enemy. Isabel looked so feeble and unwell, the two burly guards at her side seemed ridiculous; she could hardly run away in that state. She wore khaki shorts and a similar-coloured T-shirt. A military look which said 'fight', yet her passionless face said only 'surrender'. Her bony knees were the fattest part of her legs, and her hair had been cropped so short she was almost a skinhead.

She watched Isabel take her seat. Beside her, her lawyer's place remained conspicuously empty. Isabel stared at the vacant spot, even reaching out a hand to touch the unoccupied seat, and then turned away with both hands folded on her lap and her eyes downcast. She didn't even look around for her friends as she had done before.

Judge Donato cleared his throat before speaking. Then he launched into a lengthy monologue which Piper did not try to understand, as the translator would no doubt communicate the message to the mostly foreign court when the judge had finished talking. After twenty minutes had passed and Judge Donato had barely paused for breath, Piper began to feel terrified.

Half an hour later, the translator was translating the standard court preliminaries. Piper scribbled, so well-trained that she could take notes automatically even when her head was not really processing anything she was hearing.

Eventually proceedings progressed to the case. With no representation, Isabel did not even look up when the judge called her name. He asked her questions, asked her to help herself. She couldn't or she wouldn't. Piper watched Isabel drawing out her sentence again and again with her lack of cooperation.

The atmosphere was growing rowdy. She knew it was Tyler they were arguing over. The court, even the witnesses and the jury, wanted to wait for him to appear before sentencing Isabel. The one small gesture they could give her before they destroyed her.

The courtroom was stifling. Piper felt faint. She saw a vision of her brother, Tyler, and was unsure if it was a hallucination. Fuzzy at first and then scarily focused and clear.

He had arrived.

Pandemonium broke out in the courtroom and Judge Donato had to repeatedly sound his gavel before order eventually returned. Tyler was summoned to talk with the two judges before it was decided if he would be allowed to take the stand.

Tyler kept his composure. 'Let me present to you an alternative version of the events leading up to the murder of Mr Charles Sweet. Now, the prosecution have been claiming, all this time, to be Sweet's family friends. People who have always helped him out. Early investors in his company. Conveniently for them, all the accounts and company documentation have apparently been destroyed. It seems they just didn't know where to look. Well, I, with the help of a small team of private detectives, have been able to locate the relevant papers and accounts of the various business interests of the late Charles Sweet, which the prosecution have now entirely taken over.

'These papers show that far from being early "friendly investors", they only became partners on the 29 September last year.

During the yacht trip. The very day before he was murdered. These papers show that Sweet effectively relinquished all control of his assets and that the signatures were obtained on the very same trip on which he was killed, just before the murder took place.'

An official bought the documents over to the judge for inspection.

'Furthermore,' Tyler said, 'the evidence I have collated, and the witnesses I have uncovered – who are prepared to swear under oath – will prove beyond a doubt that the business partners claiming to be "family friends" were actually his worst enemies.' Tyler paused dramatically and took a sip of water.

'There are a number of elements that are particularly strange in this case. Firstly, why have the prosecution denied having any contact with Mr Sweet in the lead up to his death when he signed their papers only the day before? And secondly, why did Mr Sweet sign the papers when the deal was not favourable to him financially? Now, I believe I have the answers to these questions, and I will answer them shortly, but first I would like to clarify related affairs.

'First, I must let it be known that I have spent the last months in Miami and in Bolivia, pursuing my client's freedom without communicating this fact to her or to anybody else. Not even to my sister, to whom I owe a lot for generating some invaluable leads through her investigative journalism. I have gone against my client's noble wishes and delved into her family history, even though she did not want me to, because she was trying to protect those closest to her. She chose to save her family over herself.

'Let me explain how my client's family history is directly linked to this case and how it has led me to discover who was, in fact, the real murderer of this extraordinarily evil man.' He looked carefully around the captivated court, lingering on the prosecution and the witnesses, but avoiding Isabel's panicked stare or his sister's amazement up in the gallery.

'Now, a question which has preoccupied the court a great deal and to which, as yet, my client has been unable to provide a satisfactory answer, is that of where she was on the night of 15 June when she was scheduled to be in Cap Ferret with her friend and then business partner, William Austin. The court has concluded that she was pursuing an affair with Mr Sweet at this time, but let me put you straight as to where she really was.

'I would like this court to know that she was in a hospital in La Paz, Bolivia, undergoing a liver transplantation in order to save her twin sister's life.'

Isabel gasped while the translator translated and the court exploded into incredulous laughter.

'Enough!' shouted Judge Donato in English. 'Because of the astounding lengths you have gone to to seek the acquittal of your client, I will allow you to continue with this absurd proposal, but you'd better be sure.'

Tyler nodded. 'When my sister, who is composing an in-depth article on Mr Sweet, and who has known Isabel since university, informed me that Isabel had a child and that she had seen the photographs, I demanded to see them for myself. As soon as I saw the pictures, I spotted immediately that although their features were the same, there was something in their eyes that was very different. The effect that my client has on me is such that …' He gave an embarrassed cough. 'What I mean to say is that I have come to know my client well and to confuse her would be impossible. For she is unique. I knew that the woman in the picture was not her, and therefore a twin, even though she has always been adamant that she is an only child. I knew then that the key to finding out the truth in this case would be to find the twin who Isabel was so desperate to conceal. And that is what I have been doing for the last few months.

'My sister's leads took me first to Miami, where together we have uncovered many truths about both the late Mr Sweet and the prosecution, and these I will soon come to. But the crucial, missing piece of the puzzle was not to be found in Miami. The twin sister was the key, and she was hidden so well that only Isabel could tell me where she was.'

Isabel gasped again. Still, Tyler refused to look at her.

'And she did tell me. In her sleep.' He got out a dictaphone and played the unintelligible message. 'Ten Spanish translators could not tell me what was being said here, but knowing there are many ways of speaking one language, I phoned a Bolivian translator, and she was able to tell me that the chanting on this recording was not a phrase but a place. A place Isabel needed to go to in her dreams. "I will go to Boyuibe", she was saying over and over again in her sleep. And that is what I recorded and, armed with the photographs discovered by my sister, I went to this place, inquired about the mystery twin and knocked on every door of every possible hiding place until I found her.

'And now, let me call a special witness to the stand.'

The judge nodded and the courtroom door flew open. In walked a young woman who was the spitting image of Isabel before she had been incarcerated. She wore a simple white dress and held hands with a boy of around eight.

The crowd stirred in excitement until the judge demanded silence. He called for the newcomer to leave the child with a court official and come forward to be sworn in.

'I, Gabrielita Sebastien Lopez, do solemnly swear ...' she repeated after the man in her heavily accented but confident English. Her hand lay reverently on the Bible and she fingered the thin gold chain with a cross pendant hanging at her neck. Her son was struggling against the kindly female official who was trying to keep him still. He spotted Isabel and shouted. He gestured frantically, as though desperate to run to her, screaming, 'Evita! Evita! Evita!'

Isabel never took her eyes from the boy. Then her sister began to speak.

'When Evita and I were younger—'

'Evita is your sister? Known to the court as Isabel?' asked Tyler gently.

'Correct.' Gabrielita's voice began to shake. 'When Evita and I were three years old, our mother and father were killed in a car crash in England where they were working as diplomats. My sister and I were brought back to Bolivia to live with our grandmother, but she died just weeks later and so we were put into an orphanage. We spent a few years there and, as we got older, there were all kinds of stories about how our parents had been very successful and had travelled all around the world to exciting places, even being stationed in London, where we were said to have been born.

'But we both hated it there, at the orphanage. All we did was read. We found we were good at reading and maths and learning. We began to learn languages because we dreamed of other places. Of escape. That's why we read, too. All we wanted to do was escape.

'When we were twelve we left the orphanage and went to live on our own.' She paused and closed her eyes tight, as though trying to block out a painful memory. 'I didn't want to work hard for nothing. I wanted to have what I believed was mine by birthright, and I wanted to travel and see the world, and see the country my parents had lived in. I met a man, an older man, and he became my boyfriend. He was very possessive. He became obsessed with me, with controlling me. Before long I was working for him. Swallowing latex balloons filled with cocaine and transporting the drug halfway across the world for him. As I grew older I realized what I had got myself into, and saw the effect that these drugs had on people's lives, what animals they became when they took them. And I saw the darker side of the trade; the murders, the beatings. I understood that what I was doing was gravely wrong. But by then it was too late. It was a case of keep going, or be killed. They would kill me if I asked to stop, rather than risk me getting them into trouble. I had seen this before. They even took photographs of those they had killed, or planned to kill. On the photographs, they would tear the heads off the bodies and send the fragments to the victims' families.

'And then, at the worst possible time, just when I was trying to work out what to do, I became pregnant. By Miguel who I loved and who loved me. But one day, before he ever knew he was to be a father, he confronted my bosses to try to set me free. And …' She began to cry. 'And they killed him. The very same week they ordered me to carry more cocaine than they had ever asked me to carry before. For the first time in my life, I knew that I could not take that risk. I could not risk a balloon exploding in my belly and killing me, because it would not just be me who would die, it would be my little unborn child.

'So Evita said that she would pretend to be me and make this final trip while I was pregnant, and then we would try to work out how to solve the problem once and for all.

'I trained Evita up and when she was sent to London with a passport given to her by the boss, circumstances conspired that she was not properly met at the other end and was essentially left alone in London. She brought an untraceable pay-as-you-go phone and we discussed the situation. We figured that if the bosses thought I was alone somewhere in England and would not come back to headquarters in Bolivia to rock the boat, then they would probably just write me off, forget about me. All I had to do was disappear from the area and stay low-key, and all Evita had to do was stay out of Bolivia and also keep a low profile for a while.

'For Evita – now Isabel after the name on her new passport – things were very different. She continued to read and became very learned. She enrolled in a school in London for sixth form and eventually gained a place at Oxford University. From there, we all know what happened, how she went on to set up a successful business. Of course we worried slightly about her becoming too successful, too famous, but we figured that the Bash Boys wouldn't take any notice of what was happing in British cultural life.

'Everything was going to be so great for her, and I was so proud, until I became gravely ill.

'It was still not safe for me to come completely out of hiding as I was still at home in Bolivia and more vulnerable than my sister and, similarly, I was reluctant for Evita to return to Bolivia and risk drawing any kind of attention. The Bash Boys had been growing and becoming more and more successful in the criminal underworld. They were even branching out internationally, and the word on the street was that a lot of it was being organized from Miami as well as home. Now it wasn't just drugs; it was girls too. I told Evita not to come. By now my son was a healthy young boy, and I knew that if I died of my liver cirrhosis, at least he could now live, he too could go into an orphanage, though the thought was horrible. But when Evita heard about my liver, she insisted that she must donate part of hers for the operation, which had to take place immediately if I was to have a chance of survival.' Gabrielita began to sob. 'Evita flew back to Bolivia for the first time in years, risking everything, though she tried to keep a low profile and turned off all her phones and anything which would mean she could be easily traced. We were worried about her travelling on her passport just in case they were tracking flights into Bolivia, but she decided to risk it. We thought she could be in and out in days without the alarm being raised.

'And things would have been fine if the nurses had not been so moved that they decided to tell the press. After all, the operation was the first of its kind ever performed in Bolivia. And then the whole country knew about us. Even though we used fake names, our faces were identifiable. I had had a long affair with the big boss and I knew he would recognize me and realize I was still around and had a twin sister who also knew everything. And with a bigger criminal operation, there was much more at stake for him now.

'Evita managed to escape back to the UK, but once again, I was desperately hiding in Bolivia.'

The prosecution lawyer, who had been slumped stupefied on her bench, suddenly snapped back to attention and got to her feet.

'This is a sad, sad story indeed, and thank you for furnishing us with a long list of other offences for which we can prosecute you and your sister.'

The judge held up a hand to silence the lawyer and called to Tyler to corroborate the witness statement.

'All of the aforementioned is correct. Can we have video A please?'

On the projector screens was a recording of Bolivia's most famous chat show, with coverage of the two girls waking up at the hospital looking dazed, fragile and terrified.

'And so you see, Isabel has been so reluctant to inform the court, even when the information is to her advantage, because she has always been thinking of protecting her sister and her nephew. But now she need not worry that her sister has been exposed without the ability to protect herself and her son, because the people she needed to protect herself from will soon be put away for life.

'In fact, they are right here in this room. The head of the Bash Boys is called Fernando and he is currently in the team trying to secure the prosecution of my client for a murder he organized, thereby allowing him to silence his new international business rival, Charles Sweet, take over his money laundering operation to add to an already flourishing drug trafficking operation and, in framing Isabel for the murder, he could silence her and punish her and her sister for their deception years earlier. All he would then still have to do was go after her twin.'

The focus of the court shifted to Fernando and his surly henchmen, who all smirked.

'You know we were nowhere near the boat when the murder happened and we have watertight alibis.'

'You may not have been there,' said Tyler, 'but your honey trap certainly was. If there's one thing that can be said about the murder victim, it is that he liked to spend money, and no better way for him to show off his wealth than to lavish expensive gifts on his lady friends. This is how our "not so innocent" witness, Candi, managed to persuade him to buy her a rather fetching little dress in one of the designer shops of Capri. Only when Sweet signed the bill and the lady at the till casually asked him to sign the guarantee too, he signed immediately, without even reading it, assuming the short document was just one of the many such extras one is often asked to sign by stores. The document was in Spanish but, to an untrained eye, would have looked like Italian. Nothing out of the ordinary there, being in a reputable Italian store. He was in a hurry, Candi was at his side pushing for him to complete the transaction and move on, and this is what he did.

'What the local police department can confirm here, as they already have done to me, is that shortly afterwards a lady called Luisa Sabbieti reported that she had been blindfolded and locked in a cupboard at the store she worked at for an hour. Enough time for Candi's accomplice to take her place behind the till and get the papers signed. Luisa was then unlocked and found that all was left pretty much as it had been at the store.'

Piper was mesmerized looking out from the gallery. It was all falling into place. She shook her head with pride at her brother as she remembered how she and Bryan had been unable to work out why the police had arrived after Sweet had taken Ginger and Candi shopping in Positano. They had tried to find out themselves but had gleaned little information.

'Once the contract was signed, and Sweet had officially handed over his business to you, a business which concealed a far more lucrative undercover operation that you planned to takeover, there was no more need for Sweet to be alive, and the murder could go ahead as planned.' Tyler was hitting his stride.

'This is just conjecture. Why did Sweet invite Candi on the trip in the first place if she was working for the enemy?' barked the prosecutor.

'Your clients' honey trap had seduced Sweet prior to the trip, as planned. That was not hard as it was common knowledge that Sweet loved beautiful women. Even his bodyguards were gorgeous women and Candi is a skilled seductress.'

A woman is the way! Piper thought back to Fernando staring at Sweet in Hakkasan and then saying 'a woman is the way'. 'OK, let's get real. And how do you suppose that Candi carried out the attack with your client's shoes as the murder weapon?'

'Yes, indeed.' Tyler glared. 'One piece of information my client did give me and which I have made clear already was that the Missoni heels, bought for her by Natalya Ozolin, went missing shortly before the crime was committed.

'As I've made clear, the evidence points to the fact that your client is lying,' the prosecutor shot back.

'Well, here's the thing.' Tyler was incredulous. 'One thing your honey trap couldn't resist doing when she found herself on the 300 foot super-yacht, was to take a few show-off photos of herself to post on Facebook. Now I've searched the Facebook pages of every single one of the witnesses time and time again and wondered what was weird about Candi's pictures. On the ninth look I realized. Just a hint of glove peeking out from under the lid of her suitcase. And tights. Who needs gloves and tights when the temperature is forty degrees?' He paused. 'A murderer, that's who. Somebody who planned to leaf through other people's suites without leaving a trace, and steal shoes and underwear covered in someone else's prints. Tights were needed to slip her foot into the shoes without leaving a trace, so that she could plunge her heel into Sweet's neck. Quite probably, had I been able to open up that suitcase in the photo, I would also have seen the razor sharp coil she had fastened to the heel.'

'Nonsense,' responded the prosecution. 'And how do you suppose Isabel came to have Mr Sweet's blood on her person?'

'The evidence shows more than one point of piercing of the skin. Not only at the neck, the source of the fatal injury, but also on the mouth – an injury that occurred significantly earlier, according to the forensic report. It is virtually impossible that the same attack would have lasted the entire duration of the time – two hours – over which Mr Sweet's tongue was first bitten and he was murdered, without anybody else on the boat noticing. Therefore there were two separate encounters. The first encounter did indeed involve Isabel, who we now know to be called Evita. Mr Sweet, a known sexual predator, attempted to kiss Isabel, presumably against her will, and she bit down on his tongue in self-defence. If we could replay Exhibit A again, the video evidence used by our "honey trap" in her witness statement, please? But this time, look closely at the colour of Isabel's lips.'

The video was duly shown.

'The red is unevenly applied to her lips. A closer look will show that this red is not lipstick, but, in fact, blood. The very blood that poured forth from Sweet's tongue when she bit it to save herself from an attack. What must then have followed is that Isabel runs back to her bed and attempts to sleep but is so traumatized by the attempted attack, that she rises and plots to escape from the yacht. At this stage, Candi is also putting the finishing touches to the murder. She decides to gather more incriminating evidence on Isabel, having been watching closely all of that night's events. She sneaks to Isabel's door and secretly films her in her torment. Seeing that Isabel's suitcase is packed and she is preparing to leave, she returns to Mr Sweet's cabin, wakes him with the news that she thinks Isabel is planning to leave, and lures him out on deck through a separate exit to wait for Isabel's appearance. But before Isabel can make her way out on deck in order to exit the boat, Candi, dressed in the stockings, whip and stilettos that he likes her to dress up in from time to time and indulge his well-known taste for sadomasochism, orders him to lie on the floor so she can punish him. He, always ready for a sexual act, obliges, lying down on the teak floor in excited anticipation. Within seconds it is over – Candi steps down hard on his neck and he is instantly killed. She throws the stockings overboard, leaving the shoes covered in Isabel's prints, and calls the police anonymously just before Isabel makes her way out on deck. The sight of Isabel standing over the body is the first thing the police are confronted with and she is arrested shortly afterwards.'

Candi began crying and Fernando got to his feet in anger.

'She did it!' he yelled, pointing at Candi. 'It had nothing to do with us; she hated Sweet and she did it.'

Candi shook her head. She knew the game was up for all of them.

'The allegations against me are untrue,' Fernando carried on. 'I am not a criminal and I've never met Candi before or instructed her to kill anyone for me.'

'Oh yes you have.' Tyler grimaced. 'With the help of information about the Bash Boys, given to me by Gabrielita once I had found her, I was able to seek them out and, with the help of a team of private detectives, we discovered enough evidence to put away all of the gang for twenty lifetimes.'

Now the noise of sirens could be heard outside the court. There was a frenzy of activity as the three key gang members were rounded up and arrested, with simultaneous arrests happening at that same moment around the world. Isabel, Gabrielita and her son were escorted into a temporary holding cell to await their new fate.

Two hours later, Tyler walked into the holding cell to meet with the girls. He carried with him a wide slim case.

'Isabel? Evita?'

'Evita,' she replied quickly.

'Evita, Gabrielita, for your drug trafficking offences ten years ago you must be tried separately and sentenced, but as you were both young offenders and, Gabrielita, your testimony has led to the conviction of a serious crime gang, it is likely that you will be sentenced to a maximum of ten months in jail, and with good behaviour you should be out within two months. Evita, the six months you have already been detained will likely exempt you from further incarceration for your offence. But you were both forced into situations beyond your control, so my guess is that we can get you both cleared of any wrongdoing.'

Gabrielita and Evita fell into each other's arms, trembling with relief and gratitude.

'There's one last thing,' Tyler said. He opened the case to reveal the two Sam Fire paintings Evita had asked him to look after while she had been in jail. 'You should take these back. They are worth millions now.'

Evita took the paintings out of his hands, stood up and walked shakily to him.

They regarded each other solemnly. Nobody said a word. The cell seemed to vibrate with tension. When the silence became unbearable, Evita broke it. 'When you didn't send word to the prison. I wanted to die.' Her voice was hoarse and broken, her face stricken. The colour drained from Tyler's face and the dreadful silence followed once more. But neither could avert their gaze from the other.

Tyler took a slow, deep breath and began to speak, but Isabel silenced him with an urgent kiss. He kissed her back, tentatively at first, and then as long and passionately as he'd wanted to from the moment he saw her.

When they returned to the courtroom, there was rapturous applause. Piper, Will, Chloe, Ol, Sam, Anna and the other interns ran to meet them.

'Piper,' Evita said, looking in the eyes of the girl whose investigative journalism had helped to free both her and her sister. 'I'm sorry.'

'Don't be an idiot.'

'And thank you.' Evita reached for one of the two Sam Fire paintings and turned to Sam. 'May I give Piper the most valuable gift I have to give?'

'I'd be honoured,' said Sam.

'Piper, this is for you.' Piper took Evita in a long embrace.

Next, Evita picked up the second painting and gave it to Chloe, who couldn't control her sobs.

'No,' Will said, when Evita turned to him holding the chain at her neck. 'I'll share Chloe's painting'.

'You know I don't need anything.' Ol smiled, hugging her as she turned to him.

'Nor me,' said Sam with a sly grin. 'I've become pretty successful.'

'You!' Evita said, incredulous that Anna and the other interns had flown to Italy to support her.

'We saved all your things to stop them being seized by the police when they raided your offices.'

'Please, keep them all,' Evita said. 'Consider them long overdue payment to you, and the table has a very special signature underneath.' She glanced at Sam while hugging Anna. With each material possession offloaded, she felt lighter. All she needed were the people she loved. Speaking of which. She turned again to Tyler.

'I'm so sorry for everything I put you through,' she said.

He simply stared at her, with longing in his eyes.

For the first time since she'd known him, Tyler was completely out of words.

Epilogue

And so Isabel's story is no longer one of tragedy. It is a story of hope. Of happiness borne of heartbreak. It is the tale of a feisty and heroic businesswoman who helped to bring down a little-known but hugely powerful international crime gang, with her sharpest weapon: a pair of Missoni heels …

Piper put the finishing touches to her cover story for the *San Francisco Eye*. She read it through one last time to be sure she was happy with it. Then she attached it to an email to her editor and pressed send. It was done. Her first cover piece.

She moved away from her laptop and picked up another cover piece. Chad had finally made the big time with his latest film alongside Jake Jendar and she had attended its premiere with him. There, blown up for all to see, was a gigantic photograph of the two of them. Their eyes shone with joy. The picture was in America's biggest national magazine and would be syndicated all around the world. To think people had once thought she'd made up her boyfriend! Nobody would think that now, not that it even mattered anymore.

'You're too far away,' he teased, sitting at the other end of the sofa. She turned to look at him. She'd never felt more contented.

'Well, we'd better do something about that, hadn't we?' She collapsed into his arms. She was home.